By Jennifer Stevenson

THE BRASS BED
THE VELVET CHAIR
THE BEARSKIN RUG

TRASH SEX MAGIC

The Bearskin Rug

Jennifer Stevenson

BALLANTINE BOOKS • NEW YORK

A Ballantine Books Mass Market Original

Copyright © 2008 by Jennifer Stevenson

Smoking Pigeon copyright © 2008 by Julie Griffin

Published in the United States by Ballantine Books, an imprint of The Random House Publishing Group, a division of Random House, Inc., New York.

BALLANTINE and colophon are registered trademarks of Random House, Inc.

ISBN 978-0-345-50024-3

Cover design and illustration : Tamaye Perry

Printed in the United States of America

www.ballantinebooks.com

OPM 9 8 7 6 5 4 3 2 1

For my babe, Rich

CHAPTER 1

Jewel Heiss sat white-knuckled in the back seat of her aged Tercel with her ex-con-artist partner in front and her sex demon at the wheel. It was a steamy Chicago Monday in late summer. They were headed for the Eleventh Ward, responding to a consumer complaint. This one had come down from the Fifth Floor. The complainant had gone to her alderman, and her alderman, knowing what was good for him, had brought it straight to da mayor, and from there it trickled down to Jewel's Hinky Division.

Today's mission was to make the consumer's problem go away, without publicity. That, and to get out of this car alive.

Jewel sat in back with the files, so that Clay could take the risk of a head-on with Randy at the wheel. Randy's model for driving was obviously a Hollywood chase scene. He had flair.

"Here's the turn. Jazus, Randy, slow down!"

Wordlessly, Randy slewed the Tercel into a squealing halt.

Jewel put a hand on her throat. "That was way too exciting. I hope I didn't pee my pants." If it hadn't been ninety degrees in the shade, she'd have been ice-cold with terror.

In the rearview mirror she caught Randy smiling at

her. "I'll wager you'd no notion you could get such performance from this vehicle."

"Clay, you're supposed to teach him how to drive like a normal person, not a cop-show rerun."

Clay showed her an innocent face over the back of the front seat. "Well, we're sort of cops."

"Sort of! As in, not really. In fact, where traffic is concerned, we're not cops at all, and we do not get to drive like idiots. Ever."

Clay made his pouty lips into an O and twinkled at her through his shaggy blond bangs. "I think he's doing very well."

"It's sabotage. He'll be busted and grounded within a week of getting his license. Which we cannot afford."

"Getting busted and grounded is the best education for a new driver. Worked for me when I was sixteen," Clay said. "Hammers home the rules."

"Which you ignore for the fun of it," she said. "Difference being, you were a citizen on a learner's permit, and Randy can't even get a learner's permit until he has an identity. You were going to fake up ID for him, remember?" Jewel hated to think how many laws she was breaking, the longer Randy stayed in her life. "If he gets busted, he'll be deported." Did the Immigration and Naturalization Service have a special way of dealing with hinky wetbacks? She shuddered. "He could end up in hinky Guantanamo." She didn't know which would be worse. "For nasty experiments."

"No, he won't. He'll end up in a bed somewhere," Clay said, which didn't reassure her at all.

"I shall be on my guard," Randy said, his smile gone now. Randy had once been an English lord—pedigree, gold, estates, and all—and then he was turned into a sex demon by a mistress who thought he needed basic nooky training. And then, two hundred years later, he'd turned up in Jewel's life. Gorgeous, arrogant, now brilliant in bed, dirt broke, and unemployable in the twenty-first century.

Clay had turned up in her life at the same time. It was testimony to his con-man skills that he was now her partner and not behind bars. Jewel never worried about Clay.

But the competition thing worried her.

It was barely seven o'clock, but the complainant had a funeral to go to that morning, and she'd insisted on speaking to an investigator. Jewel led the team up to the house, a solid red brick two-story bungalow with beautiful stained-glass windows in front, and knocked on the door.

"Best behavior," Jewel said sternly. The door opened. She said, "Mrs. Othmar?"

A tough-looking old battle-ax in a long black cocktail dress looked her up and down. "I am."

"I'm Senior Investigator Heiss with the Chicago Department of Consumer Services. We're responding to a complaint you made through your alderman."

Mrs. Othmar said stuffily, "I made no complaint."

Oookay. Jewel backed up a step and checked the house number over the door. "Pardon me, ma'am, but it came down to us from the mayor himself. We take your concerns seriously."

Mrs. Othmar seemed about to shut the door in their faces and then she didn't. "Come in."

She led Jewel's team into a dim, cool living room full of antiques. She thawed when she got a load of Randy's dark blue Armani. "Please sit down."

Jewel took a deep breath. "According to our report, you told your alderman that a man from the Department of Inspectional Services came to your door two days ago and asked to see your smoke detectors and electrical boxes. He found something unusual in your basement—"

"There's nothing down there," Mrs. Othmar snapped, and Jewel thought, *Uh-huh. Not anymore.*

"And when he found it, he told you he would condemn your property if you did not remediate within ten days. He also said that remediation probably wouldn't work."

"He said it would cost ninety thousand dollars!" Mrs. Othmar said indignantly. "That's ridiculous! Even asbestos remediation doesn't cost that much."

Patiently Jewel resumed, "Then he suggested that since you couldn't afford remediation and it wouldn't work anyway, you should sell your property to a man he knew who buys such houses and remediates them on the gamble."

"Search my house," Mrs. Othmar said in a shrill voice. "You won't find any such thing."

Randy had a faraway expression. Clay tapped his knee. Randy shook his head.

Jewel said, "That won't be necessary, Mrs. Othmar. We'll take your word for it."

That made Mrs. Othmar blink.

My sex demon is a walking hinky detector. He would know if there was anything on the premises.

"Do you happen to recall the man's name? The man who visited your home? Or the name of the man he said would buy it?"

Mrs. Othmar was still blinking. "I think Joseph? Samuel? Something biblical. It was on a patch on his windbreaker. The windbreaker was blue," she added helpfully.

"Did he show you any identification?"

"Naturally. I insisted." More blinks. "But unfortunately I don't recall—"

"How about the guy who buys hinky—who buys houses?"

"He gave me a card for that man. I've been looking for it."

Jewel's hopes collapsed. "If you find it, will you phone me? I'd like to see it." Mrs. Othmar still seemed upset.

"Do you happen to know if he visited any other homes on your block?"

"I asked around," Mrs. Othmar said. "He hadn't. That's why I complained to my alderman. It was as if he chose me to bilk." She was plenty mad about that. "He must have expected a fool."

"Well, he knows better now," Jewel said.

That pleased her. "Of course I complained immediately."

It took twenty more minutes to get out of there.

On the way to the car Jewel said, "She got rid of the pocket zone after she complained and before we got here."

"Ten four," Randy said.

She socked him on the arm. "I'm cutting off your television privileges until you can drive sanely." She got them onto Lake Shore Drive. A faint haze of pink smog hung over the Drive, promising a doozy of a morning traffic jam.

"What *is* a pocket zone, anyway?" Clay said. "Other than something the city can condemn your house for."

"A pocket zone is a little patch of unreality. A—a hinky spot." She still found it hard to say the word *magic*.

"How big a spot?"

"Depends. They say Pittsburgh started with a pocket zone on a single seat on a commuter train. They don't know if some guy died there, or if a teenager had her baby there, or what. It spread through the train, and they think somehow the train spread it across the city. Pocket zones formed in places along the rail lines and the expressways. Nobody knows for sure, and the people who know the most are behind the yellow-striped barricades."

"That makes it kind of tricky to gather information, doesn't it?" Clay drawled.

"Don't get me started on how the feds 'fix' things."

"So the city will condemn a place with a pocket zone on it?"

"First I've heard about it. Inspectional Services should have reported it directly to me." She frowned out the windshield at two teenagers in Grant Park who were holding up lighters and giggling, trying to coax a pigeon to bring a cigarette butt close enough to light it. "But if it's hinky, it stays hinky, doesn't it? Randy? You didn't feel anything on her premises?"

He shook his head.

"So somebody has figured out how to, what? Fake a pocket zone? Let's report to Ed. I need coffee."

They were stopped dead at the light at Jackson Boulevard.

"I thought I was to drive," Randy whined. "How may I acquire a license without practice?"

"Oooh, all right." Out of misguided pity, she switched seats with him. While she made notes on her clipboard, she overheard snatches of conversation from the front seat.

"Darn, she's moody. You didn't stork her, did you?" Clay said to Randy. "Go straight here. You can get off at Randolph."

"Give her a slip on the shoulder? No."

"You're awfully positive."

"A sex demon knows these things. I see every part of her."

"Too much information. Turn right here. Wait, wait! Wait for the light!" The car jerked to a stop. "Now you can go." The car jerked forward. "Wait for this guy to turn." The car stopped. Clay called from the front seat, "Stay calm back there! We're just building a little right-of-way awareness!"

Jewel shut the file, laid it on the car seat beside her, and covered her eyes.

She wasn't calm. She was jonesing for coffee, tired, hungry, annoyed, afraid for her life, and, under all of that, horny. Maybe it was sitting in a car with two men she'd had sex with recently. Clay claimed he didn't want to mess up their work partnership by sleeping with her, but he'd had two shots at it on their last undercover case. He wasn't bad, either. And he never, ever stopped competing with Randy.

Randy, of course, did her with mind-blowing magical sex-demon tricks every single night.

For some reason, dating two guys was exhausting her. Since she'd hit the city she'd dated uncountable men, bedded and dumped them. When that got scary she stopped, and, just when the pressure had built to the internal combustion point, she'd found Randy and rescued him from sexual slavery to a brass bed. And now he was *her* sex slave. Though Jewel might as well be his slave, since he lived with her, worked with her, and haunted her dreams.

Add a manipulative sneakypants for a partner. Put them all in a car. Clamp the lid on and shake—

The car bounced heavily. She bit her tongue. "Ow!"

"My apologies!" Randy called.

"Be careful!"

The car hit a pothole. Jewel almost swallowed her tongue.

"My apologies!"

CHAPTER 2

By eight they had made it to the Kraft Building. Jewel left Randy with the car and dragged her butt and her partner into the Department of Consumer Services staff room, only to find every one of her colleagues plastered against the east windows.

"Gimme the field glasses."

"C'mon, I saw them first!"

"There goes her shirt! Hoo boy!"

"Me, me, let me see!"

Clay strolled up to the nearest peeper, who happened to be their boss, and calmly took the field glasses out of his hands. "Where are they?"

"Hey!" Ed said, turning.

"Eighth floor of the Darth Vader building," Digby said, indicating the seventy-story black-glass condo monster across Lake Shore Drive, which had earned its name by looming dark and ugly against the shoreline.

"Third time this week," Sayers said.

"You people are disgusting." Embarrassed for the anonymous naked people in the Darth Vader window, Jewel turned away.

She poured herself a cup of stale coffee and took a cinnamon cow plop off the pile of pastry next to the coffeepot. The coffee sucked, as usual, but the plate-sized pastry disk was so sensuously cinnamony, so addictively crumbly and crunchy, it made her swoon.

"Gimme those." Ed snatched the field glasses back from Clay and trained them on the black curve of the Darth Vader. "Damn. Those rings in her nipples?"

"You wouldn't catch me piercing myself. I fainted when they did my ears," Britney said.

"Ouch," Tookhah agreed.

"Pussy," Lolly said.

"That's harassment," Finbow grunted, cupping his hands around his eyes and fogging up the window.

"Girls can call each other pussy. *You* gotta watch your mouth," Merntice said, folding her opera glasses and tucking them in her cardigan.

"Jewel, you gotta see this," Jason called.

Jewel yawned. "I don't have to watch sex, Roller Skates. At least *I* know what it looks like."

"Clay leave you any sleepytime?" Britney said. "Or was it that hunky Englishman?"

"Hunk," Jewel said. Clay looked at her with annoyance in his face. "I don't sleep with my partner," she added, putting out her tongue at him. *Much*, she thought.

Ed stuck the field glasses up in the air with both hands. "Jesus mother Mary, don't you women have any discretion?" He came away from the window, glaring at Clay. "Can't you do nothin' about her mouth?"

Jewel looked at her boss with patience. "You are so lucky I am not recording this conversation."

"Get in my office," Ed said.

In his office he slapped a file across his desk to Jewel. "That shit out there." He made an Italian gesture with thumb and two fingers. "Been going on all over town. Some broad from a real estate company complained anonymously over the weekend to three-one-one," he said, referring to the city's hotline for consumer concerns.

"They had a orgy in her office four days ago. She thinks the boss put Viagra in the coffee urn."

Oh, brother. Why did hinky stuff so often come coupled with sex? "This is not my problem."

Ed looked at her under his bushy eyebrows. "She says people were flying around the conference room naked."

Jewel's heart sank. "So the boss put Viagra and LSD in the coffee urn."

"Nope. Lab test came back negative."

"Actually flying," Jewel said.

"It's hinky," Ed said flatly. "Yours. We wouldn't of taken the case at all, only the PD was in there that very day for a disorderly. No charges filed."

"Why not?" Clay said.

She said, "Yeah, if the cops thought it was worth coming out for, why didn't they send the case over at the time? How come I get it stale?"

"The owners of the company are connected."

"Oh, God." Jewel groaned. "What do you want me to do?"

"Go in undercover. Sniff around. You find anything beyond this isolated incident, it's your problem. Otherwise find out who filed the complaint and smooth her down, shut her up."

Jewel grumbled under her breath, but she took the file, feeling more cheerful. She'd been undercover twice in the past month and loved every minute of it.

Ed leaned forward. "Now, what did you get in the Eleventh Ward?"

"A wash," Jewel said. "She doesn't have a pocket zone and she never had a pocket zone and she wouldn't know a pocket zone if it bit her on her Junior League heinie, but she's thrilled to be of assistance to the Department."

"She give you any names?"

"Nope." Jewel tossed aside the orgy file. "What gets me is, it sounds like IS really did pay her a visit. And they had the balls to diagnose a pocket zone and threaten to condemn her place within ten days, as if that was, like, Policy, which it totally is not. How come I never heard about it?"

The Hinky Policy was, "Cope, Don't Tell." Jewel's tiny division enforced it.

Ed said, "*They're* in violation of Policy. All hinky investigation should come through your division. Trouble is, nobody talks about the Policy, so it kinda slid by."

"Fake pocket zones. How can you fake that? And why?"

"Money." Clay shot Jewel a keen, blue-eyed glance under his bangs. "Somebody wants to buy that specific property cheap so he can sell it high."

Ed grunted. "And it's a snap it ain't his first victim. Mrs. Whatserface was just the toughest nut they met so far. If they keep at it, we'll catch up with 'em."

Leafing through the file, Jewel said, "Any feds involved?"

"Nope. But if we get too many pocket zones, even fake ones, the feds'll find out, and the whole city could end up with a yellow-striped necktie. That would be bad," Ed said heavily. "Only last week, they closed off four square blocks of Hollywood, California, best part of the tourist district."

Clay's eyes widened. "That's expensive real estate."

"So this means what?" Jewel said. "Somebody covets Mrs. Othmar's lobelia bed?"

"Da mayor wants it worked out on the quiet. Since the key is the hinky stuff, you're elected."

"I know, I know."

"Let me look into it," Clay said. "I'm good at following paper trails."

Ed nodded. "At's what I figured. Both of youse can track the pocket zones, and Heiss can take the orgy thing."

Jewel dragged herself back to the coffee urn for a refill. The cow plops were gone, so she scored a doughnut.

The peep show seemed to be over. Her coworkers were off to their rounds: Weights and Measures to the delis and gas stations, Taxis to O'Hare inspection or home to test response times, Immigration to their undercover stings, Credit Card Fraud to burrowing into their mountains of paperwork. Maxwell Street detail went back to the land of hot dogs and cheap tee-shirts, Child Support to their phones. Target Investigations was wrapping up a big identity-theft case, organizing evidence for indictments.

Jewel had been like them once, rotating from duty to duty, learning new scams, busting new crooks, keeping up with every possible way Chicago could protect its citizens from chicanery, sharp practice, and other forms of financial abuse.

Now she was going undercover to find out if some secretary had been dropping acid, or if the wave of daytime sex enlivening the summer had its root in something hinky.

Later that morning Jewel presented herself at the offices of Baysdorter Boncil, a real estate development firm located within eyeshot of Neiman Marcus. It was like walking into a cigar box. The walls were rare mahogany below the chair rail and ornate, tan-flocked, Skokie-baroque wallpaper above. Every window office had a kind of corral in front of it made of the same expensive wood, and inside every corral sat a beautiful girl at a computer. Checking out the secretaries in their flirty little I'm-a-virgin-but-I'm-desperate-not-to-be dresses, Jewel knew her navy polyester pantsuit was not adequate.

In fact, it seemed nothing about her was adequate.

The complainant was a Ms. Sacker, who turned out to be the office manager. As arranged, she interviewed Jewel for a temp job—Jewel's cover—behind closed doors. Maida Sacker had that pinched blondeness that doesn't age well. Her pastel skirt suit was just a shade over into the desperate zone, with white eyelet at her suit collar and in the bosom of her low-cut, hot-pink shell. Her makeup was perfect, if bland. Jewel felt more like a dairy-farmer's daughter than ever.

Ms. Sacker said, "It is very important, Ms. Heiss, that management doesn't know about your presence at Baysdorter Boncil."

"Good thing, if one of them put Viagra in the coffee. You were present for the incident?"

Ms. Sacker said, "I wasn't involved in the—the incident. I discovered it."

"You don't seem comfortable. Shall we meet outside of work?"

Ms. Sacker scowled.

Boy, that must have been some orgy. "I understand that there were, ah, hinky elements. Magical," Jewel added, when Ms. Sacker raised her penciled eyebrows. "You suspect that management was involved."

Silence.

And now Ms. Sacker doesn't want to talk about it. Jewel said, letting understanding into her voice, "If there is a corporate culture of abuse, I'm not the right officer to prosecute it, but I can certainly go between for you. *Is* that a problem here at Baysdorter Boncil?"

Ms. Sacker pressed her bloodless lips together.

Okay, that was an admission that some shit was going down. Jewel realized she was dealing with a tricky legal moment. As a woman and as office manager, over the girls but under the men in the window offices, Ms. Sacker was in an equivocal position.

"Are you telling me there was a rape? Were you"—she tried to soften her manner—"were you raped, Ms. Sacker?"

"No!" Ms. Sacker turned her head and glared, apparently at a Lucite teamwork trophy sitting on her sideboard.

Through the floor-to-ceiling window by the door, Jewel spotted a dark suit, a pale face. "Date rape counts. Coercion, even subtle coercion without the threat of force, counts. If your employer exerts pressure—"

"There may have been drugs," Ms. Sacker burst out.

"Date-rape drugs also count."

"I can't discuss that here," Ms. Sacker said.

"O-kay. Can we proceed with the portion of this discussion you are willing to have?"

The door burst open. A sleek, forty-something man in an expensive suit swept in.

Ms. Sacker snapped, "I'm busy, Mr. Tannyhill."

"This won't take long, Maida," the man called Tannyhill said. He flicked a glance at Jewel and then away, as if she didn't register on his people-o-meter.

Maida Sacker looked up at him. "This is the new temp. You remember Mr. Boncil said we might—"

"Mr. Boncil approved it. I didn't."

Jewel pretended to be fascinated with the teamwork award.

"Mr. Boncil is the firm's principal," Ms. Sacker came back.

There was a prolonged silence. Jewel noticed a Band-Aid on the back of Maida's left hand.

Without breaking eye contact with Tannyhill, Ms. Sacker handed Jewel a glossy maroon folder with *Baysdorter Boncil* embossed on it.

Jewel looked in the folder. It was empty except for a yellow sticky note: *Billy Goat at six*.

"Are you the boss now, Maida?" Tannyhill said nastily.

Jewel thought for a minute that Ms. Sacker would cave. Then the woman stood up slowly and looked Tannyhill in the eye.

To Jewel's surprise, Tannyhill left.

Maida Sacker turned a face of covert triumph to Jewel. "It's difficult for me to talk about possible negative aspects of our corporate culture. Part of my job is keeping those aspects under control and preventing them from becoming public knowledge. Those are two very different tasks. Depending—"

"Whether the cut-up is a boss or a secretary. Or both."

Maida closed her eyes. "Administrative assistant. Let's get on with our entry interview." Her lips twitched. "Can you type?"

Luckily for Jewel's patience, Maida handed her over to Sharisse, one of the secretaries, *I beg your pardon, administrative assistants,* for orientation, after it was established that, yes, Jewel knew her way around a computer. Sharisse showed Jewel her own corral and made sure she could find the files she would need. Pretty girls in fragile, girlish, well-tailored outfits passed by, one at a time. Sharisse introduced the new temp. Jewel felt like a milch cow trying to pass for a racehorse.

Sharisse was the assistant of Hugh Boncil, surviving partner and now the only principal since old John Baysdorter had handed in his dinner pail. In a confidential tone she informed Jewel that Mr. Tannyhill, who had been "First Senior" for years, whatever that meant, would soon add his name to the company.

"Lovely. And I care because?" Jewel snarled before she could get control of her mouth.

Sharisse looked at her with huge, shocked eyes. "But you're Steven's temporary assistant."

Jewel whistled. Maida hadn't had the nerve to tell her this. Either that or Maida had a sadistic sense of humor. Jewel stared at Sharisse and wondered which of them was getting punished, the undercover temp or Mr. Tannyhill. "That dickhead is my boss?"

A tiny smile creased the corners of Sharisse's mouth.

Jewel whispered, "I don't suppose you drink mudslides."

Sharisse dimpled. "Maybe Wednesday lunch?"

"It's a date."

Sharisse was a lot more relaxed after this, and Jewel began to see past her glossy finish to the shy, earnest girl underneath. She sat with Jewel in her new corral and

helped her puzzle through the paperwork stacked up in
Steven Tannyhill's assistant's tray.

Steven showed up at length, striding right past Jewel
into the window office behind her, swinging a briefcase
as if it were a tennis racket. In spite of his attempt to
bully Maida Sacker this morning, his taut, well-groomed
machismo appealed to Jewel. He gave off the message, *I
can have any woman in this room.*

This was not to be encouraged.

"Yo, temp," he commanded casually, sticking his head
out of his office. "Call me a cab."

Sharisse glanced sideways at Jewel.

Jewel called back to him, "Is your finger broken? Call
it yourself."

Sharisse gasped.

Steven stared at Jewel, his head showing past the door
sideways like a hound dog peering around a fence. A
puzzled smile crossed his face. He sighted along
his pistol-finger. "Bang." Then he disappeared into his
office.

"Holy shit," Jewel said. "That guy is spoiled rotten."

Sharisse tittered. "C'mon on, Jewel, tell us how you
really feel." She seemed more shocked by Jewel's language than by her defiance to the next partner of BB. She
whispered, "He doesn't treat his girl near as nice as the
other guys do."

Jewel would have asked a question, but at this moment an older man walked up to her corral and laid an
age-spotted hand on the top rail. He said cozily,
"Sharisse, honey, did I give you that Franklin letter?"

Sharisse looked up with a dazzling smile. "You did,
and I finished it. It's in your briefcase."

"Thanks. No, don't get up, I'm fine." He patted the
mahogany rail as if it were Sharisse's head. "You just
keep on with what you're doing." With a pleasant,
denture-assisted smile, he strolled on.

"My boss," Sharisse said with pride. "Mr. Boncil." There was a funny little tone in her voice, and Jewel turned to look searchingly at her.

Sharisse raised her eyebrows. "What?"

"You're sleeping with him," Jewel blurted. Then she shook her head. "Never mind." She'd never get the informant outside of a pitcher of mudslides this way. "Sorry I spoke."

Sharisse went back to the file she was sorting. "I'm a single mother," she said quietly.

"I see," Jewel said, wondering what the hell she had stepped into. And, because of those yet-undrunk mudslides, she added, "Of course."

CHAPTER 4

"Might I indeed be arrested for driving with too much spirit?" Randy said to Clay as they waited in Jewel's Tercel for Jewel to get off work.

Clay shrugged. "I guess."

"But on television only criminals and comely women are detained for driving."

"Sadly, life is not enough like TV. I wish she wasn't doing this stupid job." In Clay's view, undercover should take place only in the haunts of the rich and famous.

It was four-thirty. Men in fancy suits came out of the office tower, looking at their fancy watches, talking on their phones. They jumped into cabs or private cars or marched briskly into the bar on the street level of the tower.

Clay drummed on the steering wheel. "Where's all the women?"

"Is that why I am not permitted to drive this evening?" Randy said with an edge in his voice. Good, it was about time he started acting needled. Clay had been needling him for nearly three weeks, since the end of the last job. He'd begun to think the haughty Englishman had no nerves at all.

When Clay didn't answer, Randy said dryly, "Perhaps I drive not too badly but too well."

Bingo. *The mark takes the fly.* "It's rush hour, dude," Clay said in a kinder tone. "You'd hash it, and she would hate that. Didn't they have traffic cops when you came from?"

"We had no traffic control of any kind. Bow Street Runners had more important things to do than to harass gentlemen for the speed of their horses." Randy was silent a moment. "I once drove from London to Brighton in four and a half hours. Not at 'rush hour,' as you call it. By moonlight, before dawn. Match bays, two teams, one stabled in town, one on the Brighton road." He sounded wistful and off-guard.

"Fast, huh. How fast was considered fast?"

"Sixteen miles an hour at a canter. Faster if you put 'em along, but one could not, of course, spring 'em in town."

"And you never hit anything?"

"I was no whipster," Randy said with amusement. "Any man may own blood cattle if he can afford them, but he won't drive them hard more than twice. Horses are tricksier than cars."

"Cars are hard," Clay said indignantly. "Try handling a clunker like this on the expressway in the rain at rush hour."

"It's not raining now."

Clay let that remark lie between them a couple of beats. "Don't think I don't know what you're up to."

"I want to drive. There is no subterfuge."

Clay huffed. "Criminy! All right, all right." He switched seats with Randy.

Randy settled behind the wheel with a satisfied little wiggle.

"Seat belt," Clay said.

"We are stationary."

"Seat belt."

"Such petty tyranny," Randy said.

"It's the law."

"Which you honor so much."

Clay said with as much annoying patience as possible, "A con artist has the sense not to get busted for a lousy seat-belt charge."

At that moment the office building started tossing out dozens and dozens of women. Out they poured, fat ones, skinny ones, tall ones, short ones, every single one dressed like a real female, high heels flashing, all legs and hair and flirty clothes, chattering and giggling and shouldering against each other through the door of the bar on the street level.

Clay sighed. "Ed should have sent me in there."

Randy looked at his watch. "She's late."

"She's the boss. And she won't let you drive."

"She wants me to acquire independence."

"The least you could do is stay home once in a while and, like, do the laundry or something. Run the vac. Cook dinner."

"If you have tired of teaching me," Randy said pointedly, "I will ask her."

"All right, all right. Let's work on your identity. What's your social security number?"

"Two zero four, nine one, nine eight five three."

"Born?"

"Guam, 1980."

"Employment?"

Randy paused. "Companion," he grated.

"I'm thinking we change that to houseboy," Clay said thoughtfully. "A companion doesn't skank off and bone the suspect in the middle of an undercover operation and then disappear for days when the person he's companioning needs backup," he said, referring to how Randy had messed up on their last undercover case.

"*You* found my absence convenient," Randy said, now sounding pissed off.

"I certainly did. Jewel knows who she can count on. Plus, she's good company," Clay said, alluding delicately to the fact that he'd got Jewel into bed twice while Randy was waiting for Jewel to rescue him from being magically trapped in the suspect's bed. "I was surprised you gave us a chance for quality time—surprised and grateful."

Randy grunted.

Clay pushed. "I've been meaning to ask you, how many times did you do my stepmother while you were haunting that bed?"

"I never kiss and tell," Randy said dryly, and Clay felt himself go hot. "She's a charming woman."

Sheesh! So Clay had a little Oedipal something for his stepmother. Randy sure knew where to stick the knife in. Clay said with less than his usual finesse, "One thing Jewel told me. She can't wait to get you shut of this curse thingy. She's sick of having you underfoot."

"I'm sick of the curse myself. Perhaps when I am shut of it, and can support myself, I'll be able to woo her in form."

"*Woo* her!" Clay blurted. "Is that what you call it? Sending her to work bowlegged every morning?"

The one area where he felt definitely outclassed was this sex-demon thing. If Jewel had been one of these giggly virgins clattering out of this office tower on high heels, she'd have tried Randy for one night and never slept on that brass bed again.

On the other hand, if Jewel was one of those virgins, Clay wouldn't be the least bit interested.

"Do you call what you do wooing?" Randy sounded genuinely curious.

Clay didn't have an answer to that one. He'd put off closing the deal with Jewel a hundred times this summer, blaming Randy's eternal underfootedness. He couldn't pursue his interest in her until Randy was out of the way. Could he?

While he pondered this question, Jewel opened the driver's door of the Tercel. "Out."

"Clay said I might drive," Randy said, sounding like a four-year-old.

"Not after yesterday's performance. Out." She seemed to be in a temper.

They played musical car seats. Clay got out and got into the back seat. Randy took the front passenger seat, looking smug.

Clay felt pretty smug, too. *Let him think he has an advantage, sharing the front seat with her when she's like this.*

Randy could take the edge off her.

And then Clay could soothe her.

Jewel got in, handed her purse to Clay in the back seat, and banged the door. "Morons."

Nobody said anything while she turned on the traffic report, then switched to "Ask Your Shrink."

Ask Your Shrink was taking call-ins. "—*Wife is never interested! Is that fair?*"

"*No, it isn't,*" said the soothing voice of Your Shrink. "*You could take her to dinner or a spa. Offer her chocolate. Get her drunk.*"

"*It's ruining my marriage!*"

"*Or, if the marriage is more important than the sex, you can try taking saltpetre to match your libido levels to hers—*"

Jewel slapped the radio button to off.

"How was your first day at work?" Clay said.

"Sucked. My boss is hot and knows it, the girls screw their bosses, and the office manager is a wimp. My best informant so far is taking child support, and pipe, from a man forty years too old for her."

"It must have been bad."

"Why do you say that?" she said dangerously, changing lanes and cutting off a taxi.

"You're driving crazy."

"Fucking moron!" she yelled at the taxi.

"And swearing."

"Forced abstinence. Those girls—" She snorted. "I'd call them women, but they're so desperately afraid to seem adult. They get sexually harassed, they dress up like ice cream frappès to fucking type and answer the phone, they sneak and they backbite and they get chewed up in politics between the white guys in suits, and then they lose their rag because I cuss a little."

"Sexually harassed?" Randy said.

"So is that where the orgy came from?" Clay said.

"I have no friggin' idea. The slick willy I work for is part of it. What do these motherfuckers *think*? This is their own personal private stag movie? Sunday driver!" She slapped the horn and leaned on it. "Jesus Christ on a bicycle!"

Clay leaned forward from the back seat and slid his hand over her mouth.

She shut up.

"It must be bad," he said. "You're channelling Ed." He pulled his hand back, peeked—her lips worked— then he slid his hand back over her mouth.

Randy said critically, "Ed's diction during a seizure is more elaborate."

"Funkier," Clay agreed. "More creative."

"Sometimes he fails to blaspheme," Randy said.

"And when he's really upset Ed doesn't use the F-word. I think he actually forgets it," Clay said.

"Difficult to believe," Randy said.

Behind Clay's hand, he felt Jewel smile. He took his hand away and relaxed into the back seat. "So, the orgy. What do you know?"

She drove silently for a minute. "I don't know. There's a woman I can talk to at lunch Wednesday. Maybe more, once I've been around the place. I made a lot of friends by telling Steven to call his own cab today. Of course

that's why I may not be working there by Wednesday."
She looked at her watch. "Plus I'm meeting the complainant at six at the Billy Goat."

"What is sexual harassment?" Randy said.

This should be good, Clay thought.

"It's something you could learn more about, roomie,"
she said to Randy. "When someone puts unwanted moves
on a coworker or subordinate." She stopped the Tercel
at the light. "Any kind of unwanted advances, a look, a
verbal approach. Touching, exhibitionism, showing her
feelthy pictures."

"You see me as one who tampers with chambermaids?"
Randy said, going lord on her.

Jewel said calmly, "I think that a guy who has been a
stealth fuck to more than a hundred women over the
past two centuries might not realize how important consent is to a woman."

In the back seat, Clay's ears flapped.

"I always obtain consent," Randy grated.

"Oh, bull. You can't take 'no' for an answer. Prying
into her dreams—and disguising yourself as whatever
she wants—is not the same thing as asking, in English,
under circumstances that allow her to refuse freely—"

"I take 'no' from you!"

"—Allow her to refuse *without consequences*," Jewel
said, raising her voice. "I'm not going to argue this with
you."

Randy shut up.

Darn. Just when Clay was getting a nice clear view into
something he'd been dying to know about for months.

Clay glanced at her in the rearview mirror. In her navy
polyester, with her chin sticking out and her eyes ablaze,
she looked all cop. Very hot.

After a million years they got to the bottom of Michigan Avenue and Jewel surrendered the car, not without misgiving, to Randy. She took the ferry stairs down to Lower Mich and made her way through the bowels of the Wrigley Building to the Billy Goat, a newspapermen's hangout that was everything Dick's Last Resort wanted to be: rude, grubby, greasy, smoky, and short on elegance. Way at the end of the bar, Maida Sacker perched on a stool, knees together, in front of a double highball.

Jewel ordered a beer and then lunged for an emptying booth. Maida joined her.

"Okay, tell me about the orgy. Who was behind it?"

Maida leaned forward. The highball was full, but her breath was 180 proof. Her second, then. "I have an educated guess. Since Mr. Baysdorter passed away, the corporate culture has become a little, um, destabilized."

"You mean Baysdorter kept the boys in line?"

"He must have," Maida blurted. "Steven—Mr. Tannyhill has always expressed himself very freely." *Translation, he propositioned all the girls.*

"So it was Superstud Steven?"

"The pressures on him are much higher, now that he's in line to be second partner." Maida frowned. "And recently he inherited part of Artistic Publishing Company— a family business." Her mouth soured. "He always comes back from there in a poor humor. Mr. Boncil has remarked on it."

Jewel thought of single-mother Sharisse. "That reminds me. Mr. Boncil is doing his girl, too. Don't make a face, she didn't say anything. I just saw it. It was in his smile. The way he didn't touch her. Who else, besides those two?"

Maida covered her mouth with both hands.

"You're positive it's Steven, then?"

Her eyes pleaded with Jewel.

"But you don't know how he did it, or why it was hinky."

No answer. *I'm screwing this up.*

"Listen, you really might want the EEOC. I'm here because you said there was something hinky about the orgy. That's my division," Jewel said bitterly. "If it was just Viagra in the coffee, you could get a harassment expert, but since it was magic, you get me."

"No! No one else! I can't risk it." Maida took a deep breath, then a slug of her highball, then another deep breath. "He—it was under control for a long time. I don't know what's got into hi—them."

Jewel caught the slip, but she didn't pounce. She said as gently as she could, "You can't just hire me to throw a scare into the white guys, Maida. You've called in the city over hinky phenomena. That doesn't go away. Regardless of the stink, I'm here until I find out what happened, and decide that I can be reasonably sure it won't happen again."

Maida sipped. "Understood."

"And you can't blame yourself for the way bosses behave. Though I admit I'm a little sickened by the dress code. Those girls dress like victims."

Maida glanced at Jewel's navy polyester pantsuit with a shudder. "Perhaps you're right."

"Okay, I get the message." Jewel rolled her eyes. "I'll find something girly to wear tomorrow."

An almost-human smile twisted on Maida's lips. "Don't bother. Even in appropriate attire I expect you'd, uh, stand out. Telling a senior to call his own cab!" She tittered. " 'Is your finger broken?' " She seemed thrilled and horrified.

"That's made me, huh?" Reluctantly Jewel grinned.

"Maybe you're helping more than you think."

"Even if I dress and talk like a cop?"

With a sigh, Maida said, "You might put heart into the girls," as if that was the one thing she hoped Jewel could accomplish. She slugged back her highball and got up. "I can't be seen with you." She put a twenty on the table and whisked away to the ladies' room in back.

Interview over.

She may not have meant me to interpret that last remark as blanket permission to interrogate the employees. But I'm gonna assume she did.

CHAPTER 5

"You once told me," Randy said that night, as they put clean sheets on the bed in Jewel's apartment, "that you had a family attorney in Homonowoc who became your lover."

"I don't remember telling you that," Jewel said guardedly.

"You said he was a septuagenarian. Now you say that this young woman has accepted the patronage of her employer, who is 'forty years too old for her.' That troubles you?"

"So?"

Randy looked at her across the half-made bed. "In what way," he said patiently, "is her situation different from yours?" He twitched the sheet out of her hand and shook it out.

Jewel smiled. *Old Liddy Lidheimer.* There was a forgotten name. Her belly softened at the thought of him.

Randy flicked the blanket over the bed. When the pillows were covered and piled up, he stepped out of his clothes and slid his big, wedge-shaped body between the sheets, looking at her expectantly. "Come, you are not so irreflective as you pretend."

Jewel got naked, slid down under the covers, and let her head sink into the pillow.

"I was seventeen. My grandmother died. Liddy, the

lawyer, Mr. Lidheimer, had been coming around, setting up a power of attorney for Gram. That was so I could keep the farm running while she was sick. I don't really know how it happened."

She turned out the bedside lamp and stared at the lines of streetlight striping the ceiling through the venetian blinds, remembering. She smiled.

"Liddy was there for me. He joshed me along when I was desperate. He liked me strong, you know." She turned her head on the pillow. "That's different from this poor girl at this office. She's so, so *flat*. So docile."

Randy didn't say anything.

"After Gram died I guess I did flatten out," she admitted. "Liddy cured me. He saw me through grief and panic and feeling abandoned. And he kept the farm title tied up in court while I sold the last crops and reduced the herd to a manageable size. And he nursed me—"

Her throat closed suddenly. She paused.

"Nursed me through selling the farm." She took a deep breath. "Liddy made me see I had to let it go. He helped me realize that I didn't want to be a dairy farmer. I was just holding onto it so I wouldn't feel so lost. He got the best price, a crazy big price, and he kept the law off me until I was legally of age to sign things. And he made me go to college." She looked at Randy, begging him to understand. "He *made* me go. He wanted the best for me."

"For a price. He was seventy. He despoiled a school-girl," Randy said in a critical tone.

"You're over two hundred and you've slept with more than a hundred women," she said, relaxing. "You've never said if any of them were jail bait."

"May I ask something?" She nodded, and he said, "How long were you faithful to him?"

"How do you know I was faithful to him?" She frowned, remembering. "He died while I was in college. It was in my first year, in spring. He hadn't even told me he was sick." She said in a harder voice, "Everybody who loves me dies."

"That's my line," Randy said, and she did a double take at the phrase. His big black eyes glittered. "So Liddy died, and you drowned your sorrows in a rakish career."

"Who the hell are you, my shrink?"

"What is a shrink?"

"A head-shrinker. A psychiatrist. I have no idea if they had shrinks in 1811, so I don't know what you would call it."

"A confessor." He laughed, and bowed his head. "I will not tease you to confess to me."

She smiled weakly. "Besides, you have other skills I need you for."

Now he looked serious. "Yes." He reached for her.

No sooner was she in his arms than Jewel began twitching. It was a mental twitch, invisible, she was sure, to Randy, but horribly perceptible to herself. Then the twitch moved into her legs, then in her arms, then her back. He pulled her close. The hairs on his thighs tickled hers, and then the twitch swooped into her crotch, where it stayed and drove her nuts.

I thought I was getting used to him!

She groaned aloud, a deep, sad groan with a lilt of panic at the end, because she knew what this restless feeling was about.

I can't be tired of him. That is simply not an option here.

If things were normal, if *he* was normal, he would be gone in the morning and she'd be free, free, free to have her life back. If things were the way they used to be, she could kick him out tonight, no comment, no questions asked or answered. He might call her for a few days, but she could choke him off, no problem. If he was a normal guy.

He's two hundred years old. He can see right through me.

Very tenderly, he touched her face with one hand.

He's trying to get closer and I'm terrified.

"I want it hinky tonight," she blurted.

His hand stilled. In the dim bedroom, with only street-light from twenty-three floors below coming across the ceiling through the slats of the venetian blinds, she thought his eyes got bigger and blacker.

Oh, right. He's a lord, too.

She tugged at his shoulders. "Come o-o-on. Take me to demonspace. You know I love it." When he didn't move, she added, "Pretty please?"

Now I'm catering to his ego. What's next? Playing dumb while he talks about da Bears?

But Randy relaxed. He drew his hand over the crown of her head, down over her face, his fingertips brushing her eyelids. "Sleep, Jewel."

And bang, she was asleep.

Snow, she thought, trudging naked up the front steps of the Field Museum over dirty old crusts of snow. *I'm sick of snow.* It was bone cold. A breeze off the lake carried icy razors in it, blowing six hundred miles down the lake from Canada.

Hope the museum's open. She couldn't feel her feet. She got to the enormous brass doors and peered through the glass. The museum was dark.

Turning, she saw the long front steps were empty, the exit for Roosevelt Road empty, Lake Shore Drive empty and bleached white by road salt. The breeze picked up and blew cold salt into her eyes until they watered.

The door opened behind her. Gratefully, she went in.

Somehow she was on the second-floor mezzanine, look-ing at the Malvina Hoffman bronzes of primitive man, as they called him back in the thirties, from around the world. The bronzes were her favorites, all rich red-brown and naked, every one seeming at peace in a world that made sense to them.

She reached out and rubbed the shiny bronze nose of a Podaung Burmese woman, proud in her rings and rings of necklaces, her eyes downcast as if saying, *See how much it'll cost you to marry me?*

One gallery was lit.

She wanted to keep walking around the second floor, visiting her old friends the Hoffman bronzes, but the light pulled her.

She walked under a marble arch and was instantly in warmth and light, in a long gallery she'd visited before, with glass cases in a rick-rack pattern that made nooks.

In the first nook, behind glass, Liddy stood, his old tweed jacket slung over his wrinkly birthday suit. His lawyer briefcase hung from his hand, one shoulder lifted higher than the other like always, and he smiled that old sweet smile that said, *Wanna make trouble?*

Her heart caught. Her belly went cold. Her eyes met his. She saw that he was twinkling at her. He was alive in there.

Her chest tightened. She backed away. For a flashing instant she dreamed she was running down the cavernous dark halls, screaming for a guard. *Didn't you know he's still alive?*

But she didn't run.

Feeling horrible but unable to face Liddy any longer, she moved to another nook. Here was a guy she'd dated in college. Smart-mouthed grad student from her dorm who'd thought that women got turned on if you insulted them. He stood naked in his glass case, prouder of his erection than he should have been.

She walked past.

The next case held another naked guy from college, a face only faintly familiar. His lips shaped her name.

Alive in there.

In the next, the pledging class from the Phi Kap house posed like so many statues of horny bare-assed Greek athletes. They grinned at her. Behind them stood cheerleaders all in a row, naked except for their pom-poms, giggling and shoving.

Oh, yeah, the cheerleaders. Lot of punch at that party.

The itch between her legs was turning hot and hard.

She walked faster.

Every case held somebody she'd dated.

There were dozens of them.

They were all alive.

This gallery had to end sometime. She knew it did. For one thing, she'd quit dating last year and spent six months in celibate hell. So this had to end somewhere.

She broke into a trot.

There, an opening at the end of this row. She ran toward it and found herself at the bottom of another long gallery just like the other one, full of glass cases full of naked men. They were all alive. They all looked at her. Beckoned to her. Showed her their rampant dicks. Some were crying. Some threw themselves against the glass and slobbered on it, beating it with their fists, yelling her name.

She picked up her feet and sprinted.

She burst out of the exhibit onto the mezzanine and bolted for the stairs. There was a uniformed guard at the corner of the stairs—well, finally—and he turned reproachful eyes on her.

Not a guard. A Chicago cop. One of maybe forty she'd dated.

As he reached for her she jinked past his outstretched arms, skidded, and leaped down the stairs two at a time, past marble statues that came to life as she passed.

Sobbing for air, she vaulted the turnstyle and escaped

into the freezing evening air on the front steps. The lake spread out before her, frozen, flat, and still. A full moon rose, splashing orange light over the ice. Untouched snow lay on the steps. Orange moonlight seemed to skip over the snow.

Someone stood on the verandah with her, half in the moonshadow of a big pillar, naked and shivering. His back was to her. He was watching the moonrise.

She breathed more slowly. Panic left her.

Okay, okay, I get it. They never go away.

He didn't move. *Have you ever wondered what my gallery might look like?*

No. Aren't you cold? she said.

He didn't answer.

Her body steamed. She took a step forward on the verandah. Snow melted under her foot.

He didn't turn when she slid her arms around him, but his shivering stopped.

She touched the front of her burning body to his back. His flesh felt chilled through. Pulling him back against her, she tried to pour the heat radiating off her straight into him. She stroked his face and down over his cold, bare body. When her hands reached his groin, she found all his heat.

He knelt, and she knelt with him, never letting go. Side by side they lay on the cold stone, the snow going to puddles under them, and she stroked him and pulled him warm. When she thought he would climax, he turned in her arms. *Finally.* She was aching for penetration. But he rolled over her until she was spooned, her back to his hot chest, looking out on the frozen lake, and he worked her with his hands while his schlong branded her back like a hot poker and the moon rose higher. His fingers dipped into her, penetrating, teasing, withdrawing, and extra hands tickled her nipples, and his teeth nibbled both her earlobes at once and his tongues licked into the hollow of her collarbone. She squirmed, *no, please, please fuck me*, and he flicked her clit with his thumb in a slow rhythm that made her arch like a fish. The moon seemed to swoop down out of the starry sky.

Now, for God's sake! Her eyes closed.

And in he came, long, thick, impossibly long, because he must be bending clear underneath her bottom, his chest pressed against her back.

With that deep penetration she heard a crackle like thunder. Her eyes flew open. The sky was sapphire clear. The moon pulled at her blood.

Please, she begged.

One more time, he did the impossible. Inside her his cock swelled, moving ever so slightly, not *hard* enough, not *far* enough. She arched again, squirming against his belly, whining. Then he shrank a bit, *oh, God, no*. Then his cock swelled. And shrank. She felt herself stretching, felt the blood pulse in her temples, felt her eardrums pop, as he pulsed larger and smaller, beating like a heart inside her, until she tightened around him.

Oh boy. Here it came.

Just as she was about to beg, his hot hand settled over her mound. A clever finger pressed down on her trigger.

She spasmed. His cock pulsed inside her. Thunder crackled, and a hundred miles of frozen lake convulsed, sending shards of ice high into the air, then falling, and frozen moonlight melted in slivers all over her thawing heart.

Afterward Jewel lay on her back, feeling the throbbing sink and fade while sweat dried on her skin.

Randy seemed asleep.

Reluctantly, she thought about his suggestion.

Was that really why she'd started her rampant college fuck-a-thon? Because Liddy had died, abandoned her, just like her parents and her grandparents? Would she have horndogged through the past seven years if he hadn't taken her to bed? If the family lawyer had been a woman? Would she even have sold the farm?

Maybe not. She might at this very moment still be wearing out her strength trying to keep the damned thing going, her back sore, her hands cracking from the contact with wet steel and the teets of stupid, needy cows.

To be fair, would Liddy have been able to distract her with anything besides sex?

She smiled at memory. He was so dry and funny, and he had enjoyed her youth and her smart mouth so gaily. He took this shell-shocked kid and coaxed her back into her humanity.

Randy spoke critically of a "price."

But Liddy hadn't made it seem like payment. He'd reminded her how to be alive. He taught her to feel her own pulse pounding and the sap rising in her veins. He'd told her to live gratefully.

Don't you ever do it for anything but the joy, my girl, Liddy had said. *The world runs on sex. There's no life without sex. Make sure you have fun at it.*

Liddy had taught her everything she ever learned about sex, the good parts anyway.

Until Randy came along.

She listened for Randy's steady breathing, felt his dense body weighing down the mattress beside her, and thought, *What the hell have I gotten into here?*

Twelve extremely irritating hours later, while she was at BB wrestling with a copy machine the size of her car, Ed phoned her.

"Heiss, get your ass up to the Kraft, right now. And call your partner."

"I'm in the middle of copying these damned proposals. Eighty pages, double-sided, two hundred copies, collated and stapled. Oh *shit*, another misfeed!"

Just then Maida Sacker walked past, holding a coffee cup as if it were the Sunday offering basket. As Jewel's cussword rang out, her head swivelled. She leaned into the copy room and shook a finger. "Language, Ms. Heiss."

"Myeh myeh myeh," Jewel muttered after her.

"I'm not kidding. This is an emergency." Ed sounded upset.

"Okay, okay. Let me get this d-arned thing piled up so I can figure out where I left it when I come back."

"Now. I need you here an hour ago. I need you yesterday."

"Okay!"

"Bring your driver." Ed ended the call.

Jewel frowned at the dead phone. In the three months Randy had been around, this was the first time Ed had expressed a desire for his company. "Why do I think this is not gonna be good?"

Clay and Randy met Jewel and Ed in the basement of the Kraft Building.

"What is this place?" Randy said.

Jewel never came down here. The basement was used as a lair by departmental retirees who had no life to retire to.

Clay wrinkled his nose. "Funky smelling."

"It's the locker room of the old cop shop," Ed said. "Ain't been PD property since before the Kraft was demolished. We kind of took it over."

"Not me," Jewel said, looking around fastidiously. The walls were painted that turkey-turd tan you always saw in cop shops, and the ranks of tall, battered lockers were bilious green. Flyspecks dotted the flickering fluorescent lights overhead. "Do you suppose this grime is from, like, all eighty years before the Kraft came down?"

"Gross," Clay said.

"Never mind. Take a look at this." Ed led them to a corner in front of a mangled locker door. He paused dramatically, looking over his shoulder at them, his black caterpillar eyebrows working. Then he opened the locker and leapt back as if it were full of rabid weasels.

Jewel came to stand next to him. "What—?"

On the floor of the locker was a pile of magazines.

The top shelf was packed full of crumpled white paper bags.

And in between, gyrating slowly like some kind of X-rated ballerina in a music box, a small, glistening, naked female figure danced, wiggled, simpered, beckoned, and silently giggled, like a burlesque movie with the sound turned off. She stuck her forefinger in her mouth and pulled it out slowly, sucking on it with pouty red lips. She raised one knee and stroked herself against her other thigh, arching her back, lolling her head, swinging her wheat-blonde, old-fashioned curly mane so that it played peek-a-boo with her heavy breasts. She had Marilyn's lush figure, and apparently a complete lack of shame. She was eighteen inches high.

Jewel was shocked, but it was actually kind of sweet. There was something hilariously wholesome and innocent about her sexual gyrating, as if the girl next door had just found out what sex was for and couldn't wait to show her boyfriend.

Clay whistled behind Jewel. "What is it? Three-D projection?"

The girl in the locker seemed to hear him. She cocked her head, looked straight at Clay, and laughed, shaking her mane at him, dipping and wiggling her breasts as if to say, *You silly boy, come over here and stick a twenty in my—*

"Holy. Shit." Ed sounded flabbergasted.

Jewel said, "It's a poppet. You get 'em in the really bad places." She'd never seen one this close before.

"Pittsburgh," Clay said.

"Shit," Ed repeated.

Jewel agreed. With a poppet in the Kraft Building, there was no longer any question whether the place was hinky enough to be condemned. The feds had shut all of Pittsburgh down for just a handful of these things.

Randy reached past Jewel and casually dipped his fingers through the figure. Jewel gasped. The poppet's image swirled and de-formed as if he had scooped up some honey. Then, when his fingers were gone, she slowly re-formed into her old shape.

"Magic," Randy said.

"Urk," Ed said.

Clay backed up. "How did you find this?"

"Remember O'Connor?" Ed said to Jewel. "Used to do immigration until he got too fat to move around. Then he phoned taxis from home."

Jewel remembered. "He's a wreck." O'Connor was the kind of drunk who never actually fell down, but he was never sober.

"He used to be a good investigator," Ed said. The Department was loyal to good people. "He came in once a week to collect his check. Sometimes he sat down here all day and played cards, shot the shit with the older guys. Smartened up the young kids if they was smart enough to let him."

"He's helped me a couple of times," she admitted. Then she noticed the past tense. "Oh."

"Yeah. He was found dead in his apartment this morning. One of the guys thought he might of left some gin money in the locker, so he bust it open."

Jewel cracked her first smile all day. "Let me guess. Sayers?"

"Yeah." Ed snorted. "Poor unlucky fuck."

A laugh escaped Jewel. She watched the naked girlie-girl in the locker do indecent things with no more props than her own outrageously proportioned body. "Did Sayers stroke out, or just stroke?"

"Talk like a lady, dammit." Ed frowned. "Sayers came up and told me, like he should. What I want youse to do is deal with this. Then go over to O'Connor's apartment and see if there's any clues. Find any more of it." Raptly, he stared. The tip of his tongue touched his lower lip. Then he shuddered. "Just deal with it! And come up to my office when you're done."

When he'd stumped out, Jewel looked at Clay. "Any ideas?"

Clay shrugged. "How should I know? Does it move from locker to locker? Can we just shut the door and forget about it? How did it get down here, anyway?"

"You're a big help."

"This is a pocket zone," Randy stated.

"Got it in one," Jewel said.

Clay watched the show. "Is it alive?"

"That remains to be seen," Randy said crisply. He shut the locker door as much as was possible—somebody had pried it open with a crowbar, destroying the combination lock in the process—and opened the adjacent locker, which was empty. Jewel watched with fascination. Randy ran his hand over the wall shared with the infested locker, then tapped it lightly, as if testing for stickiness. Then he opened the pocket zone locker again and stared expressionlessly at the small, very womanly figure inside.

"Well, Sherlock?" Clay said.

Ignoring Clay, Randy squatted and gingerly pulled out one of the magazines stacked in the locker. He handed it behind him.

Jewel grabbed it before Clay could. "*Girls, Giggles, and Garters*. What kind of magazine is that?"

Clay took it from her. "Tame porn." He flipped through, and she caught a glimpse of bare skin, black lace, red lace, bold eyes, bulging breasts. "Very, very lame, very tame porn."

"O'Connor was kind of a sweetheart," she said absently. She watched Randy tease a crumpled white bag out of the top shelf of the locker. Standing, he was much closer to that dancing *thing* in the lower compartment.

Jewel saw the poppet reach for him. It put its hands right through his jeans.

"Ohmigod! Randy!" Jewel shrieked.

Randy looked down and backed away, far too calmly in her opinion.

The girl in the locker pouted, looked sly, beckoned, and flirted at Randy with girl-next-door blue eyes.

Slowly he shut the door on her. "We must keep people out of here for now."

"That's a big yes," Jewel said. "Did you feel anything?"

Randy frowned. "Hard to say."

"Where the hell did Clay go?"

"Here," Clay said, coming back into the locker room with a roll of gray duct tape. "Will this do?" He tore off a strip.

Randy sealed the gaping steel edges shut. "Temporarily."

"Let's get upstairs," Jewel said. "See what else Ed knows."

Ed was sitting behind his desk when they came into his office, but he jumped up, looking relieved. "Shut the door. You're okay?"

"Peachy," Jewel said. Her skin prickled. "I don't think it can get any worse."

"It's already worse. That douchebag Bing Neebly called today. OED is interested in the Kraft." Ed looked at Clay. "Office for Economic Development. You know how we got this building?"

"Sure. It got torn down and then it came back like magic."

"Don't say that word," Ed said automatically. "And after all the legal shit settled, the city gave it back to Consumer Services, because everybody else was scared to move in. If you'd a seen the old quarters in River North, you'd understand why the Commissioner said yes. Like a sardine can."

"Shit," Jewel said, comprehension flashing on her. She turned to Clay and Randy. "This land is worth a lot of money, developed. But like this? It's just home to dopey old Consumer Services. OED must be slavering to get their hands on it."

Clay said, "So I don't get it. What's the scam? We have use of the building because everybody's scared because it, like, magically reappeared after demolition."

Jewel winced. "Don't say that word."

"But now that it seems to be safe, this OED wants to take it over and sell it," Clay said.

"Right," Ed said.

"But it isn't safe." Clay pointed at the floor and made a va-va-voom shape in the air with his hands. "So we won't lose the building after all."

"Not necessarily," Jewel said. "OED could call in the feds and have them condemn the building, thinking maybe they can nip in and cash in."

"Only with a poppet in the basement, that would backfire," Ed said. "If it's too hinky, the feds don't let you reuse the property. Could end up a bajillion-dollar hole in the ground."

Jewel scowled. "I can't believe they would do that. You can't get taxes out of a hole in the ground. Da mayor wouldn't thank OED for taking a property that rich permanently off the tax rolls."

"You don't know Bing Neebly," Ed said gloomily. "He used to work here, eight-ten years ago. Mumped freebies and peddled influence and sold favors all day. Everybody hated him. Then Taylor comes in and re-forms the department. Neebly cried woof to da mayor and moved over to OED just in time to avoid indictment. He'd put us out for a bent nickel."

"Everybody would lose," Clay mused, with an all-too-familiar, there's-money-in-here-somewhere-for-me look that Jewel dreaded. "The situation has possibilities."

Jewel shook herself. "Let's get over to O'Connor's place."

"And bring your hinky radar," Ed said, pointing at Randy.

Randy looked eager. She began to think he might earn his keep after all.

CHAPTER

7

Merntice gave them the address of O'Connor's apartment, and Jewel phoned ahead to the landlady, who sounded hysterical. The address was a yellow brick two-flat on north Kedzie in a formerly Bohemian neighborhood. The landlady and her husband met them on the front steps.

"Thank God you came. My husband had heart attack," she said. "I don't know vot to do!"

"I did not have a heart attack. You had a heart attack when you saw that thing. 'Cause you're a prude," her husband said.

"We're not paramedics, ma'am," Jewel said. "Do you want us to call you an ambulance?"

"No, no, ambulance already came and took away Mr. O'Connor." The landlady flipped her apron up to cover her eyes. "Go look. Up there. I give you the key."

"I'll show 'em," her husband said.

"You vill not! It's disgusting!" his wife said. She retreated behind the screen door of the first-floor flat.

Her husband gave a growl and mounted the stairs to the second floor with the key in his hand and Jewel's team on his heels.

"Whoa," Clay said, first through the door. "Funky."

Jewel pushed past him. It was beyond funky. The bachelor smell of old sweat socks and stale beer thwapped her like a county-jail pillow in the face. Magazines and newspapers were piled everywhere. Girlie posters wilted on the walls in the August heat. Jewel wouldn't have sat on the sofa for money, though clearly it had been O'Connor's favorite spot.

Over the funk, she smelled a sweet, flat, musty odor she recognized from hospitals, the smell of death. O'Connor had died here. She remembered him as a shapeless old fart hanging around the coffee station upstairs, and then, later, never getting above the basement lair where the other senior investigators gathered to play cards. He'd always winked at her. She hadn't minded.

"He was a great reader," Randy said, reaching for a magazine on a stack.

"Don't touch that!" she said too late.

As he lifted the magazine, another poppet sprang up. She looked just like the first one, blonde and wholesome, with innocent blue eyes, and a very naked body that she twisted and stroked. Jewel wanted to look away, but the poppet was too—too *much*. She felt herself blushing. She wished the landlord would stop leering at the damned thing and go downstairs.

"More smut," Randy said, leafing unconcernedly through the magazine. He turned it sideways, tipping his head at the fold-out. "Remarkable." He flipped past the centerfold.

Jewel eyed the poppet nervously. "Will it hurt us, do you think? Hey, Lord Perv. Can we do some work here?"

He looked up. "This is abysmally badly written."

Clay turned from picking over the piled bills on a huge wooden spool table. "You're *reading* the porn?"

Jewel rolled her eyes.

"Aubrey! You are coming down here!" the landlady screamed from the bottom of the stairs.

"You can go now," Jewel said to the landlord. He went.

Randy still couldn't get over the stories. "Moreover, this is grossly improbable. One would suppose, if they had nothing but sex to write of, they could make it plausible."

Clay said, "That's that lame porn again."

"What makes it lame?" Jewel said, to talk about anything except the teasing, flaunting pin-up poppet.

Clay said, "It's tame. It's old-fashioned. It's, like, porn for prudes. Nipples! Big whoop."

"And unlifelike drivel to boot." Randy rolled up the magazine, stuffed it in his back pocket, and squatted to face the poppet. "Nothing unlifelike about you, is there?" he murmured.

Jewel squinted at him. "This from the guy who did me on the porch of the Field Museum in the snow by moonlight?"

Clay glanced up suddenly from tossing through an overflowing wastebasket.

Jewel bit her lip.

"I," Randy said, without looking away from the poppet, "can make the impossible completely real. Not only do these illiterates have no imagination, but I suspect they don't even like sex." He reached out a finger and the poppet leaned forward to rub her round little breasts against it.

"You're pretty critical for a guy who would rather read porn stories than look at the pictures," Clay said unpleasantly. "You couldn't do any better."

"On the contrary," Randy began haughtily.

"I'm not staying here to listen to your antlers clashing." Jewel went into the kitchen.

Clay followed her. "You indulge him. He's getting unmanageable."

"Not like you. Good grief, look at this mess." The kitchen was worse than the living room. "Didn't the old guy eat anything besides danish?"

Clay closed the fridge. "Don't look in there."

"Why?" Her blood ran cold. "Is there another pocket zone?"

"No, but it's really gross. Randy's a good guy and all, but I get the impression he misinterprets our role. I mean, he's not even a city employee."

"And you behave like such a good citizen," she snapped. "Don't forget, you're getting him some fake ID papers."

"Now, is that what a good citizen does?" Clay said.

"The way you've taught him to drive, he could get arrested or deported, or worse!"

"Okay, okay," Clay said, soothing. "Consider it done."

The landlady came up the back stairs. "This is horrible. Ve wanted to move up here so ve could renovate first floor. Now ve can't use second floor!" She peered through the kitchen door into the living room. "It is still there?"

Jewel took a deep breath of stale danish and re-entered the living room.

Randy was walking from pile to pile of the magazines, tapping them. Poppets sprang up wherever he tapped. "Interesting. My touch seems to summon the apparition."

Clay said, "Could that be because you're, uh—" He glanced over his shoulder at the landlady. "English? Jewel, you try."

"No thanks."

The landlady said tremulously, "Have you look in bedroom?"

Euw. Jewel got the icks just trying to imagine the bedroom. "Clay, how about you look?"

"I'll save you, little lady," Clay said in a deep voice. He threw his shoulders back and opened the bedroom door.

"They persist as long as one engages with them," Randy said thoughtfully.

"What do you mean, engage?" Jewel said.

At the bedroom door, Clay gasped.

"What?" She came to stand behind him.

"It's—it's full of—" Clay turned away, pushing her back.

Randy straightened.

"*What*?" Jewel demanded.

Clay pinched his nose. "Sweat socks."

She shoved past. The bedroom violated the Clean Air Act, but Clay was right. It was G-rated. Dirty laundry lay ankle-deep, but she saw no girlie posters, porn, or poppets.

She came out and stood looking around at the stacks of porn and their dancing, twirling, teasing, laughing poppets. She turned to the landlady. "Do you have a dumpster? Or just those little garbage cans?"

"Deli on the corner hass dumpster," the landlady said.

"When do they swap out for a new one?"

"I ask my Aubrey!" The landlady went downstairs.

Jewel called a huddle. "Randy, what do you mean they persist if you engage with them?"

"I believe your term is 'interactive.' They are autonomous but responsive only. That signifies a message of some sort."

"So?" Jewel said.

"So if one doesn't ask them to appear, they will not appear. Probably. If one ignores them, they subside— vanish. O'Connor must have known what would happen, for he never threw away the old magazines."

Jewel bit her lip. "So did he, like, *make* them appear? I mean, did he make this happen?"

Randy looked around the room. "I don't know."

"I know something else you don't know," Clay said.

Jewel looked at him impatiently. "Yes, Mister Comic Relief? You have a contribution?"

"These bakery bags." Clay took a white ball of paper out of the overflowing wastebasket and uncrumpled it. "Have you looked at the address?"

"Hoby's," Jewel said. "My favorite."

Clay yanked the rolled-up magazine out of Randy's back pocket. "They're from the same place as this lame porn." He flipped through the magazine and pointed at fine print. "Nine sixty west Washington Boulevard."

"I've seen that address recently." Jewel frowned. "Huh. Obviously we're gonna have to pay this porn company a visit." She licked her lips. "And buy some pastry while we're at it."

While Jewel phoned in their discovery to Ed, Randy gathered up armloads of magazines and hauled them to the dumpster behind the corner deli, and Clay got the landlady and her husband to show him around O'Connor's apartment and describe how they were going to redecorate. As the magazines went away, the landlady cheered up.

"Ve never haff cockroaches, you know." She dug Clay in the ribs. "That's something, in neighborhood vit deli. Plus Mr. O'Connor vas no neatnik."

Her husband came up beside her and put his arm around her waist. "That certainly was something," he said sadly, watching the magazines go out the door in Randy's arms.

"Oh, you." His wife slapped him gently on the hand.

Jewel pushed the moment while they weren't fighting. "Tell me, have you been approached by anyone else from the city about—about all this?"

The landlord pinched his wife on the behind and she squealed. "Nope. You're it. I'm thinkin'," he said to his wife, "we put the bed in this room, eh, honey? It's bigger and it gets more light." He bumped his shoulder against his wife's and she giggled.

They got personal. Jewel looked out the window.

Clay came upstairs with his phone in his hand. "Ed says we can go over there tomorrow."

"What about my other job?" Jewel said, air-typing.

Clay shrugged, stuffed his phone in his pocket, then did a double take at the landlord and his wife, locked in a clinch. "Whoa."

"Let's give 'em their privacy. Randy's done here." She led Clay downstairs. "That was interesting. Randy isn't scared of this stuff at all."

"Randy's hinky to the bone himself," Clay said. "Why should it scare him? Come to think of it, that could be a decent job for him."

"Removing hinky stuff to disassemble pocket zones?" Jewel nibbled her lip. "I'd feel better if I had the slightest clue how they worked or what makes 'em." She glanced up the stairs in the direction of the now-porn-free apartment. "Do you suppose it's safe for them to move in there?"

"I'm sure it won't hurt them," Clay said.

Jewel wasn't sure at all, but she didn't know how to find out. And she didn't know how to protect them without taking their home away from them.

CHAPTER 8

That night, she broached the idea of hinky-stuff removal to Randy. "You'd get on the city payroll. The benefits are great."

He lay under the sheet, his schlong making a tent. He scowled. "You would make a dustman of me."

"What's that?"

"One who takes away filth. This is not a career."

She slid under the sheet beside him. "Nnno. But it pays. It's safer for you to do than for anyone else I know. Ed would sign you onto the payroll without a murmur. No close scrutiny of your paperwork."

"By this you mean proof of my citizenship."

"Right."

"I think not," he said casually, turning out the light.

She sat up in bed. "Look, it's hazardous waste removal. That's not garbage detail. It's high tech. You could charge whatever you wanted."

"No, thank you."

She punched his shoulder. "Hey! I'm trying to get you an income here!"

"Clay is teaching me better skills."

"Great." She wanted to ask what had happened to the money Clay said they'd got when he and Randy raided the bank accounts of a serial black widow. But that whole thing made her honest soul so crazy that she couldn't even bring it up. Since Randy hadn't mentioned that money, and he was still hitting her up for cash for clothes, she assumed it was one of Clay's jokes. "Does he ever bother to tell you he's teaching you something illegal?"

"We have been most careful." Not the answer she'd hoped for. Randy rolled over, propping his head on his elbow. "Currently I am earning micropayments from a pay-to-read company. I worked out the algorithm for the click-bot," he added proudly.

Internet wasn't her expertise, but it sounded crooked. "And this pays what?"

"So far it earns in the realm of twelve dollars a day."

She threw up her hands. "That's not an income!"

"But I don't have to sit and click all day," he pointed out. "I arm my click-bot and set it running. In the meantime I can learn other skills, or take other positions."

"Okay, this totally sounds like a scam. I'll have Clay shut it down tomorrow."

Randy's voice rose. "But I'm earning money!"

After the stink she'd made about him living off of her, she supposed she should be more sensitive.

"Okay, I'm sorry, okay. I'll talk to Clay and find out what the deal is." She yawned and slid down under the sheet again. "Let's just have sex and go to sleep, okay?" she said, laying one hand on his muscular thigh.

He said stiffly, "If my efforts to achieve solvency inconvenience you, I humbly beg pardon."

"Yeah, yeah. You're such a drama queen." She stroked his thigh. "Sex? Sleep?"

He lay rigid under her hand.

Oh, jeepers. What now? "Randy?"

"You have no use for me but one." He sounded mortified.

"And what a fabulous use it is," she said, trying for lightness. He said nothing. "Don't be mad."

"I cannot batten on you forever, trading *favors* for bread."

"Why do you care? You're a sex demon. You can't help yourself."

"I am trying to break a habit of centuries."

She rolled her eyes. "You say yes to every woman who gets you alone! You make *me* say yes in my *sleep*. You love it."

"I was not always a sex demon. In bed, yes, I am. But since you freed me from sexual slavery," he said with an ironic note that pissed her off, "I am reverting to the man I was."

"A lord. A snotty, bossy, privileged—"

"Just so," he said quietly.

Suddenly she realized that she was being dismissive and impatient, while he was exercising restraint.

Even his restraint criticized her.

She took her hand off his thigh. "Oh, all right."

Her bad-girl brain said, *I don't have to put up with this*.

Grumpily she turned over and put her back to him. She still wanted sex.

But his message was coming through. He felt exploited and taken for granted. *Every night for three solid months*. He was fabulous, magical, powerful, totally swoony and explosive, and she rather thought she was getting addicted to him. And now, naturally, he expected something more of her.

In her heart, she knew he was right. It was time for her to bite the bullet and make an effort to get used to this . . . relationship.

Ugh, that word.

She wondered how much relationship talk they'd have to do tonight before she could get laid and roll over.

Okay, now you're being insensitive, Heiss. Go to sleep.

Jewel wanted to spend Wednesday investigating the link between the tame porn and the poppets in the pocket zones, but when she called in to Baysdorter Boncil to claim a sick day, the receptionist transferred her to Sharisse, not Maida.

"Maida's out today. When are you coming in?"

Jewel began, "Uh, I was thinking maybe not—"

"Steven will be here. You want to get him on harassment for the EEOC, right?"

What makes you think I'm with EEOC? Jewel wanted to say. Maida was right. Her navy polyester had done its evil work.

If she was to accomplish anything, she'd better do it soon. "We still on for lunch?"

"You bet."

"Okay." Jewel drew a deep breath. "I'll be there in an hour." She hung up and told Randy, "I have to go to BB. Stay out of trouble. Call Clay over to work on your identity."

"I'm sure he would prefer to hear that from you."

Jewel faced her sex demon squarely. "Look. You two can lock horns on your own time. I can't be bothered trying to handle you delicately. Got me?"

He aimed huge black eyes at her. "When is my own time, Jewel?"

She did a double take. "What?"

"Clay works eight-thirty to five with you, except when he is undercover. What is my workday?"

She opened her mouth to say that, while she was at work, he could visit the zoo or take up tai chi, she didn't give a rat's patoot, but she stopped. They both knew he might zap into a bed at any time. He'd already zapped into a bed in a department store and the back seat of a junked Camry, to name two. He couldn't afford to stray far from her side, and she couldn't afford to let him go places where retrieving him could be embarrassing.

So he stayed with her, or he stayed home, or sometimes Clay babysat him.

And Randy hated it, which was reasonable.

"We'll get you a real job soon. I promise."

She threw on the navy polyester pants but compromised on the top: a white lace-edged cami layered under one of those drapey scoop-necked tops that look so demure in Lane Bryant until you get them on a woman with major boobs. Also, the scoop top was red. She felt like all she needed was a scarf with stars on it and she could be a walking tribute to the American flag.

He called after her. "I thought you wanted to see my pay-to-read click-bot." He looked like a hound dog watching Mom get ready for work, knowing he would be left alone all day.

With her hand on the doorknob, she said guiltily, "I'm sorry. I just don't have time right now."

She shut the door before he could make her melt.

The Baysdorter Boncil office was humming. Girls whispered over the mahogany rails of their corrals. Girls whispered over the coffeepot and the copy machine.

Jewel found her way to her corral.

Sharisse met her there and handed her a bulging folder. "Steven will be back after lunch. He left this stuff to go into the lease package spreadsheet. Remember how I showed you?"

"Yeah, yeah. What makes you think I'm, uh—"

Sharisse rolled her eyes. "Oh, please," she said, lowering her voice. "We all know you're from the EEOC, investigating what happens to Steven's girls. Believe me, we're rooting for you."

What happens to Steven's girls? That was a whole new wrinkle. Jewel frowned. "I'm not—"

"Shh, here comes my boss. I'm being Maida today. Let's talk at lunch."

"Sure."

Jewel's morning passed frustratingly slowly. She typed stuff into spreadsheets. She answered Steven's phone. Girls walked by and smiled at her, or looked curiously at her, but nobody stopped to talk. *Dammit to hell, I've been made. Nobody wants to be seen with me.* She was ready to give up the whole undercover thing as a waste of time and go back to the pocket zone crisis, when Sharisse collected her and took her downstairs to the noisy grillroom for lunch. They were joined by two other BB office girls.

The Bennigan's was jammed. Daringly, Jewel ordered a pitcher of sangria. The girls giggled, but they filled their glasses.

Geri, a striking brunette with a street-smart air, reported all the current rumors about Jewel. "One, they think you're a cop, cracking down on harassment on the job. Two, you came in after the orgy as an excuse to catch Steven in the act."

"Three," Tonia said, brushing her hair away from her face with long, elaborately painted fingernails, "you came in because of what happened to Maida's daughter."

"What?" Interesting that Maida hadn't mentioned that.

"You didn't know?" Geri leaned forward. "It happened almost two years ago. Maida's daughter worked for Steven for maybe a month, and they did *not* get along."

"She didn't understand the deal," Sharisse said.

"Who didn't understand what deal?" Jewel said. She slurped some sangria and the other girls drank, too.

Tongue loosener did not seem all that necessary. They were dying to dish.

Sharisse said, "Lena, Maida's daughter? Apparently she didn't know that old John Baysdorter was sleeping with Maida."

Jewel's jaw dropped. "Our Maida? See-no-evil, hear-no-evil, speak-no-evil Maida?"

"Yeah," Tonia said. "For, like, twenty-plus years. Maida could have been a partner herself if she'd of had cojones. But she didn't have the education, wouldn't fight for her rights, so she's stuck at office manager level."

Geri said dryly, "Worked fine until he ups and dies on her. She thought she had 'til he retired, but he died at sixty-three."

"*What*," Jewel demanded, "happened to Lena Sacker?"

"Well." Sharisse leaned forward. "We kind of hoped you knew. It was Steven, for sure. Lena hated Steven. They had a screaming fight the day she left, and then she had one with Maida, and then she walked out at one-thirty in the afternoon and never came back. As far as we know, she still isn't speaking to Maida, or Maida to her. Steven must have pulled *something*."

"*I* think she found out about old John Baysdorter and her mother, and blew her stack," Geri said.

"Lena was no prude," Tonia countered scornfully.

"No lie." Geri snorted, and Jewel thought she was about to say more, but Sharisse interrupted.

"I think Lena knew about old John being her dad."

Whoa! Jewel would have liked to probe further, but she'd better stay on task. "I can't believe this still goes on. God knows I can't afford to be a prude either. But I had no idea."

"Oh, Steven is the only real offender," Sharisse said. "Until he started bucking for partner after John Baysdorter died, it was all pretty consensual. Old John put Lena through private school, finishing school, and

college. I couldn't make ends meet without Hugh's help.
Precious, of course, is playing Mike Redpune for what
she can get, but she's also playing Steven, which will get
her canned someday."

"Precious is spying on Steven for Mike," Tonia said
positively.

"Precious could be spying on Mike for Steven, and
Mike would never know. Mike's too butt-dumb arrogant," Geri said.

Jewel waved a hand. "I don't care about the white-guy
politics. I want to know who put the Viagra in the coffee at that staff meeting." *And I want to talk to this
Lena.* Anyone who had dirt on Steven should be interesting.

The girls looked at one another. "You first," Sharisse
said to Geri.

"Okay," Geri said, "I have zero proof, but *I* think
Steven doped the coffee to discredit Mike."

"That's dumb," Tonia stated. "Nobody could have
imagined what would happen."

"*What happened?*" Jewel burst out. "Were any of you
there?"

Sharisse looked at Tonia. Geri raised her hand, looking from Tonia to Sharisse with her chin in the air. The
other two hunkered down on their swivelly bar stools to
listen.

Geri said, "The thing is, we've all been on edge for
months. As in, horny. Even Precious didn't take up with
Mike until this spring." The subtext, audible to Jewel,
read, *And Precious is a total skank*. "It was like the air
conditioning stopped working. Know what I mean?"
She looked Jewel in the eye.

Jewel said, "Girl, there's whole weeks go by and I just
need it all the time." *Years.*

Geri put up a palm and Jewel high-fived her. "I can't
speak for anyone else, but I was *ripe*. I could blame

Precious, I guess. She always makes such a production out of these rollout meetings. Coffee and pastry, low light, a music track on her PowerPoint. She does it to impress Mike, and boy, did it work this time. He was dancing around with his laser-pointer like a monkey on crack. He got *all* worked up."

Geri sipped her sangria. "And the funny thing was, we were all getting worked up, too. I mean, we're talking condos going into a downtown Omaha landmark bank building with a strip mall rehab on the side. When Mike put his pointer down we actually clapped, and he turned to Precious and said something like, 'Great job!' and gave her a big wet one, and she threw her arms around his neck and gave it right back, and the next thing I know, I'm hugging Anna from Accounting, and Hugh Boncil jumps on Diane from Marketing and two other girls are rolling under the conference table." Geri shrugged. "It just snowballed. I can't explain it."

Jewel hated to interrupt. "Steven wasn't there?"

"Nope," Geri said.

"It must be killing him he missed it," Sharisse said.

"Huh," Tonia said. "I think he did it. Whatever it was. Viagra, Ecstasy, Spanish Fly, whatever."

"Oh, I do, too," Geri said. "It was Steven. He's been smug ever since, which just shows you. Zip-lipped, but smug."

"Then what happened?" Jewel said.

"I walked in," Sharisse said, "late, because I'd been notarizing and filing some stuff at court for Mr. Boncil, and when I saw all the bare skin I just shut the door and walked back to my desk and sat there, shaking."

"I heard there was something hinky about the whole scene," Jewel said. *Here we go.* Mentally she crossed her fingers.

"Other than Mike Redpune banging Precious against the ceiling like it was a king-size bed?" Geri said tartly.

"And bringing the ceiling tiles down? And two of the girls turning into dogs and humping?" She looked at her fingernails. "Anna sprouted two extra tongues."

Jewel realized her mouth was hanging open. She shut it.

"Then Maida walked in and gasped, and it felt like she sucked all the air out of the room at once. Mike and Precious fell off the ceiling. Maida almost passed out. She, like, staggered and leaned on the table and one of the girls who was an actual dog bit her on the hand. Hugh Boncil looked up from on top of Diane from Marketing and said, 'Close the door, Maida,' and Maida screamed, and the bitches turned back to normal. And Maida left."

"Good grief," Sharisse said faintly.

"What about you and Anna?" Tonia said, her nose shiny with sweat.

Geri fluttered a hand. "Oh, that. That was days ago. I think it was just the heat of the moment, know what I mean?"

"So who called it in?" Jewel said. *See who knows.*

"Maida, of course," Sharisse said. "Everybody knows that. Steven's hit on every girl she hires for him, and when he has no girl of his own he hits on the rest of us. He's gotten, like, totally out of control. She wants you to scare him straight."

"Fat chance," Tonia said.

"Bloated," Geri agreed.

"Shit," Tonia said, and Sharisse looked at her in shock. "It's twelve-thirty."

That broke up the sangria party.

CHAPTER 9

Jewel bailed on BB for the afternoon to pursue the clue Clay had found in O'Connor's apartment. The boys brought her Tercel to the curb on Michigan Avenue. Jewel moved Randy to the back seat so she could sit in front. "Clay, you drive. I'm still high from lunch."

"You smell like a party," Clay remarked.

"Sangria with the girls. I was pumping informants." She rubbed her head against the headrest, yawning. "I didn't tell you to bring him," she muttered.

"He wouldn't stay home," Clay muttered back.

Jewel groaned aloud. "You two clowns behave, hear?"

"Naturally," Randy said from the back seat.

"Naturally," Clay said.

"Where's our paperwork?"

Randy handed a file over the seat back.

Clay said, "Ed says the majority stockholder died about two years ago, and the new owner hasn't re-registered the place as Adult Use."

"What does 'adult use' signify?" Randy said.

"It means," Jewel said, "that unless they're grandfathered in, they have to go through Revenue and Zoning to register as an Adult Use business. And even if they're grandfathered in, we have to establish that they haven't been out of business for any interval since the original registration. Plus, if they've diversified, i.e., if they have any dependent divisions, those have to register separately."

"Gibberish," Clay said.

"It's perfectly clear to me," Randy said. "Even in this republican state, one's grandfather is important."

"Right. Except Cook County is solid Democrat," Jewel said.

"So they register and then they kick us out," Clay said.

"No, no," she said. "You don't know the game. It's an excuse to get us in the door. Once we're in, they're wide open."

They found the address soon enough, but parking sucked, and they had to weave through the meat packing district looking for a spot.

"This area is one of my favorites," she said as they crawled through a neighborhood of low brick warehouses and about a million trucks. The sidewalks and streets here were used as extensions of the loading docks. Burly guys carried whole dead pigs on their shoulders. Lidless boxes of dead fish gaped open on the sidewalks. People in rubber waders hosed down the pavement with hot water, and blood literally ran in the gutter, along with lettuce leaves, oranges, and discarded plastic gloves. Jewel sniffed the air and smiled.

"You have strange tastes," Clay said.

"It's all real. Stuff is being bought and sold. Food is being prepared and put in trucks and taken someplace where somebody will eat it. It's not pork futures, it's real pork. It's not a law office, it's actual sharks getting skinned and sliced. Wow, you ever seen so much zucchini in one place?"

She maneuvered them through a steaming maze of

trucks, loaded pallets, and workers in gore-stained white aprons.

"Strange place for a porn company," Clay said.

"Good place for one," she said. "You won't find a bunch of soccer moms protesting in the meat packing district. Although condo creep is moving closer every day."

They parked illegally in half a space by a locked-off lot that hadn't seen traffic in years. Jewel put her OF-FICIAL BUSINESS tag on the dash, and they picked their way through the detritus of the City of Big Shoulders.

The Artistic Publishing Company was a five-story red brick building occupying half a city block. The name was carved into limestone over the front door, and it rang a bell for Jewel. Who had mentioned this company to her recently?

"What's that aroma?" Randy said. "Cinnamon?"

Clay pointed to the corner of the Artistic Building.

Jewel gave a heart-cry.

"Hoby's!" Her stomach rumbled. "I need pastry! I need it *now*." Leaving the boys on the street, she ran into the bakery.

Hoby's Bäckerei was a room-size pastry bong smelling of melted chocolate, browning butter, cinnamon, toasting pecans, and fresh coffee. A guy in white rolled in a big rack of hot cow plops. Jewel bought three and ran back to her team with her white bag.

"These," she said, handing them out, "are fresh cinnamon cow plops, the finest non-chocolate pastry money can buy." She bit into the edge of hers. It was so hot, the crunchy crust sizzled against her tongue. "Ohmigod, it's fabulous."

"Cow plop." Randy looked dubiously at his. "I suppose there is a facetious resemblance." He nibbled. "Good."

"I wouldn't eat anything made in this building," Clay said.

"You eat 'em at work every day," Jewel said thickly. "Be done in a minute." She looked at her half-eaten cow plop. "No, I won't. If I finish this one I'll want another. Here." She handed the rest of her cow plop to Randy, who put it all back in the white bag. "Business before pleasure."

"Must I stay in the car?" Randy said.

"I'll watch him," Clay said.

Jewel shook her head. "I just realized, we need his hinky radar." She scanned the building. "They've been here for ages. Wide open in a dozen ways. Their only hope is to make nice."

"We're nice," Clay said.

"Exceptionally so," Randy said.

Jewel put on her cop face. "Let's go."

There was a security guard inside the entrance. You could either turn left and buy porn at wholesale, or you could sign in and go right to a set of blank gray double doors or to the elevators, or straight up a grand staircase. Jewel gave the guard their names and titles. He phoned upstairs.

"Go on up to four. Miss Tannyhill will see you."

Jewel elbowed Clay. "Tannyhill! Holy shit, do you suppose there's a connection?"

Clay muttered, "Don't curse. It puts off the marks."

On the fourth floor they were met by Miss "call me Onika" Tannyhill. Onika was a sixty-something old bat with hard miles but an excellent repaint job. She wore her dyed orange hair in a smooth Hillary, tons of striking makeup, white mink on the collar of her deep blue suit, and diamonds on her long cigarette holder. Her eyes were as blue and snappy as her suit. She ushered them into a vast, hypermasculine office full of dark wood and leather wing chairs.

They sat in the leather wing chairs. Onika said, "What can I do for the City of Chicago today?"

Jewel explained about Adult Use registration. Then she said, "We were surprised to find that Chicago had another adult publishing company."

Onika fitted a cigarette into the jeweled holder and lit up. "Don't mistake me for Christie Hefner. I don't have her brains or her money. She went to Brandeis for *summa cum laude*, I went to the Bahamas for a tan. I'm just a bad girl who got handed a great big fun toy." She grinned around the cigarette holder.

"So Artistic is a family business?"

"Yep. My grandfather founded this company almost a hundred years ago." Onika sucked in smoke, coughed, sucked deeper, and coughed again. "My father took over in seventy-six. I got it—" She paused and coughed horribly for a minute, then croaked, "Oh, hell," and stubbed out her cigarette. After a sip from a glass she said, "I've only been in charge two years. You'll forgive me if I don't know what the kumshaw runs to these days."

Jewel said, "We don't do shakedown in my department, ma'am."

"Guess that'll have to wait, then," Onika said, unruffled. "Did you want a tour?"

"That would be great," Jewel said, keeping her temper. Everyone stood. Something caught her eye. *Bingo!* "Who's the blonde beauty in the painting?"

There she was, the minx they'd seen in poppet form both in the locker at the Kraft and in O'Connor's apartment. The oil painting made her look classier. Jewel was reminded of the nude who reclines full-length over the bar in a cowboy movie. It was a nice painting. The blonde's blue eyes sparkled, and she seemed to say *Peel me a grape* from clear across the room.

"Sweet, huh?" Onika said in her gravelly voice. "The

original model was named Teüschnelda Wilmerding, but everybody here calls her Wilma. She's our mascot. You'll be seeing a lot of her." She put down her glass, which contained Scotch by the smell of it, and shepherded them all out of her office.

CHAPTER 10

Onika showed them layout and editorial. She showed them photo production. She showed them accounting, MIS, and website management. In the elevator, they felt a deep, rhythmic thump. "The presses are old and slow, so they run twenty-four-seven when we're on deadline."

Wilma was everywhere. Framed paintings of Wilma from the Year One, wearing a lacy corset and high button shoes. Tattered posters under glass of Wilma in abbreviated pink gingham undies, pinning a rose on a WWI doughboy. Wilma cooing over a puppy held between her perky naked breasts. Wilma roller-skating naked. Naked Wilma laughing while she roped a snorting, bucking Brahma bull from the back of a bucking horse.

Yeah, it was total fantasy, but it had energy and wholesome appeal. Wilma was out-of-control sexual, yet adorably innocent.

Jewel felt herself blushing, which embarrassed her and made her blush hotter. *Darnit, I'm too sophisticated to let lame porn bother me.* The pages of the current issue tacked to the corkboard in editorial were considerably raunchier than Wilma. She swallowed.

A young woman with horn-rimmed glasses and her dark hair in a bun came up to them.

"This morning's online orders, Onika." Her dark suit

was so severe, it was a parody of Jewel's navy polyester. She was the picture of everything Jewel couldn't measure up to at Baysdorter Boncil: trim, sleek, and pseudo-virginal, as if she wore her virtue like a carnival mask.

"Honey, this is Jewel Heiss and her team from Consumer Services downtown. This little gal's my right hand."

The brunette nodded at Clay and dimpled demurely at Randy. Jewel felt her hackles go up.

"Of course that's not what you've come to see. Honey, tag along."

The assistant handed off her folder and fell in beside Randy. Clay took Jewel's elbow, and they went down a big marble staircase. More Wilmas hung in the stairwell.

Onika gestured grandly. "A hundred years of smutty pictures. My inheritance." On the ground floor, she pushed open the gray double doors. "And this is the money shot: the old studio, where we take feelthy pictures—stills only, of course. Who's the talent today, honey?"

"Flash Titty and Sancho and the Tokyo Twins."

"They won't mind company." Onika paused at the door to the studio. She grinned wickedly at her guests. "You wanted to see it all. This is what everybody wants to see."

Randy bowed. Clay smiled. Jewel squeaked, "Sure."

"Cigarette," the assistant murmured. Onika swore and put out her cigarette in the ashtray by the door.

"Who writes your salacious stories?" Randy said as Onika ushered them in.

"Bunch of dirty-minded newspapermen," Onika said. "We need new blood. Care to try?"

"As a matter of fact," Randy began.

Jewel said, "Oh, hush."

All four of them stopped in the shadows outside a brightly lit tableau.

Under bright lights, three people were moving around on a huge, red-plush, heart-shaped divan, or bed, or something.

The women wore peasant blouses and bright ruffled red skirts bunched around their waists, kneeling side by side on the red velvet thingy.

Sancho wore only chaps, big fancy ones, allover fringe and shiny silver medallions, and silver-tipped cowboy boots. He was kneeling behind both women, hard at work with flesh and with plastic.

In spite of Jewel's sophistication, her temperature rose.

The twins howled and barked and bayed. Sancho preserved a thoughtful, almost abstracted expression.

The camera flashed. The photographer yammered in a breathless monotone, "Dumi, twist right. Duyu, twist left. Sweet. Good action, Sancho. Duyu, grab your right cheek and look back. Dumi, how about a frig. Atta girl. More elbow. Love it." Somehow that was even sexier than the sex.

Speechless, Jewel found herself looking at the women more than at the man. They were impossibly skinny. It was fascinating, and somehow appalling, and she realized half of her discomfort was because the women were also beautiful. *I would look like potato salad doing that. Potato salad with cellulite.*

Onika said to someone standing nearby, "Flash Titty, this is Jewel and Clay and Randy."

Jewel shook hands with a totally naked, totally gorgeous woman who believed in truth in advertising. Clay was warm and friendly and didn't look at her below the neck, which Jewel thought was carrying chivalry too far. Randy shook hands, too. In some way Randy acted more polite than Clay and yet something, his taut posture or the sparkle in his eye, told Jewel he was fully aware of Flash Titty's qualifications.

The naked woman smiled at Randy. "Can I have a cappuccino?"

"They're not assistants, they're just rubbernecking," Onika said.

"I once knew a beauty," Randy remarked, "who claimed that coffee was ruinous to the complexion."

"Baby," Flash Titty said, "they're not looking at my complexion."

Jewel wanted to pull her hair.

"I'll get your cappuccino," Onika's assistant said. She lifted her eyebrows at Jewel as if she'd heard Jewel's thought.

God, I am such a bitch! Jewel felt like one solid blush.

She paid attention to the contortionists so she didn't have to hear what Randy said next. Those women sure were limber. Skinny, exquisite, shameless—it embarrassed Jewel to discover that the shamelessness she prided herself on was small-town stuff. On the red velvet dais, the panting Tokyo Twins offered the camera proof of their high level of satisfaction. The photographer leapt and snapped and yammered. Sancho pulled out his, holy crap, his ten-inch thing and experienced his moment of triumph, which seemed like an anticlimax, all things considered.

Jewel reluctantly turned back to see what her sex demon might be getting up to with a porn star. She found Clay watching her.

"Bored?" she blurted.

He shook his head, smiling at her.

"I can't believe you're not looking at this."

"Seen it. My dad's collection is legendary."

"Oh." There didn't seem to be much to say to that. She leaned closer to him, and he put his arm around her. That felt nice. She might be the fattest woman in the room, but somebody wanted to cuddle her.

"Okay, we're done!" somebody yelled.

Sancho and the Tokyo Twins got up and calmly wiped themselves down with pop-up moist towlettes.

"They seem to like their work," Jewel said lamely.

The assistant checked her watch. "Onika, I'm due upstairs."

"Go, go." Onika shooed her off.

Flash Titty moved languidly to the dais. A man in a bear suit already stood waiting for her. The suit had a very realistic bear head and claws, but a human body part poked through a hole in the bear's fly. Another man was getting into a weird outfit that looked like a porn version of a Disney version of a Brahma bull. The bull guy had not, Jewel noted, been circumcised.

"They love their work. Hard to believe, I know," Onika said, eyeing Jewel with irony. "Nice girls should have more shame."

Jewel laughed uneasily. She felt like her blush system had blown a circuit breaker.

To her profound relief, Onika led them out of the studio. "Come upstairs. You must have some questions by now."

In the elevator, Jewel said what had to be said. "You know, I always thought I was this balls-to-the-wall horny city girl. I mean, I've been around. But I sure feel small town here."

"It's the concentration," Onika said. "There's just so much of it in one place. I was a bad girl myself, back when I was young and fuckable." She elbowed Jewel and dropped her growly voice another notch. "But half the fun of being a bad girl is being the only one in the room, yah?"

Jewel burst out laughing. Clay smiled a discreet smile. *Girl talk doesn't embarrass Clay*, she remembered.

Randy was brick red. He stared rigidly at the elevator doors, his lips pressed together.

In Onika's office, Jewel accepted a gin and tonic from their hostess. Clay took a beer. Randy refused refreshment.

Jewel sighed. "Okay, I admit I had other expectations. I mean, frankly, that stuff is kind of tacky and it didn't turn me on," she lied. "It was so, I don't know, mechanical? But it wasn't horrible."

Onika jabbed the air triumphantly with her cigarette holder. "That's because that stuff is for men. Our print stuff is still done for the male readership." She put a cigarette in the holder and drew flame onto it. "But upstairs." She sat back and blew a smoke ring and grinned, sipped her Scotch, blew another ring, and started coughing. "Hell." She hit a button on her phone. "Honey, get me a press goodies bag for Hot Pink Studios."

"Ma'am, please, no." Here it came. *What did you expect? You go on a fishing trip, you have to dodge bribes from the fish.* "We can't accept—"

But Onika gestured and the assistant handed the bag to Jewel.

"Ma'am," Jewel began again, holding up a palm.

"*Miss,*" Onika corrected. "I want to give you these so you can see what I'm trying to do with this company. It's not a brand-new idea, but it's new to Artistic. You know the old joke? What's the difference between porn and erotica? Porn is what turns you on, erotica is what turns me on. Well"—Onika leaned forward—"the real difference between porn and erotica is, porn pays ten times better."

Jewel thought. "Because more men than women buy porn?"

"Nope."

"Because men have more money?"

"Nope. It's because for a long time nobody figured out that *women* have more money, and they *will* buy porn— if it isn't tacky and mechanical. Those were your words, weren't they?"

"I'm not trying to insult—" Jewel began.

"Go home and watch it. We're making erotic film for women. It's respectful, it's enjoyable, it's made with the kind of sex women like. Not the calisthenics you saw downstairs."

Jewel felt a smile coming on. "Sex women like?"

The twinkle was back in Onika's eye. She said, "Men like quantity. Women like quality. Men like it fast and talk-free. Women like it slow, with lots of foreplay and conversation. Men like to break the rules. Women do, too, but they also like to break down a man's emotional resistance." She blew smoke. "Some of 'em. I've heard tell there are some girls so modern, they like sex any old way."

Jewel's pulse sounded in her ears. "I get you."

"I'm not asking you for any favors. I just want you to look at what we're doing and decide for yourself if it deserves a chance. You saw what we do downstairs. Now let's go upstairs."

CHAPTER

 11

On the fifth floor, they went into a room full of sound mixing consoles—"sound is almost the most expensive part, which is why the sound for a lot of porn sucks"—with a long, low window looking out and down onto a scene of intimacy.

Down there, inside a circle of artificial light, was a fake living room in a fake ski lodge. A fake fireplace flickered. Squat oil lamps sat on old-timey tables around a big white fake bearskin rug—"I have a thing for bears"—and on the rug lay a fully-clothed couple in ski duds, including boots and snowsuits.

They were kissing very slowly, touching faces, looking into one another's eyes.

Jewel frowned. She felt like she'd walked into a spy-hole on somebody's private bedroom.

"I wrote the first couple scripts, but my contract gal wrote the rest. She's good. She has to live with 'em, so it's only fair."

Jewel watched the man slowly unzip the side of the woman's snowsuit to reveal perfect skin, tawny in the fake firelight, all the way down to her ankle. He looked in her eyes the whole time. The woman said something, and her murmuring came through a speaker in the ceiling of the sound booth. She took the man's hands in hers and pressed them against her cheeks. He smiled, shaking his head, and drew her face very slowly to his for a kiss.

"That's freaky," Jewel said.

"Beeecause?" Clay said.

"It must take forever to get down to business." That wasn't why it felt freaky, but she couldn't think straight.

"That's what makes it good," Onika whispered. "Going slow."

That's what's making me antsy as hell, Jewel thought. She'd been horny all through this visit, but in a casual, volleyball-on-the-beach kind of way. Now she squirmed.

Onika whispered, "I have a meeting in accounting. Stay as long as you like," and went out.

"You should not be here," Randy murmured in Jewel's ear.

She turned on him. "*What* is your problem?"

"You are vulnerable to certain kinds of magical influence," he whispered. "In one summer alone, you have met with a genie and a magical beauty machine—and with me."

"So what's the friggin' magic here? It's just sex. Not even *sex* sex. For pete's sake, look at them, they're touching each other's *hands* now."

"I don't know where the magic is. I feel it. There is something hinky in this building," Randy said, lifting his head and letting his eyes roam over the ceiling. He looked at her. "I feel your state."

She set her teeth. *What state?* she would have said, but she knew. Randy was attuned to her level of arousal all the time, like, *all* the time. It was like owning a dog who could hear you think the word "suppertime." From across town.

"This is not an appropriate moment for you to be tuning in to my state, buddyboy." She didn't want to think about sex with Randy here.

"Can we have it quiet?" said a guy plastered up against the window with headphones on his head.

"Sorry," she whispered. She moved away from Randy.

Clay sidled up to her other side. "Uh, think I'll run downstairs to the printing plant, give it a quick sweep."

She squinted. "Why? You don't have hinky radar."

Clay pecked her lips lightly with his. And out he went.

She felt abandoned. *I'm on my last nerve here and my team is playing hooky.*

Clay felt that things were moving along nicely. Randy thought he was so smart, flaunting his ability to read her mind, talking about it right there in front of strangers. He didn't know Jewel, even if he could see into her deepest sexual desires.

Clay knew Jewel. This was a woman who liked skaggy old men's porn better than the touchy-feely stuff going on at Hot Pink Studios. Sex for Jewel was an athletic event.

And relationship was her four-letter word.

It might take Clay longer to get where he was going, but he would stay there longer than Randy ever could. Because Clay knew how and when to back off.

Randy would never get that. He'd spent too many years wading around hip-deep in the sexual swamps of women's minds. He was bad at consent. And the thing Jewel hated most was being crowded.

Clay had set Randy up to push too hard. If he'd done it right, Randy would even now be digging his grave.

And Clay wouldn't even be there. She couldn't know he had made it happen.

Sweet.

As he descended the basement stairs he heard the presses thundering. He went through a set of scarred Plexiglass doors and the noise increased tenfold. A friendly young man with snaggly front teeth asked him if he needed help.

Clay thanked him. "Just checking the noise level!" he shouted, holding up the back of his cell phone and peering at it. "You ought to be wearing ear protection!"

The kid pshawed visibly and wandered off. *Second quickest way to get someone to ignore you—fuss over them.*

Clay wandered, holding his phone in his palm by his waist.

Yep, this was still a porn company. Photos of bare flesh flashed through the old-fashioned presses every half-second. The press room's lower walls had centerfolds taped against them, and the upper walls bore porn posters from bygone decades. These posters were raunchier than the stuff in *Girls, Giggles, and Garters*, but there were plenty of Wilmas on the walls, too.

It was fascinating, how much effort had gone into varying Wilma's pose and costume, and yet how carefully the artists of succeeding decades had preserved her wholesomeness. She could have been Miss Idaho Potato of 1900 or the Daisy Queen of 2000. From every wall Wilma beckoned, promising everything he'd ever wanted.

Everywhere, printers with happy grins greeted him. They seemed to love their work.

Clay checked out the men's room. The smell hit him first, so bad that he tripped over the cracked black-and-white tile floor. More pin-ups covered the walls, one over each urinal. And—he stepped into a wooden stall— yep, the stall had its own fleshy wanton taped against the inside of the door, with a suspicious and unsavory stickiness coating the lower half of the poster. For some reason he didn't feel like sitting down.

Jewel's lucky she didn't draw this duty.

He wandered out into the press room and kept moving, following the walls to stay out of the way of men clambering around the greasy presses, loading huge paper rolls or grabbing handfuls of naked pictures off huge stacks and snapping them in the air, for all the world as if they were making a bed with sheets of porn.

"Why do you do that?" he shouted, fascinated.

"So they won't stick together!" shouted the lucky paper-wavers.

Clay didn't really expect to find anything hinky. So, when he saw the ancient men's room door with the brand-new board nailed across it, he almost walked by. The doorway was vaulted, as if this hadn't always been a men's room. It was hung with neatly printed signs. KEEP OUT. OUT OF ORDER. HEALTH DEPARTMENT WARNING. DO NOT ENTER.

Huh. That's a lot of signage for one busted sewer pipe.

He tugged at the board. It came loose easily. The nail at the top end had been yanked loose before, and then slipped back into its old hole. Many times, by the look of it. Hm.

With a swift glance around, he yanked the board free, let it swing down, whisked inside, and shut the door behind him.

"I want children someday," said the brunette beauty on the bearskin rug. "Does that seem crazy to you?"

"Yes," Jewel muttered. She wanted out.

Onika appeared at Jewel's elbow. "That's Velvita Fromage, our contract girl. Isn't she gorgeous?"

"Gorgeous," Jewel said hollowly.

Onika looked at her watch. "Conference call time. I'll be in my office," she whispered.

Jewel forced a smile.

Okay, okay, she was getting the picture. These were movies about nice, good-hearted porn queens who got slow, affectionate licking from their studs before they took all ten inches in some orifice. He had to say "I love you" before he got to stick it in. BFD. *Get me out of here.*

She wondered where Clay was. Randy stood in a corner, glowering. Jazus, was he mad at her for being turned on? That was another first. She fidgeted silently until she couldn't take it anymore. Then she went out of the sound booth in search of a place where she could scream.

Across the hall she found another sound booth, this one looking out on an empty stage and one bare light-bulb on a stick.

She hugged herself, grateful for the dark.

But here came her sex demon, looking as he so often did like a hanging judge. He flicked on the light as he entered.

"Jewel, I beg you listen—"

I am so not up for a fight. "No, you listen. I've had enough. I thought I could take this. I thought I was so smart and sophisticated and big city. Well, I'm not. There, are you happy? You broke me down. I'm just a small-town girl with small-town morals, and I think it's—it's disgusting." *And disturbing. And it makes me feel weird about myself.* "I want to go home!"

"Then go!" Randy exploded. "I met with less hypocrisy from a nun than I have seen in you!"

"Oh, really!" she said, stung, her voice rising. "Where did you meet *her*? In bed, of course?"

He jerked his head back as if he'd been slapped. "Of course. That's what I am. I'm good in bed."

Oh, great, now he was insulted. She tried to soothe him, but frankly she didn't want to. She wanted to slap him.

"Yes, you are, you're terrific in bed. Can't you see, it's the difference between what I do with you and that—that fake sex that bothers me?"

"It's not fake sex."

Whoa. If Randy said it was real, it was real.

Double ick.

"That's even worse. They're having fun out there and people are watching, they're *taping* it, they're *listening in*. And then a million creepy old farts like O'Connor are gonna mess up the upholstery on their couches, watching—"

"Or perhaps a million respectable women and their husbands," he said with mystifying sarcasm.

"What's the difference?" she yelled.

"I don't know," he said, tight-lipped. "What is the difference? How does all this differ from your own behavior with me?"

"Those people are being paid to have sex!" she screamed. "I never did that!"

She'd never seen him so bleak. "But I do it every day."

She gasped. *Now that was an insult.* "I do not pay you for sex!"

"But you do. You house me, feed me, clothe me—"

Frantic at his expression, she put out both hands. "Randy, you were in trouble. I couldn't turn you away. You're still in trouble. I'm not *making* you." She stopped, remembering their argument the other night.

Let's just have sex and go to sleep, okay?

Sensitive she wasn't.

He said in a brittle voice, "Yet it's fortunate, is it not, that I have one skill that permits me to be of service to you."

She sucked a long breath through her nose. "Tell me." She pointed at the closed door and that bearskin rug across the hall. "Tell me that what you and I do and what they're doing are the same." She said through her teeth, "And I will *kill* you."

A look of sadness and shame crossed his face. He closed his eyes. He bowed his head. And then he faded away.

His clothes sank, empty, to the floor.

Jewel stared in horror.

This had happened before. She knew exactly where he must have gone.

And what it would take to set him free.

And what he would be doing in the meantime.

She put her hands over her mouth to hold in a scream.

CHAPTER 12

Clay shut the door covered with keep-out signs behind him, groping for a light switch. He didn't find it, but he found a book of matches. He lit one.

Tiles, black and white underfoot. Tile on the walls. Urinals. Wooden stalls. It was a men's room after all.

But a much older, fancier men's room. The tile was classier. The urinals were molded with a fanciful, ornate shape on top. The posters on the walls were behind glass. A narrow ledge ran the length of the men's room at elbow height under the posters, and on it sat some votive candles, unlit.

The match burnt out, scorching his fingers.

He lit another match. This time he used it to light three of the votive candles in their red glass holders. The flames sprang up, throwing a wobbly red glow through the glass.

In a few moments his eyes adjusted to the red gloom. Now he saw that the ledge was piled with dried flowers and cheap-looking costume jewelry and scraps of fur and lace and the ruffly satin lids of chocolate boxes.

In spite of his breezy assurances to Jewel, he felt the hairs rise on the back of his neck.

He looked up at the posters.

They were all Wilmas.

The one hanging over the dead roses was naked. She

had one hand between her thighs and one on her nipple. She wasn't so much posing as standing there, as if the painter had caught her in a moment when she wasn't "on." She seemed relaxed and happy and decent and kind.

She looked so sweet. Like a kid sister. He could imagine her saying, *They pay me for this, can you believe it?* and *Let's have fun!*

By thick red candlelight, he imagined that he saw her wink.

Chuckling, Clay fished a nickel out of his pocket and laid it on the ledge.

"You're a grand girl, Wilma," he said, his voice big and echoey in the tiled room. He put his hands in his pockets and smiled up at all her images.

The Wilma on the poster moved. She took her hand off her breast, kissed her fingers, and reached down to press them to his lips. Her fingers were warm.

His mouth fell open in astonishment.

She leaned forward, then stepped down off the wall, dipping her fingertips into his open mouth, running her hand over his throat and down his arm as she walked behind him. She put both palms over his eyes.

Clay held very still.

He felt her lips touch his ear. A voice sounded in his head, not in the room.

Hey, baby. Tell me what you want.

His dick got hard. This was really spooky. For two cents he could run screaming.

But not yet.

His body felt light and peaceful. A certainty spread through him that everything was going to be all right.

C'mon. Tell me what you want.

Now Clay understood the candles and things. They were offerings. He imagined the snaggle-toothed boy without ear protectors coming in here and laying those roses on the ledge, saying something like, *There's this girl, she doesn't take me seriously, I want to marry her.*

Wilma's lips moved against his ear again. *Tell me more.*

Suddenly he let go of his irony and his Buddha-calm and his con-man aloofness. He had come to the shrine of Wilma and made his offering, and Wilma was prepared to answer his prayer, if he had the courage to say one.

He closed his eyes behind her palms and spoke humbly. "There's this girl. She doesn't take me seriously. I want to marry her." That wasn't so scary. "She has another guy in her life. He's, like, really good in bed. Really, really, really, *really* good. It's taken him two hundred years and a lot of magic powers to get this good. I think I have a chance, but—" His voice cracked. "I can't compete with that."

Hush, hush, you don't have to compete with that. You have what you need.

"You don't understand. He can give her anything she wants. Anything."

You have yourself to give.

"I'd give her anything," he blurted, wondering if that was really true. "But I don't have magic sex powers."

Her palms slipped from his eyes and rested on his shoulders. He could feel her behind him like a wavering warmth, like a bit of music the size of a human hand brushing up and down his body, making him hum back at her.

Hm. Then we can make a deal.

"A deal?"

She slid around to face him. Her eyes seemed huge. *You can give me something I want.*

A guy would give her anything if she looked at him like that.

He licked his lips. "What?"

The door burst open. "Clay? Are you in here?"

The candles went out.

Wilma vanished.

Clay turned toward the blinding fluorescent light in the doorway.

Jewel was silhouetted there, panting with a little sob in the back of her throat.

He ran forward. "What's the matter?"

"Randy's gone! He's in bed with those porn stars!"

She threw herself into his arms.

"You can't go in there!" somebody said from the doorway.

Jewel looked over her shoulder, hyperventilating.

"Come outta there!"

Clay shepherded her out into the bright light of the printing plant.

An old eight-fingered printer scowled at them. "Look at this door! What does it say?"

Jewel looked at the keep-out signs. Clay was impressed to watch the changes cross her face: blankness as she put her hysteria aside, then a questioning frown, then curiosity, then comprehension. By the time she looked at the printer, she was all cop.

"Why?" she said in a sinister voice.

"Because it says keep out!" The printer picked up the barricade board and tapped it into place with his fist, using, Clay noticed, the same old nail hole.

"Clay Dawes, Consumer Services." He showed the printer his badge. "If you don't mind, we'd like to have a word with you."

The printer's coverall said *Vincente* over the pocket. He looked at the badge. Silently, Jewel showed him hers. He swallowed. "Come into my office."

Clay followed him to a grubby, wood-partitioned workspace.

"It was the old men's room. We had the posters up, same as everywhere else. We all have a personal feeling for Wilma," Vincente said, and the hairs rose on the back of Clay's neck. Vincente looked from Clay to Jewel, frowning, and Clay could imagine him wondering how to explain to a nice-girl-slash-cop what happens when you light a candle in front of a Wilma poster in there. "It's too dirty."

"Gross," Clay said, helping him along.

"Yeah." Vincente seemed to struggle for words. "So we boarded it up. Nobody goes in there now."

"Unless they really feel the need?" Clay suggested.

Jewel frowned. "What need? What are you talking about?"

Vincente cut his eyes to Clay.

Clay said, "Remember O'Connor's sofa cushions?"

"Euw." She wrinkled her nose.

"You don't even want to see the men's room they use now."

A panicky look flickered across her face. "Was it the same as O'Connor's apartment?"

He nodded and stood up. "We'll probably have more questions later. Thanks for your time." He shook Vincente's hand, and a look passed between them that was strictly male.

"I'm always here," Vincente said.

Jewel blamed herself all the way back to the office. Clay was driving, so she had both hands free for tearing her hair.

"This is horrible. How am I gonna get in there? I can't." *Ugh!* Her skin crawled with heebie jeebies. "I can't go back in there and—and let him—oh, *ugh!* And meanwhile," she added angrily, "every minute he stays in that bearskin rug, he's doing Velvita Fromage or the Tokyo Twins."

"On another note," Clay said, "I wonder if your new employer orders their staff meeting pastries from Hoby's

Bäckerei. You've realized, of course, that the pastry bags in O'Connor's apartment and his locker come from the same address as his porn collection. If you're looking for a hinky vector—"

Jewel's jaw dropped. "You're shitting me." She blinked. "*Hoby's?* What do you mean? Hoby's stuff can't be hinky." The implications were staggering. "Oh, no! Hoby's is a Chicago institution!" she wailed. "I don't believe it!"

Clay shrugged. "I'm just saying."

Hoby's cow plops too hinky to eat? "Ow. This is not happening."

"I'm sorry," Clay said.

"Oh, God. It could be true."

"Well, don't panic. We'll experiment."

"Good idea." Her brain veered off to her real worry. "And how the hell am I going to get at that rug?" She imagined Randy and Velvita Fromage on the white fake bearskin rug—Randy and Velvita and Sancho, Randy and Velvita and Sancho and the Tokyo Twins—oh, and she mustn't forget Flash Titty—could he do multiple women? Of course he could—plus the guys in animal costumes—she put her hands over her eyes. "Argh! I need to steam-clean my brain!"

Clay patted her hand.

She sniffled. "I guess we'd better report to Ed."

At the DCS offices in the Kraft Building, Ed seemed to be holding a meeting. Most of their fellow investigators sat or stood in the staff room. Jewel and Clay slid into the back.

Ed looked gray and grim. "Assistant Commissioner Neebly from the Office for Economic Development will be comin' around to look the place over. So no clowning around. I need all youse to get busy. Wherever he is, you fill it up. Mill around. Move boxes outta storage and pile shit around on desks and stuff. Everybody cuddle

him up with hoops a steel by jowl so's we squish our-
selves through the halls like fuckin' lemmings inna mosh
pit in spawning season, know what I mean? Make it
look like we need every inch. That's all. Go back to
work. Heiss, Dawes, get in my office."

Jewel followed Clay, feeling a certain amount of unfo-
cused dread. "What was that all about?"

"Those OED sons a bitches. I'd like to tell him to take
a hike."

"Why don't you?" Clay said. "OED has no clout in
this department, has it?"

"Can't." Jewel shook her head. "Bing Neebly went to
high school with our commissioner."

"What's he inspecting for?" Clay said.

"Hinky shit," Ed said succinctly. "They demolished
the building, and then it came back outta thin air. What
if they sold it, and it did something hinky again? God
forbid it should vanish before the bonds clear. The feds
would be all over us like a cheap suit. Da mayor would
not be happy."

"Ed," Jewel cut in. "What do you want us to do?"

"I dunno. Think of something." Ed's caterpillar eyebrows worked with the effort of thought. "Maybe if we
could make the place look just a little hinky. But not *too*
hinky."

Clay said, "I get you. Make him doubt his eyes."

"Yeah. Scare him. Speaking of which, where's your
driver?"

Jewel said guiltily, "Uh, he's detained."

"Undercover," Clay said, and she sent him a sharp
look. "We got some intel on the pocket zone downstairs, by the way." He filled Ed in on the possible connection between Hoby's, Artistic Publishing Company,
and the pocket zone poppets in O'Connor's locker and
apartment. "It could be the pastry is involved somehow.
Contaminated."

Jewel shuddered at the very idea.

Ed looked skeptical. "I ain't takin' their danish away from those women." He gestured toward the outer office. "They'd kill me." Of course, Ed loved Hoby's, too.

"Oh, and get this," Jewel said, "Randy packed up O'Connor's porn and moved it out of the apartment, and the pocket zone went with it. Mrs. Othmar must have done the same, which just shows she has more balls than I have."

Clay crinkled his eyes at her.

She said, "So our hunch about how the pocket zone got there looks good. Inspectional Services is involved, so it has to be someone in the city. That kind of points in a certain direction. So can you get clearance from the Fifth Floor to give us the lists of properties the city wants to buy?"

Ed said, "I'll try. They're tight with that shit."

"Great," Jewel said. "And I think we may have found a way for the city to employ Randy. He can move hinky stuff for us."

"Don't get carried away." Ed waved both hands. "I got no clout. You know that."

"Hey, if pocket zones become a regular issue in Chicago, the Hinky Division will definitely need a toxic waste removal guy."

"He got papers? I ain't crossing the Immigration on this."

"Of course he has papers," she said, and sent Clay a look intended to drill straight into his skull. *Randy needs that ID, stat!* she tried to beam at him telepathically.

CHAPTER 13

Clay suggested Thai food and a movie and Jewel let him come back to her place. They sat on the sofa and pigged out while she fretted.

She felt very sorry for herself.

She felt pooped, stupid, fat in the can, and, what was most unfair, guilty. The sadness in Randy's face as he faded away wouldn't leave her.

"What did I do wrong?" she wailed.

"Couldn't tell you," Clay muttered, nose in the pad thai.

"He always acts so insulted! I never met anybody so worried about his dignity all the time! Swear to God, if I worried about his precious lordly feelings, I'd end up tiptoeing around like I really am his milkmaid or something." She stabbed a pot sticker with her chopstick and bolted it. "I can't stand thinking of him in that place where those women are—are *working*." She noticed Clay wasn't saying anything. "I'm sorry. I won't rant anymore. I'm totally wiped."

Clay put his chopsticks down and scooted closer to rub the tendons on top of her shoulders. "Save your worries, worrywart. Tomorrow's another day."

"You should get on the system at work and find out what you can about Bing Neebly. Use Ed's ID."

"You're loosening up," Clay remarked, his hands working wonderfully on her back.

"Mmm, thank you."

He said, "Two weeks ago, you wouldn't have encouraged me to use a supervisor's access code to snoop on a city official."

She moaned under his squeezing fingers. "I'm broken. My integrity and my common sense are shot. Plus, it turns out I'm a milkmaid after all. Lowborn *and* provincial-minded." She thought of the scene on the bearskin rug and shuddered.

"What's with milkmaid? Did Randy call you that?"

"You wouldn't understand. I guess it's because he knows my family owned a dairy farm. He told me recently that if I was back in eighteen-whatever, when he was a lord, he wouldn't even give me the time of day. I'm too low. I suppose he wouldn't bother to fuck me if he had his druthers," she added gloomily.

That was the worst part. She faced this every single time he did a zapper into some other woman's bed.

She'd got used to Randy's sexual services. Perilously comfortable with his magic mojo. Scarily satisfied, probably addicted.

And she wasn't good enough for him. Oh, good enough to save his butt when he got stuck in a bed somewhere. But long term? If he ever got free of the curse?

"Let me get this straight," Clay said, his hands pausing on her shoulders. "He *told* you that if he was walking down the street in eighteen-whatever and saw you, he'd just walk on by?"

She sniffed. "Yes. And I could see what he was thinking, too, because that was before you fixed what that Venus Machine did to me, when it gave me telepathy about men and sex? And he thought I was a *milkmaid*. I mean, with the yoke and pails and a big white stupid hat like some girl in a beer ad!"

Clay turned her on the sofa to face him. "You do know that machine was a fake, right? It didn't work."

"I only wish."

He looked exasperated. "Jewel, you can't afford to be credulous. We're supposed to be catching frauds, not buying into the con."

"I suppose you think you can teach me all about that," she said, stung. "Mister Yeah-but-I've-never-been-indicted."

"Well, yes. That's more or less what Ed said when he hired me." Clay seemed miffed.

Was he cheesed off because she was obsessing about Randy?

"I could see what you were thinking, too." She lifted her eyes to his. Suddenly he looked very not-frivolous and unsmug. "You would look at me, and I'd see a white picket fence and a golden retriever."

A moment of panic flickered in his eyes. He pulled away. "Tell me again what you thought you were doing."

"Reading men's minds. Randy put it into my head," she said with venom, "and then that stupid Venus Machine zapped me, and then whenever I made eye contact with a man, *euw*. Randy was like a sheet of glass, I always understood what he was thinking. But then, I almost always do. You, I don't know. I never figured out the dog and fence thing. Probably you thought I was a bitch, or else I was trying to keep you inside the law, or something. But random guys on the street, euw. Thank God you were able to fix the machine and reverse the effect."

Clay made a sound in his throat.

She frowned. "You had this whole explanation about chakras and vibrational frequencies. Don't tell me you've forgotten."

In a troubled voice, he said, "That was sympathetic magic. You thought it would work, so it worked."

"Is that like real magic?"

He shook his head, watching her face. She'd never seen Clay look so serious for so long. When he wasn't trying to put one over, he seemed like someone who'd been fighting a losing battle all his life. A sweet boy, too young for war.

While she watched, his eyes darted to hers and crinkled up in a mischievous expression. Kid to con artist in four seconds.

He held up a cellophane-covered square.

"Wanna look at feelthy pictures?"

So she let him play the Hot Pink movie Onika had given them. She was too tired to argue. Sheer surprise at having an intimate moment with Clay Dawes when she wasn't the one on the defensive had thrown her off balance.

She was so off balance, in fact, that she let him get fresh on the sofa.

Onika's porn for women came across cute and sweet and sexy, sort of like Wilma, the blonde mascot of Artistic Publishing. The story was about a lady librarian in hornrims and frumpy clothes who hooks up with a geeky male professor-type in hornrims and a tweed jacket, while researching Tantric sex in the limited-access shelves. Once they were naked, of course, they proved to be physically perfect. But at least the professor didn't have a foot-long schweinstücke. And the camera spent more time on their faces and slow caresses than on jackhammer genital action. He even wore a condom.

At some point in the middle of a silly yet tender scene where the professor tried to put his ankle behind his own head, Clay slid his hands up under Jewel's red knit top. She let him.

I shouldn't sleep with my partner. More than a mantra, it's a good idea.

Jewel was sick of being responsible. She hadn't had sex

in forty-eight hours, her incubus was doing somebody else, possibly this very porn star, damn her scrawny ass and perky tits, and Clay, as usual, was just Clay. A normal guy. He almost fell off the couch trying to kick his shoes off, and she laughed until she got the hiccups.

And yet she couldn't forget that moment of vulnerability in his face. He was so darned indirect. If she were to take his sexual messages seriously—the heavy focus on intimacy, the extreme vanilla quality, his slowness— she might almost believe he had been making love to her all this time, while she'd been having sex with him.

That unsettled her. *This is not about l.o.v.e.* Setting aside his style in bed, Clay's message came across loud and clear: *I'll go easy on you if you go easy on me.*

She would never have to work at a relationship with him.

On the other hand, she might never know who he was.

This whole train of thought gave her the willies.

They spent an hour on the sofa in front of the TV. By the end of Onika's girlie-porn movie, Jewel felt sad and unaccountably lonely. Clay did his best but, every time she looked over at the screen, she saw the girl from the bearskin rug, and her mind wandered off, picturing the dreams that Velvita Fromage might be having while she cavorted with Sancho and Randy.

In the end, to Jewel's deep shame and confusion, she faked falling asleep.

Clay took it like a gentleman. She lay still while he got up and put his shoes and shirt back on. As he bent and pressed a kiss to her forehead, she felt an urge to drag him down on the sofa with her again. She kept her eyes closed.

When the door had shut behind him, she got up, got naked, crashed into bed, and pulled out her battered vibrator, wondering why on earth she had turned down a perfectly good man when she was horny.

Maybe tonight the vibrator made her feel more in control. She badly needed to feel in control. Odd, because boffing random guys used to be her number one way of feeling in control.

Of course Clay wasn't random. Anything but. Her partner. She rationalized her decision by invoking the don't-fuck-your-partner rule, which hadn't worked very well so far.

Maybe that was why, as her little electric friend buzzed, she thought about Randy instead.

Next morning, as she checked her E-mail, she had a sudden attack of nosiness and inspected the register that kept track of Randy's activity on her computer.

The browser history was a mile long. *Hm. Have to ask Clay about this click-bot thing.* Excel tutorial. Microsoft Word tutorial. Good boy, Randy was building solid work skills there. Solitaire—he'd used the most advanced form and had beaten the computer more than eleven hundred times.

And a text file, eleven kilobytes, called "My First Month, by Randy Darner." She clicked on it.

As she read the first line, Jewel flushed. *This is private.* Her mouth went dry.

She couldn't have stopped reading for a million dollars.

CHAPTER 14

"My First Month"
by Randy Darner

I was twenty-six when my life ended and I became immortal. I didn't know at the time that this had happened. One moment, I was sneering at my mistress, my pride stinging from her complaint, and the next, I was bodiless, blind, hearing her voice pronounce a sentence that has yet to run its course. As judges will, secure in their wigs of office, she ranted a good deal, but what I remember vividly is this: *Until you satisfy one hundred women, you are a prisoner in this bed, an incubus.*

A hundred women! From my lady's complaint I was to understand that I had yet to satisfy a single one. That stung worse than ever her vengeful magicks could.

COME, RANDALL, THIS IS TEDIOUS. THIS IS TO BE PORN, NOT PULING LAMENTATION.

Of my first days as an incubus I remember little. I dreamed of whores, and the things whores do. In time, with growing dismay, I realized that the brass bed in which I lay imprisoned was situated in a brothel.

Well, at least my task should be easy enough.

So I thought.

My lady had granted me magical powers, powers to enter a woman's secret heart and sniff out, as a hound sniffs out a coney in its burrow, her hidden desires, be she never so respectable. Whoso lay in my bed, I would know her wants, and would have the power, supposedly, to render her wanton.

Yet in that unclean academy it seemed that the whores did not desire desire, not even abed. I found them distasteful. They were little better than drabs. They were dirty, coarse, and lowborn, as were their customers, and the girls were further cheapened by their work. The sauciest opera dancer was as an angel floating above the sewer where they plied their trade. They did not even serve gentlemen.

I spied on them whenever they occupied my bed. There they performed prodigies of contortion—and yet felt nothing. As my mistress promised, their desires were in my view.

But not one of them desired congress.

In a moment of hurt, I had declared to my mistress that all women were like this, though I hadn't believed it.

But what if it were true? In despair I wondered, are none of these women ever carried forward, flesh upon flesh, in the sweaty tangle of the moment? Is there no whore who jousts for jousting's sake?

I couldn't believe it.

Yet the more time I spent wading, as it were, with my coat-skirts fastidiously raised, through these women's lives, the more certain it seemed that I would never be free.

They were pathetic wretches. They went hungry. Some racked their bellies with back-alley physicks, trying to rid themselves of child. Some were beaten by their abbess or by their patrons. All were broken to their labor, broken as a dung-hauler's horse is broken, without regard for their pleasure.

Reluctantly I acknowledged that one's desire might lie in abeyance while the necessities of life went unfilled.

I FEAR MY PORN IS A POOR EFFORT. YET I FEEL
THIS HAS MERIT IF PERHAPS ONLY TO MYSELF.

That first fortnight bored me and disgusted me. I was
sure that my mistress meant me to stay imprisoned forever. Nothing could be less to the taste of a man of my
pride than to pander to whores' desires. Faugh, what
petty desires! They desired to drink themselves insensi-
ble, or to dress well, or to scratch out the eyes of some
other member of their tawdry sisterhood.

And then I met Maggie. A senior whore, she had been
stolen by the abbess from a rival, so she claimed, and
was paid better than the others, which boast got her hair
pulled. She was thirty if a day, pockmarked, with a
screeching voice, drooping dugs, and a paint-raddled
face. She constantly bickered with her fellows and stole
from their hidden stores of money. She lied. She drove
secret bargains with her patrons to cheat the abbess of
her share whenever she performed special favours. She
was none too clean in her habits.

Yet she was lusty. How my Maggie loved to bounce!
She brought first to my brass bed a man in orders, perhaps some country vicar up from his respectable village,
and fucked him soundly.

To my astonishment, I found myself attracted. O won-
derful moment! My body, it seemed, came back to me: My
heart beat again, I panted, my pulse hammered in my ears,
I felt the slide of skin upon skin and a fiery bodily urge.

At first I thought it was my own body.

Then I realized it could not be, for I'd no power over
my limbs.

Was it the stout old vicar's lust I felt?

But as Maggie threw her leg over his belly and took
him, first fore, then aft, riding as if the very devil had his
horn in her, I came to understand that it was her body I
felt: *her* heartbeat, *her* pulse, *her* unclean skin burning
with irresistible pleasure.

And I stopped thinking of her inferiority.

By day I lay like her secret shadow under the coverlet, exulting in sensations—*her* sensations—as she pleasured herself. At night I learned her trade from the inside out. I, who had condescended to patronize so many of her kind, knowing nothing of what it cost or paid such a creature, I became one with her, and willingly. For to share in her panting, the rise of her greedy hunger, the sharp peaks which visited her over and over, more often and more powerfully than those crises which had satisfied me in my proper person as Lord Pontarsais, ass that I had been—this sharing was glorious.

I was being broken to my work, like that cart horse.

I began to understand, I thought, what my mistress had meant to teach me with her terrible curse.

A woman's lusts are different. Her need is particular to her sex, and quite unlike the need of man. How pleased I was with this insight! To learn this, my mistress had sent me to a harsh school.

Had she presented herself to me, how I could not yet picture, perhaps by laying herself in this bed once more, yes, that was a pleasant thought, then might I willingly have shared her flesh, traced the secret pulse in her veins, rejoiced with her, perhaps even while another man pleasured her.

But she never came for me.

Not ever.

I had been abandoned to my fate.

In time, Maggie moved on. I never knew if she left the academy for a private patron, or retired wealthy, or, more likely, harmed herself irreparably through overwork or drink or quarrelsomeness and sank back into the stews again. She was replaced by other whores, less lusty.

But I was never again aloof from their flesh. From Maggie onward, I lay alert to the slightest stirring of desire in whatever woman had my bed. Only when that woman felt desire could I feel alive.

I was no longer a man, and not yet an incubus.

In the months to come I was to discover that I had many other powers. There is a space inside every human mind, vaster than all the cosmos, like a library, or a forest, or the stacked and ordered spheres of the heavens, and this space is constructed of all that has been put into that mind, whether by bible or by painting or by plays or mummery or by the day in, day out practices of life itself. It is unimaginably crowded.

My hundredth woman calls it demonspace. But it is no more than the inside of her mind and mine, the sum of all we have ever thought or dreamt.

Moreover, this space has no order, except as the mind imagines it. To a creature like myself, an invader creeping in at the portal of desire, all is a jumble, except for the bright, clear call of lust, like a hunting horn, showing how I may share a woman's body for just so long as she feels pleasure. While I occupy that space, I see the map to her satisfaction clearly traced. I know what other man's face she may see while she is servicing her husband. I can assume that face. I can become him and perform prodigies he never could.

This is the power of the incubus: to ferret out what pleases any woman and to provide it, however impossible. For in that space, we are as gods, she and I. Whatever she can imagine, I can perform. If she has desires even she will not confess, I can find them and make them flesh, surprising her and delighting her.

But I run ahead of my story.

These powers did not come under my control all in a flash.

The bitterest year of all my decades of sexual servitude was that year in the Cheapside academy. For as much as I came to know and sympathize with the women trapped in that loathesome life, as much as they were able to teach me, I failed them.

I pleased not one of them.

At this date, I have carried a little more than a hundred women to that jeweled isle where there is no fear or pain or shame. They have lent me their breath, their pulse, their pleasure, their release. I have made stars fall for them. I have made mares of them and mounted them as their stallion. I have brought the dead back into their arms for one more tender tumble, and, borrowing secrets from their memories, I have made them believe that I was the departed, and that he loved them still. All this and more can I do.

But I cannot turn back the clock to repay Maggie or any of her poor sisters for the things they gave to me.

That failure will live with me the rest of eternity, I think. For surely, if the body of Randy Darner, third Earl Pontarsais should perish, in that moment I will slip into the nearest bed, wherever it may be, and serve out more shameful centuries until some angel comes to set me free.

And will she pass over my failure? Or will she grant me absolution at last?

Jewel's belly had gone hot and runny. Her head was on fire with pictures of Randy: Randy in an old-timey English cat house; Randy locked out in the darkness, slamming mothlike against the window while the girls did their job; Randy waiting for forgiveness from a bitch who would never come back to see how much he had learned. Her breastbone burned. She remembered making love to him on the snowy Field Museum porch, in view of the frozen lake, pouring her heat into him. In demonspace Randy had been cold and she burning, but the snow had come out of the depths of her own mind.

Randy had only showed it to her. Randy could always find her, no matter what frozen hell she was in.

A kind of high, soundless singing started up in the back of her head, like a choir of cicadas. It made her feel fuzzy and open and pleasantly full and a little sap-headed.

I owe him, she thought.

CHAPTER
15

Thursday was a Velvita day. When she put on the big fluffy robe and walked into makeup, Lena already felt like a porn star. It was a slow process. The body makeup. An hour on her hair and hands. Sewing the costume on her. When she looked in the mirror and licked her lips, Velvita Fromage looked back: wicked, contented, in control.

Her scene today had been developed between her and Onika the week before. It was written for Velvita and Sancho, kind of a spooky but emotional scenario about a historical re-enacter and the ghost of a Revolutionary War soldier. Velvita had doubts about some of the plotty stuff—you didn't want so much plot that it delayed the sex scenes—but once she and Sancho were in it, it flowed naturally. The situation created the characters. The dialogue cued the sex. Perfect.

This time it was a little more than perfect. Maybe Sancho was getting into the role of Zebediah. Maybe her imagination got fired up with the Puritan-girl costume. Maybe it was the tickly fake white bearskin rug.

Whatever. Velvita found herself getting *into* it.

And at the critical moment, just when she knew she was going to come her brains out and give Onika footage that would sell a hundred thousand copies, she felt herself slip sideways on the bearskin rug and slide deep into a crevasse between the hairs.

What the—?

Down, sideways, round and round like a Cheerio in a toilet bowl. Loop-de-loop like the The Demon roller coaster at Six Flags. She giggled and shrieked and squealed.

And she sailed out off the end of the invisible roller coaster and into the arms of a gorgeous, unfamiliar, naked man.

His arm circled her waist. The merry-go-round struck up a waltz. *I'm dreaming*, Velvita thought, *that's why this isn't scary.* She looked up into the stranger's face.

His big black eyes burned down into hers with compelling intensity. They danced, and the swooping music and the lift of his hand in the small of her back seemed to hit her right in the sweet spot. She remembered that the cameras would be watching, and the exhibitionist in her let out a whoop, and a cyclone orgasm whirled her in circles around her mysterious black-eyed partner.

While she reeled with sexual aftershock, he spoke.

My name is Randy. I need your help to get out of here.

Jewel reported to work at Baysdorter Boncil Thursday feeling more in control. For one thing, she'd got off last night, which always settled her nerves. Plus she was back in her navy polyester, which gave her its own brand of power.

So when Steven called her into his office first thing, she thought she was ready.

He said without any buildup whatever, "There are naked pictures of you all over the Internet."

Her mouth dropped open. "Excuse me?" Delayed shock hit her like a slow, wet fish in the face.

He checked her out with a slapworthy leer. "You have

nice nipples for a cop. They look great with clothes-pins." He rattled off the www-dot-blah-blah-blah in a gloating voice.

A hot flush crept up her back. *How did he find out about that?* And, *So he really does know why I'm here.*

She snapped back, "And you do so many cops."

"Well. . . ." He leered wider.

She felt like punching him. *What happened to Mister I'm-too-sexy-for-my-suit?* "What *do* you want? Besides a chance to exercise your Tourette's?"

"Be nice, or I'll see to it your superiors have that URL."

"Too late. It's old news in my shop. You got a better threat?"

Steven glowered. "How about I can get you fired."

"I doubt it." Her brain started working, and she calmed down. "What do you want?"

"You know what I want."

"No, I don't. I'm not nice, remember. You'll have to spell it out for me."

He leaned forward. "Kill this case. Make it go away."

She was about to tell him to go fuck himself when she remembered that the woman who ran the Artistic Building, source of Hoby's pastries and hinky porn, was named Tannyhill, too.

Was it possible that Steven knew how Wilma and the Artistic Building were connected to O'Connor's pocket zones?

Hell, he was in real estate, wasn't he? And they were looking for a scammer with ties to real estate and hinky porn.

She would have to pay Onika Tannyhill another visit.

He misread her thoughtful look. "Don't play dumb. I know exactly who and what you are."

"Yeah, but which case?" she blurted.

Steven opened his mouth. No sound came out. He scowled.

She nodded. "Work on that and get back to me."

Heart pounding unpleasantly, she walked away from her desk.

Time she touched base with her new best friend, Maida Sacker.

But Maida's office door was closed. Jewel peered through the window beside the door. Tonia from the proposal center was in there, in tears, while Maida snarled visibly.

Jewel was fed up with how these people talked to the help.

She walked in.

"Mind if I join you?" She plopped down in the chair beside Tonia. Tonia's eyes rolled, as if Jewel were a two-hundred-pound bumblebee.

"I'm in a meeting," Maida said.

"Just pretend I'm not here."

"Was there something you wanted?"

"Yeah, I was wondering if you could tell me exactly why your daughter left the firm and how long she worked for Steven Tannyhill before he did something inappropriate to her."

Tonia gasped.

Maida turned white. "You can go now," she told Tonia.

Tonia scuttled out.

Maida got up, slammed her office door, returned to her desk, and leaned forward. "What," she hissed. No more.

"What does this have to do with my case? I don't know. I come here looking into something hinky and inappropriate happening at BB." Once again she spotted someone peeping through the window into Maida's office. Jewel ignored them. "And I find a smorgasbord of options. It seems to go back a long way. Like, before Lena was born."

"My daughter has nothing to do with your case."

"Was she assigned to Steven right away, as I was? Does he get all the fresh meat?"

Maida curled her lip. "You are hideous."

"You are unmarried, and the father of your child was your boss. He was also Steven's boss. I hear great things about old John Baysdorter. A real gentleman. He paid for your daughter's education, didn't he?"

Maida folded her lips shut. Her eyes were fierce.

"In fact it might be simpler if I have a conversation with Lena myself—"

"Don't keep saying her name! Lena is dead!" Maida lifted her face and raised her voice. "I have no daughter!"

"Really," said a new voice.

Jewel felt a draft on the back of her neck. She turned.

A young woman stood in the doorway, a tall, cool brunette in a black anorak, black stockings, black miniskirt, black boots. Big steel cross. Lots of raccoon mascara. Very goth-art-student. "I told you before that you would have to take a stand." Her cultured voice had a threat in it.

She looked familiar.

"I can't," Maida choked out.

"You mean you won't."

Jewel swivelled in her seat to stare at her. Goth Girl *sounded* familiar.

"You never learn, do you?"

Maida didn't answer.

The girl looked searchingly at Jewel. Then she walked out.

Jewel wasted thirty precious seconds watching the color come and go in Maida's face. Then she got it. *The missing Lena!*

She dashed out of Maida's office.

But Goth Girl had gone.

Whoa. What was that? Jewel figured she wouldn't get anything out of Maida.

She went back to her desk.

Steven stayed in his lair all day. The only time he opened his door it was to admit Tonia. He shut the door in Jewel's face and Jewel opened it immediately, ostentatiously propping the door open with a shoe from her bottom desk drawer, which was full of shoes.

She went back to her keyboard, feeling unsettled. Now that she wasn't engaged in battle with him, she had time to wonder why Steven had gone looking for naked pictures of her on the Internet. *I mean, what, do I have "girl most likely to have dated extreme jerks" tattooed on my forehead?* He sure was proud of finding them, too. He seemed to think she'd curl up and die.

It gave her a nasty feeling to know he was looking for dirt.

Not like the dirt on me is hard to find. She'd been a busy girl, back before Randy.

Tonia came out alone, shutting the door. She brought the shoe to Jewel. "I think you're amazing," she whispered. There were still tearstains on her face, but she seemed composed.

"Hey, whose shoe is this?"

Tonia looked at it. "That's Lena's."

"After *how* long?" Jewel whispered skeptically. "The drawer's full of them!"

"Nobody will touch them. It's been almost two years."

The old "two years" song again. *I have got to get the story on this.* "Oh, another question. This company buys pastry for the break room from Hoby's, right?"

"Yeah, it's our best employee benefit."

"Do you get the same pastry in for meetings? Like, did what's-her-name order it for Mike's rollout meeting that turned into an orgy?"

Tonia blinked. "Yeah, like extra. Huge piles of it. Why?" She leaned closer and hissed, "You think Steven put Ex on the pastry?"

Jewel lifted her shoulders.

"Boy." Tonia's eyes widened. "I hope you get him for it."

Jewel stuck her thumb in the air and winked. "Thanks for the intel. Keep me posted, Agent Ninety-Nine."

Tonia giggled and went away.

Hm. Hm and hm. What was Maida up to? And were the girls right? Was it simply a street aphrodisiac? It couldn't be. Not with the girls turning into dogs, and Mike and Precious on the ceiling.

She could ask Randy if he thought the pastry was hinky.

Oh, except Randy was in a bearskin rug, doing porn stars.

With superhuman effort, she put that out of her mind.

CHAPTER 16

Jewel wasted the afternoon sticking mailing labels on envelopes, bored to the screaming point. Nobody else came up to dish. She knew she should be trying to think through the chain-o'-hinkyness: the porn, the poppet, the portable pocket zone, the publishing company, the cow plops. *Mmm, Hoby's.* She went to the break room and found some Hoby's cinnamon twists and brought them back to her desk to nibble.

Instead her brain was a squirrel cage: Randy in bed with porn stars, Steven trolling the Internet for dirt about her, Maida trying to sneak her out of proximity to Steven, Onika proudly showing off her women's porn, the slow stroke of skin on skin on that bearskin rug, Wilma dancing on stacks of magazines, that goth girl confronting Maida, Clay showing her that movie and trying to take advantage of her. She almost wished she'd let him. In spite of last night's bout with the vibrator, she felt ready to explode.

She wondered how the porn stars were getting along with Randy's special effects, and then she wished she hadn't, because that forced her to think what she'd been avoiding thinking: *Randy's diary.* And a world of guilt.

Holy Moses. The most she'd known of Randy before was two things, a wow in bed and a spoiled brat on his feet. She had never really considered what went on in his head.

That made her flush with shame. *I use him.* Did he think she was as bad as those johns back in 1811? Because it had never occurred to her to wonder if he was having fun. God, she felt horrible. He'd once said to her, *I cannot afford to be angry with you.* And she had actually said to him, *Can we just have sex and go to sleep?*

She was a horrible person. Horrible.

C'mon, he loves it.

Part of him, probably, sure. And part hated being a slave. And part—apparently he had more parts than she'd noticed—a part new to her thought deep thoughts about it all, and was actually, like, a responsible grown-up or something.

And that diary. *Failure will live with me the rest of eternity, I think. . . . I will slip into the nearest bed . . . and serve out more shameful centuries until some angel comes to set me free.*

It made her feel soft and hard at the same time. That diary was more words than Randy had ever spoken to her, in three months of joined-at-the-hip contact.

Some angel I am.

At four-thirty, she realized she was still emotional and horny, mentally replaying Randy's Greatest Hits in Bed.

Thoroughly annoyed with herself, she phoned Britney's cell. "I need margarita therapy, stat."

"I'm on it," Britney said. "But it's pouring rain."

"I'll pay for your cab. I need to talk to somebody normal."

"Thanks, I think. How was the porn company?" Britney said avidly. "Is anybody listening?"

"Probably." Jewel glanced at the clock on her desk. "Ten minutes, in the Bennigan's on North Michigan."

"Deal."

In the bar downstairs from Baysdorter Boncil, Jewel or-

dered two pitchers of margaritas and watched rain bucket
down on Michigan Avenue outside. The margaritas arrived when Britney did. "Keep 'em coming," Jewel said.

"Yikes," Britney murmured, putting her dripping um-
brella under her bar stool. "Extra limes?" she said to the
waitress.

Jewel growled, "I'm walking home. Plus I've had the
week from hell."

"Do tell," Britney said cozily. She wrapped her lips
around the straw in her margarita, and Jewel noticed for
the first time that her friend would make an acceptable
porn star.

Jewel described the porn factory from top to bottom.
Britney made suitable noises. Jewel began to feel semi-
human. *I may be a slut but at least I'm not a whore.*

"The thing is, the guy porn didn't bother me." *Much.*
"It was the girl porn that made me nuts."

"Good nuts or bad nuts?"

Jewel pursed her lips. "Itchy. Antsy." She admitted,
"Okay, it was kind of hot."

"Huh." A grain of salt clung to Britney's pretty upper
lip. She licked it off thoughtfully. "And you say it was
less skanky than guy porn."

"Yeah. Like, the actors were having real sex but they
were pretending to be in love. Really twisted my head."
Jewel's right temple felt soft and achy. "I should stop
drinking."

Britney poured her another. "Don't stop now. Tell me
about the women."

"They're perfect," Jewel said gloomily. She looked
around her at the bar, packed full as it could hold of secretaries and admin assistants, who weren't chopped
liver, either. In her frumpy navy polyester, she felt like a
sea lioness among otters. "Oh, probably you could look
at them on the street and not even notice them. But once
they're naked? Boy."

"Are they skinny? I heard they're skinny in real life."

Jewel tried to be fair. "Well, it's movies. They say the camera adds ten pounds." She thought of those naked pictures that Steven had been so glad to find, and how fat she looked in them, the one time she'd had the courage to look. Steven's cracks were getting to her, delayed reaction. She added hollowly, "I think more like twenty pounds. In person, the skinny looks really odd with those beachball boobs."

"I heard they've all had work done."

"That Velvita Fromage wasn't. Didn't. Hadn't." Now Jewel was sure that the girl in last night's movie was the one on the bearskin rug. "She looked normal, boobwise. It was freaky."

Britney emptied the first pitcher into her glass and reached for the second. "You're not making sense, Jules."

"They're whores," Jewel blurted. "They do it for money."

"I do it for money sometimes," Britney said, shocking her. "Like that time my car caught fire and burned up because a pigeon dropped a butt on it when I was filling the tank from a can out on Mannheim Road? I was flat broke. Sayers offered me money and I took it."

"*Sayers?*"

"He was really sweet. It was right after he came back from psych leave."

Jewel tried to smooth the shock out of her face. Since Britney first joined the department, they'd made a pact to accept each other's sex lives. No wigging out, no judgments.

Brit must have sensed her shock. "So, what's your point? If they've had work done, that means they're whores, and that's bad? Or is it that they look better than you, and you think you couldn't get paid for it if you tried?" She sounded cranky. "Jeez. Sayers isn't the only one who needs therapy."

Jewel realized it was time for damage control. She opened her mouth to soothe, then stopped.

Over by the door stood the goth girl.

She was looking at Jewel.

She walked straight up to where they sat.

"You must be Jewel. Randy sent me."

"Hey, Cinderella," Jewel said, as the tequila finally fired a few synapses. "I think I have a drawerful of your shoes."

The newcomer nodded. "Lena Sacker."

"Jewel Heiss." Then Jewel's eyes caught up with her ears.

Holy crow, that's the girl from the bearskin rug. Lena. Velvita Fromage. She's Onika's assistant.

And doing Randy.

Lena put her hand out. Jewel stared at it stupidly. "Velvita Fromage is my porn name."

She's doing Randy on that bearskin rug.

When Jewel didn't shake, Brit said, "Wow! Put her here! Are you really in movies? I'm Britney."

Lena shook hands coolly with Britney.

Jewel blinked. *I'm being a bitch.* "I'm sorry. Hi. Uh, thanks for finding me." She offered her hand, meeting Lena's eyes with a painfully fake apologetic smile. "I'm a recovering moron."

Lena gave Jewel a limp, three-fingered handshake.

"Margarita?" Britney said.

"Thanks." Lena slid up onto a stool.

Britney waved to the waitress for another glass. "And some curly cheese fries. And one of those deep fried onion blossoms."

"How did you recognize me?" Jewel said. It was harder to hate Velvita now that she had a real name and a mother.

"Randy showed me your picture."

"He doesn't have a picture of me."

Lena eyed her. "He can make one."

Randy could show her every dimple of Jewel's cellulite if he wanted. Jewel covered her face for a moment.

"This is the guy who's been living with you?" Britney said. "He's some kind of sex demon," she explained to Lena.

"So I gathered." Perched on the stool, Lena crossed her legs as if gravity had never been invented. The black miniskirt rode up her thighs, revealing that the black tights were in fact stockings on lacy black garters. Lena caught Jewel looking and raised her eyebrows.

Rub it in. Those legs have been wrapped around my boyfriend. And, argh, she'd just thought the B-word!

"We have other things in common," Lena said, smiling. "If you're not too much of a moron to discuss them."

Jewel realized Lena was trying to be polite in the face of Jewel's attitude problem.

She also remembered why she needed to talk to Cinder-Lena. "Steven Tannyhill."

"That's him," Lena said. The waitress put a salt-rimmed glass in front of her.

"This is your boss upstairs?" Britney said.

Lena poured herself a margarita. "Don't let me interrupt."

It occurred to Jewel that just because she and Lena both hated Steven Tannyhill, it didn't mean Lena was trustworthy. But she was three margaritas down. Her grrl-radar said the porn star was okay. And Randy had trusted her to fetch Jewel, hadn't he?

"Well, I was about to tell Britney that Steven is acting

bizarre. He seems to think he's God, or at least the big cheese of Baysdorter Boncil."

"That's Steven," Lena murmured.

"But, well, get this. He knows I'm undercover in there. Maybe Maida told him. He seems to have her under his thumb." Lena scowled. Jewel said, "I can't believe he grasps the risks. I could sue BB for a skillion frillion dollars for what he's said to me. It's like he thinks he's got the drop on me, and he's absurdly pissed because I'm not rolling over."

"He's a compulsive risk-taker," Lena said.

"Yeah, but talking about clothespins on my nipples? How dumb is that?"

Britney's breath hissed in. "I'll hold him down so you can kick him."

Jewel noticed Lena didn't address Maida being under Steven's thumb. "Today's little gem?" she said to Britney. "He found those naked pictures of me on the Internet and threatened to send the URL to my boss if I don't 'kill the case.' "

"The pictures with the clothespins?" Britney said.

Jewel said darkly, "It's a friggin' shame I'm not a lawsuit kind of girl."

Lena said, "If you don't like it, why don't you have them taken down?"

"How the heck do I do that?" Jewel grumbled.

"There's a website you go to. I log in four times a month."

"But you're a porn star."

"And, duh, my image is for *sale*. That means no one can give it away. For example, some fool got into the shoot one day about six months ago, pretending to be an electrician, and took a lot of candids. We took him to the cleaners." Lena bit a lime wedge in half and chewed. "You didn't know you could do that?"

Britney looked at Jewel with concern. "I thought you liked having those pictures up."

Jewel shook her head.

"Well, shit!" Britney said. "And here I thought—"

"Skip it." Jewel felt like an idiot. Why hadn't it occurred to her she could have those pictures taken down?

Turns out even a porn star can get protection from that crap. This is exactly what the Department of Consumer Services is for, and I'm acting like a poster child for the poor dumb helpless consumer who doesn't even know it's there.

Lena looked at Britney. Jewel felt annoyed at the degree of intimacy she detected between them.

"I thought she was tougher than that," Lena said, over Jewel's head.

"That's just an act," Britney said.

Lena raised elegant eyebrows. "Don't let Steven know. He can smell blood in the water a mile away."

First my boyfriend, then my buddy. Steam hissed out of Jewel's ears.

"One curly cheese fry, one fried onion blossom," said the waitress, saving them from a blast of Jewel's rage. "Another pitcher, ladies?"

"No," Jewel said.

"Yes," Lena said.

"Sure," Britney said.

Jewel defended her honor. "Look, I figure I'm not supposed to feel ashamed." She flushed. "I'm supposed to be a free spirit. All liberated and stuff. I guess," she said, her blush burning hotter on her cheeks and ears, "I guess I feel like I'd be betraying my—my macho if I blink."

Britney patted her hand. "Well, I feel ashamed sometimes, but hey."

Lena said, "Every woman in my industry feels ashamed. We live with it. Even when we aren't ashamed, we feel bad because we aren't. And then some jerk makes a rude remark to you, and you hate yourself, and you hate him. It's part of being a porn star."

"It's part of being a woman," Britney said. "I don't think there's any protection for anybody from that stuff."

"Wait, I understand." Lena pointed at Jewel. "You think you should feel like a guy."

"Hey!" Jewel said. "Enough already with the margarita-grade psychoanalysis."

"Guess what, guy porn stars feel ashamed, too," Lena said.

Jewel changed the subject. "There's something odd about the way Steven threw those pictures in my face."

"Who took 'em?" Lena said.

"Some guy I met in a bar. I got royally snockered, and we had dinner, and then we went back to his place. I didn't know anything about it until Roller Skates Jason mentioned the pictures to me. I guess he did them while I was passed out at his apartment."

"Jason is this dickhead at our office," Britney said.

"*Who* did them?" Lena pursued.

"I said I don't remember." Jewel felt exposed. Her blush was now all over her entire body. "I used to, uh, get around."

The whole margarita thing began to seem like a dumb idea. She felt like everybody in the bar was flapping their ears and pretending not to listen. A huge, balloon-shaped, middle-aged guy in a raincoat came into the bar. He looked straight at Jewel and turned as white as his rain-coat.

God, I've got slut written on me so big, they spot it when they walk in the door.

Raincoat Guy stared at her. Then he blundered through the bar and into a private dining room in the back.

"So what site are these pictures on?" Lena said, pulling out her phone.

"Oh, no," Jewel said. "Please. No. Let it alone."

"I can report it for you right now."

Jewel knew the URL. Even if she'd forgotten, Steven had reminded her. She rattled it off.

"Those degenerates," Lena said. "They're notorious for posting involuntaries. Many times I don't complain, but these guys are such sleazebags that I always rat them out. Hm." She looked closer at the teeny screen on her phone. "Have you looked at these pictures?"

"Not lately."

Lena squinted. "Because I think you should."

Reluctantly Jewel took the phone from her and squinted.

"Use the arrow at the bottom to zoom in."

Jewel used the arrow. "Oh. Holy shit."

The guy who took the pictures had carefully kept himself out of range of the camera, but he'd apparently failed to consider the mirror behind the bed. As Jewel zoomed in, he came into focus, his digital camera held out at chest height, giving her a clear view of his face.

He was, hello, Steven Tannyhill.

The phone clattered to the table. Lena scooped it up.

Jewel put her hands on either side of her splitting head. "I don't get it." But she could feel the pieces coming together.

"Who is it?" Britney said.

Jewel felt a rush of damp air and looked up in time to see Lena point at the front door.

"Him. That's who took the pictures," Lena said, pointing her phone like a camera at the doorway.

Steven walked in, looking like Satan in a good suit. Just like the fat guy in the raincoat, he stopped dead when he saw Jewel, and turned color.

Then he, too, swung off through the bar and into the private dining room.

"Why on earth would he do a thing like this?" Lena said, going back to studying Jewel's public shame on her phone. "Steven likes to have power over women, but he's very pragmatic. Every woman he's screwed at BB, it was for a reason, and he got leverage with it."

Britney had her cop voice on. "When did this happen? Try to remember." Jewel felt doubly humiliated. She was a pathetic victim and her ditziest friend had to play cop with her.

She shut her eyes. "It was at least a year ago, maybe two. The Cubbies were losing spectacularly, I remember. People in the bar were, like, in tears. That's what we started talking about."

"Against the Cardinals," Britney said positively. "I lost a hundred dollars on that game. That was two years ago."

"Were you on a case at the time?" Lena said.

"No. No, I was on vacation." Was she supposed to tell just anybody that? God, these margaritas were a liability. "And I was wearing this red top! That's how he recognized me." *He must have recognized me sooner than that,* she realized. Because he'd gone straight home and looked up those pictures. "Only what the lady mother is Steven so afraid of that he feels like he has to blackmail me?"

The others leaned closer over their curly fries.

"It must be something that happened when you were dating," Britney hissed.

"I would imagine," Lena said.

"Yeah," Jewel said cautiously. The margaritas were fuzzing out her edges.

There was a mystery here. She felt that if she could just sit quietly somewhere with a cold wet towel wrapped around her forehead, she could work it out.

A woman walked by with a stupid-looking white furry purse that caught Jewel's gaze.

Randy.

Bearskin rug.

Her chest filled up with tight, cold worry.

"Britney, can you find my dipshit partner outside and tell him I left already? I, uh, need to spend some more time with this source." Her head tipped toward Lena.

Plus, I have to get Randy out of that rug. She didn't want Clay or Britney along for that ride.

"Oh, are you going to the porn place? I'd love to see it," Britney said, ignoring Jewel.

"Do you mind if—" Jewel began.

"Of course," Lena said, damn her beautiful eyes.

"You guys done yet?" said a brusque male voice behind them.

Jewel looked around.

Digby, in a sopping raincoat. She was saved.

Britney dimpled at Lena. "This is *my* partner."

"Want a drink, Digby?" Jewel said, knowing he would refuse.

"No. Are you ready?" he said to Britney.

"In a minute, he-man," Britney said cheerfully. "Why don't you scram so we can finish up here?"

His face darkened. "I'll hit the men's. Then we go." He strode off to the men's like Mel Gibson with a full bladder.

Britney tossed her curls. "He's so possessive."

"It must be you, Brit. He's been a doormat for years. Who'd of thunk getting laid would turn him into an alpha male?"

"I had one of those once," Lena said. "Talk about high maintenance."

"Jazus, yes," Jewel said, thinking of Randy. Her tummy felt hot and confused. She checked her watch. "Clay should be waiting out in my car by now, wondering where the heck I am. Head him off, Brit?"

"It'll be my pleasure," Britney said.

CHAPTER
18

Jewel and Lena took a pit stop to give Britney time to engage Clay in conversation. Then they sneaked out the side door of the bar. It had stopped raining.

"I really appreciate your doing this," Jewel said, feeling hateful and despising herself for it. Lena-slash-Velvita, seen on the ground, was nearly as tall as Jewel, and all legs. Her black anorak concealed her perky, natural breasts, but Jewel could vividly call them to mind. After all, they'd been on display for a good part of the fifty-minute movie she'd watched last night with Clay. Plus the ski-lodge scene on the fake bearskin rug. She knew for a fact that Randy didn't care if a woman was a limber bombshell or if she was ninety and crippled with arthritis, because once he got her into demonspace she was as young and as hot as she felt, but the principle was ... the principle was that, goddammit, she was jealous.

I hate myself when I'm jealous.

To prove to herself she could behave better than this, she added, "Randy really hates being stuck in a bed, or rug, or whatever. You're a real saint to help me let him out. Lots of women wouldn't."

Lena flagged them a cab. "He's something, isn't he? How long has he been out of that brass bed?"

"It's hard to remember. Three crazy months, I think."

Lena smiled. She had a nice-girl smile. "He a good roommate?"

"The worst. He was a lord, back in England. I don't think he even shaved himself." Jewel scowled, then realized she was scowling and tried to smooth her expression. "I pay for everything. Sooner or later I'm gonna send him out to Mickey D's for a paper hat if he doesn't get a j.o.b."

"He feels badly about that," Lena said.

Don't tell me how Randy feels! I know all about how he feels! Then Jewel thought, *Great, he's complaining about his bitch of a roommate to this porn star. While they're in bed.* Remorse struck her. She ought to feel sorry for him. Randy was a long way from home. He could never go back to being shaved by someone else. He did his best. He didn't deserve this.

She remembered his diary on her computer at home. *Serve out more shameful centuries*, he had written.

"Do the guys you work with really feel embarrassed about their jobs?"

"Oh, yes. It takes special skills, but you'll never get the average guy in a sports bar to believe that."

"I'm a moron, remember? What special skills?"

Lena looked at her sidelong. "They have to know what a woman wants. And we have a phrase in the business. 'Waiting on wood.' Not every guy can perform on command, keep it up in front of a dozen production crewmembers until it's time for the money shot."

A smile walked onto Jewel's face. "I've had boyfriends like that. Not many."

"They're rare."

"But why would they feel bad? I would think the sports bar types would be high-fiving 'em, like, go brah."

"More likely sneer at them out of jealousy," Lena said evenly. "Most men have contempt for whores, you know. If that's your mindset, it's easy to feel like a whore. And we were all brought up with that mindset, weren't we?"

Jewel was silenced.

She must be right. Randy had written about the whores in that 1811 brothel with such wack ambivalence. Half the time he was dissing them as dirty skanks. And then the change of heart, as he found out he couldn't satisfy them, which humbled him, proving his mistress right. Then, worse, the two-hundred-year uphill climb to his current pinnacle of skill.

And what skill it is! Already she missed his magic mojo and his beautiful black eyes.

They pulled up at the Artistic Publishing Company. Jewel insisted on paying for the cab. "Have they all gone home?"

"Shooting is over for now, so, yes." Lena let them in the front door with a key. "Print production works late. They're graphic designers. No time management skills. Printing and shipping are in the basement, they won't even know we're here." She signed the security guard's register. "Good night, Harry. We'll probably be here until after you leave."

The guard touched his hat. "Right, Miss Lena."

The floor under their feet boomed, like the speakers in a car full of rap.

Jewel said, "You know a lot about the company's operations."

"Onika is grooming me to take over someday."

"Wow." Jewel thought about that. "Does Maida know?"

"I haven't talked to her in almost two years."

"Two years." Jewel was hearing that phrase a lot lately. She was beginning to wish she had a frickin' way-back machine to just go back and look. "What happened two years ago?"

"At BB?" Lena shrugged. "Just Steven being Steven. When I wouldn't put out, he told me I was John Baysdorter's bastard. He named all the girls he'd had, what he'd done with them, who else they were doing. He got physical." Lena's cool slipped. She swallowed. "I confronted my mother. She denied nothing."

Jewel thought of Maida, trapped like a cornered mink in that tiny office, watching bullshit go down with girls she employed year after year, and feeling helpless to do anything about it because her own daughter's child support depended on the boss.

Maybe she'd been a little hard on Maida.

And on Randy, too.

"You're quiet," Lena said, with challenge in her voice.

Jewel entered the elevator and turned to face her. "I'm thinking that I've been more than a moron. I've been a jerk."

A smile twitched on Lena's lips. "It's curable." Jewel laughed, and Lena smiled for real. "Now I'll tell you what you really want to know. How I ended up here."

"Jeez, am I totally transparent?"

"It's everyone's question. But you get the real answer. I started because of Steven."

She let them into the Hot Pink studio and flipped on lights. From here, the thump of the printing presses was softer.

"He's Onika's nephew and the great-grandson of the founder of Artistic Publishing. John Baysdorter did more than get his secretary pregnant. He created a macho corporate culture. I think Steven is genuinely crazy. But it's the kind of craziness the business world rewards, you know? Aggression, arrogance, the risk-taking-junkie thing."

She slapped the door with her open hand. "I'm going to take him down," she said harshly.

"You go, girl," Jewel said.

"When I walked out of BB, I was so mad that I would do anything to get him. I'd worked for Steven long enough to know that he had financial ties to Artistic, that he was dying to make partner, that he hated Onika, and that he was up to his neck in some covert deal about this building."

"Really." Jewel's ears pricked up. "The Artistic Company, or the whole building, bakery and all?"

"The building. If it goes condo, it's a hundred million."

Jewel blinked. "But would Onika sell? Seems like she's having fun with the porn."

"That's just it. She won't sell."

Jewel needed to talk this over with Clay. "We'll get to the bottom of it," she vowed. "And you'll save your mom."

Lena turned red. "I don't want to save her!"

Oops. Jewel changed the subject. "So you came to Onika?"

"She was great. She took me in and made me her assistant, and I got interested in performing, so I tried it." A smile lit Lena's face. "I love it. I mean, it's amazing. It's liberating. It's *fun.* I love being on camera. I'm such a show-off. And I get *paid* to get off. The guys are all good in bed, plus the wood thing, which believe me a girl comes to appreciate."

"Amen," Jewel said. "But it's killing Maida."

Lena said nothing.

"Listen," Jewel said. "I can see we'll have to do another three-pitcher night, but right now I've got an urgency."

"Right. Randy." Lena went to a big metal closet and pulled out the bearskin rug. "Help me get this into the sound booth. You'll feel more private there."

They dumped the rug on the sound-booth floor. Jewel stared down at the snarling fake bear head. *Well, buddy, this is a new one.*

She wondered if she could just roll the rug up and sneak it out of here.

Maybe she could leave him in the storage locker in the basement of her apartment building.

That's an awful thought.

Yet she'd thought it. She felt so mixed up. Half of her wanted to set him free like some wild stallion in a meadow or something, and the other half was pure cave woman.

Mine. Ugh.

As if reading her thoughts, Lena said, "Having this guy around must be fifty-seven kinds of evil temptation."

Jewel couldn't look her in the eye. "You have no idea."

Lena showed her the light switches and left. "I'll be at my desk downstairs." She went out and shut the door.

Jewel turned out the lights. Slowly, the blackness of the sound booth faded up. Through the window, she saw a single bulb on a stick illuminating the studio. Then she became aware of green LED lights on the consoles in front of her. Her heart was hammering.

Oh, big deal, so he was in there, like he was in all the other beds she'd saved him from. *What's so different about this?*

Duh, it was a *porn* factory. Her skin was on fire with the fact.

Her heart wouldn't quiet. Suddenly she couldn't wait to see him, see him and say, *It's all right, I know everything, you're not as stuck up as I thought.*

The rug was a thick pale patch at her feet.

She took off her shoes and stepped onto the rug in her knee-high nylons. *Randy?*

CHAPTER 19

The fake bearskin was slippery-soft. She hesitated, then took off her pantsuit and blouse, folded them, and lay them on the post-production mixing console beside her. That made her think about her surroundings.

She felt a thrill, being here. In this room they listened to porn stars sighing, moaning, crying out. Here they made those rhythmic, silly, squishy noises go away, and snipped out the occasional cough of cameraman or boom operator. She wondered what that was like, when sex, which she had always regarded as strictly recreational, became one's daily job.

She supposed that a person stopped getting horny and focused on minutiae. We're getting glare off the spit on her breast. Is the camera angle going to catch that ten-incher? Bend backward, honey, show me some pink. Suddenly she was reluctant to take off her panties, her knee-highs, and her industrial-grade bra.

The soles of her feet tingled. Randy. Waiting for her.

Looking over her shoulder, Jewel slipped out of her underthings. She laid them carefully on top of her folded clothes.

Then she knelt on the rug.

Lust hit her so hard that she slumped onto her side. Fake bear hair tickled her nose. She had just enough time to roll onto her back, and then she was sinking into demonspace, her arms outstretched and clutching for the man she'd come to rescue.

She found herself standing in the sound booth again, looking out of the long window while a technician beside her tweaked the console. In the studio, colored lights played over a naked man standing center-stage.

She looked closer at the man on the stage. Randy.

She was so relieved, she was out the door and into the studio before it occurred to her that she was naked and barefoot. The lighting man circled Randy, calling out numbers. His helper aimed bright lights at him from all sides. Randy backed away from her as she approached. Her heart thumped anxiously.

But then he lounged back on a divan covered in a tiger-print velvet throw.

A man stepped between her and Randy. *Hold still*, he commanded, and, impatient, she stopped, her eyes on Randy. The man, steadying her with one hand on her shoulder, tickled her all over with a thick powdery makeup brush: earlobes, neck, chin, cheekbones, nipples, inside her elbows, on the tops of her thighs.

She ignored him. She didn't want to lose sight of Randy. She was almost ready to pull free when the makeup man released her.

She took four steps closer to Randy, and then a voice called out, *Stop*.

She stopped.

Turn around.

She turned. The lights blinded her.

Men swooped in with lights and cameras.

Chin up. Look left. Lick your lips. Bend backward and to the right.

She did these things, realizing that Randy hadn't moved. In fact, he was waiting for her.

It was all arranged.

These men with their tickly brushes and their lights

and angles and microphones were not here to keep them apart. In fact, they meant to bring her together with Randy.

Her nipples hardened. All over her body, her skin tightened, as if her insides were swelling with every breath, making her sweat.

Snatches of conversation came through the buzzing in her ears.

Nice even breasts. Watch that shadow.

Better?

Yes. More powder.

Someone skittered the brush over her breasts. She let her eyes drift half-shut.

Lift the left one.

She was barely listening. A warm hand lifted her left breast.

Now the right.

Two hands, lifting her breasts.

Thank you. Turn?

Fingertips turned her. She realized her eyes were closed. She opened them to see Randy sitting up on the edge of the divan, his hands on either side of him, his gaze on her lower body.

He said, *May we have some oil on her cunny before penetration?*

Suddenly she realized someone else was touching her breasts. Strange eyes were watching her. She looked around wildly, staring into the face of the makeup man behind her.

He was Randy.

She looked from cameraman to boom operator to director.

Randy.

Randy.

Randy.

She looked at the window of the sound booth. The

sound man inside, Randy of course, put thumb and fore-finger together.

She put her hand on her throat.

I'm in demonspace. He can be anyone.

Randy the director spoke. *Here is the story. You are an actress. You have never performed in one of these films before. You will do what you are told. You will attempt everything, however strange. At first, you may resist, but you will do it.*

Fingertips nudged her knees apart. *Farther, please,* Randy the makeup artist said, breathing on her hip-bone. She felt a cool spritz of oil on her pussy.

Randy the director rose from his chair and walked in a slow circle around the divan where Randy the actor sat. *Your leading man is experienced. You have feelings for him, but you try not to show them. You must pretend you have never done any of these things before.* As he passed behind her he leaned forward, his lips close to her ear. *You will love every moment of it.*

Randy the director circled to stand before her, bigger and darker than she remembered, his long hair tied back in a ponytail and his eyes black with focus. She felt her knees buckle.

Do you understand?

She nodded.

You may say, "Yes." That is your only line. May we have the line?

She wet her lips. *Yes.*

Randy the cameraman leaned over his machine, his ponytail swinging forward.

Randy the boom operator moved the microphone until it almost touched her lips.

Yes, she said, and after that it was easy.

Randy the cameraman looked at Randy the director, who strode lithely to his chair and sat.

Action, he commanded.

Randy the actor stepped forward and took her hand. She went with him to the divan. *You are lovelier naked than clothed*, he said. *I think I shall always fuck you naked.*

Yes, she said obediently.

They lay back on the divan and he put both his hands around her throat, then stroked downward firmly, as if squeegeeing water off her torso. Her bones turned to butter. Tentatively, she slid her hand up his knee. He smiled. He rolled against her, slapping her thigh with his erection. It was easily as long as Sancho's. He handed her a condom.

From far away, she heard his voice say, *With your mouth, my dear.*

She opened the condom and capped his erection with it.

Have you ever fellated a man before witnesses? Randy the actor murmured.

She was going on record. Everyone would know. She felt her skin shrink, then swell again. The hot lights beat down.

Yes, she said, though she hadn't.

She bent, using her lips and tongue to roll the condom down over him. He was huge. Never again would she laugh when a guy said "nine inches." With her jaw stretched wide and her tongue working over the length of him, she was conscious of the light blazing into her eyes, his fingers twisting in her hair, the barely audible murmur of the director talking to someone else.

Her behind heated up under the lights, hotter and hotter and hotter. Randy tightened his fingers in her hair, and she forgot everything except getting him hard and teasing him.

Okay, that's enough, the director said. *On your back, dear.*

She let Randy the actor push her back onto the divan.

Show pink. Smile.

She spread her knees wide, spread her labia with her fingers. She smiled up at Randy, who was only a dark spot with a blaze of light behind him.

That's it. In you go, Randy.

She sighed with relief. She was so ready. He slid inside her and immediately began pumping. Her stomach tightened, trying to balance on the divan, then her pussy tightened and she almost passed out with lust. The light was so hot on her skin that her private parts warmed— at least, the bits not covered by Randy.

Relax, he said in a soft voice, and she let her head fall back over the other side of the divan and, daringly, put her arms over her head, too, lying wide open, draped exposed over the divan sideways, feeling Randy stroke in and out of her, feeling the lights burn her body.

The director said something, but she ignored him.

Randy held her thighs, impersonally holding her open while he drove in, in, in. Her eyelids fluttered. She could still taste him. She licked her lips, thinking, *One million copies of this at twenty-nine ninety-nine, one million horny men jacking off, pretending they can shoot it over my body*, and arched her back into Randy's thrusts.

—*Do what she's told*, the director was saying irritably. *Okay, slap her breasts.*

Her eyes opened just as Randy leaned down and slapped her breasts, left, then right, left, right, sharp little stinging slaps that made her gasp and clench around his cock. Her nipples were on fire. Randy pinched them, then pinched harder. She spasmed, and would have clutched at his hands, but he spoke in that low voice again.

Pretend you like it. Lie back. Moan for me.

She growled instead.

You like that, he said aloud, roughly. *Don't you.*

She remembered her line. *Yes!*

He slapped her breasts again, smaller slaps, but she felt them like hot brands, like ice cubes held against her puckering nipples. She squirmed, snarled aloud, and thrashed her dangling arms. She wished he would stop. She pretended a growl. He pinched her nipples ever so gently, and the zing went down through her to the point where he entered her body. She yelped.

Say yes, Randy breathed. *Make it nice.*

Yes!

Say yes. He pumped harder.

Yes!

From far away the director said, *What does it take to get her to come? You two hold her wrists.*

Hands circled her wrists. The lights shone so bright in her eyes, she couldn't see who held her.

Randy slapped her breasts again.

Suddenly it wasn't a joke, and it wasn't pretend. She had no purchase with her hands. Randy shifted his grip to her ankles and held her legs straight, stretched wide, never stopping that piledriver stroke. Her head hung down, her eyes blinded half by her own hair and half by the lights, and the men on each side of her pulled slightly, and all her muscles melted until she felt she was being pulled slowly to pieces, like taffy.

That's it. She's losing control, the director said confidently. *Plug this end.*

No I'm not, she would have said, but a cock slid into her mouth, warm and fragrant, and stopped her throat, and still it kept sliding in.

Suddenly Randy thickened. Her vulva stretched. He was too thick, in a really good way.

Pink! I need pink! the director screamed.

She was almost there. So close.

Then Randy pulled out.

She would have screamed if she could have breathed. The lights intensified. Her pussy heated up. Her heart beat in her throat. She could feel that cock in her mouth, bending with her throat, *now that's impossible*, and then it started moving, in and out, in and out, never letting her breathe, *why don't I pass out*, and panic filled her. She struggled against the hands stretching her arms wide. She wanted to kill Randy for pulling out of her pussy.

Then she felt a finger sliding into her. She bucked.

Randy's voice whispered in her ear, *Say yes. You want it. Say yes. What's your line? Say it.*

She couldn't breathe.

A second finger joined the first.

Say it. Say yes.

Her lips worked. Her throat tightened around that cock sliding in and out of her mouth, but never out far enough.

Three fingers.

She was starting to throb.

Get ready, Randy whispered in her right ear.

Okay, boys, give it to her! yelled the director.

Get set, Randy whispered in her left ear.

Four fingers, stretching her.

Now suck, baby, said Randy on her right.

Suck harder, said Randy on her left.

The director said, *Come on, somebody make her suck.* He was talking to her. She sucked, and the cock in her mouth slid all the way down her throat, into her chest, and Randy put the tip of his cock against her vulva and pushed past those four fingers to fill her tightly, and someone slapped her breasts, left, right, pinch, pinch, and a firm thumb pressed down on her trigger, and she burst open like a crack of lightning.

CHAPTER 20

Sweating on the bearskin rug, she screamed in the anechoic silence of the sound booth, just to hear her own voice. That felt so good, she gave another scream.

When her voice gave out, she stopped and lay panting against him. "That was too weird. Let's not do it again."

"Very well." Her sex demon lay beside her, propped up on one elbow. He looked so solid and hunky and real and familiar that her heart flipped over.

He looked into her eyes. "You realize that was based on your prejudices, not upon reality. A more authentic variant would be very different."

Her head was still full of those voices talking over her, monitoring her arousal, everyone watching, holding her down, helping her let go. Her body throbbed. *Randy*. She was probably smiling. A big sigh heaved up and out of her.

Randy turned up his palm. "First of all, there are many supernumeraries on the set, and several of them are women. The actress has a choice in what sex acts she will perform. The number of actors available is quite small, because of the necessity for absolute control of one's priapus, so the chances are she already knows them. She chooses her sexual partners among them."

Shaking her head to clear it, Jewel said, "Why are you telling me this?"

"Because it's part of my responsibility to you," he said, "as your incubus. Furthermore, no one directs the sex act once it has begun. There is direction beforehand, but no one interrupts the course of mutual arousal and satisfaction."

He was totally killing her mood. "So?" she said with annoyance. "I don't really care, you know."

"But I do." He raised his big dark eyes to hers. "There can be no tenderness in the fantasy you asked for."

She blinked. He'd been digging into her sewer of a libido for three months, and tonight he was *critiquing* it? She snapped, "I suppose you and Velvita have tenderness in your porno reality?"

"Perhaps not that. But there is courtesy and respect." After a pause, he admitted, "Very well, I confess, I wanted to tell you. You were dismayed by the smut and the processes for its creation. Once inside your mind, I could see why. You have so many misconceptions. I used those misconceptions to give you the fantasy you believed in." He looked earnestly into her face. "But I can't allow you to believe those things are really true."

"Why the heck not? It's my fantasy." She stood up and started putting on her clothes. "And I still don't want to do it again."

"Very well, we won't." He lay on the rug, watching her dress. He looked very comfortable naked, and yet somehow full of inner tension. It made her crazy to think of him sharing his glorious body with Velvita Fromage.

"I read your diary," she said. "I'm sorry if you didn't mean for me to find it."

His black brows snapped down. "My—oh. On the computer."

"Yes."

I was being broken to my work, like that cart horse, he had written.

She knelt and put her hand on his. "It must have been

horrible. In that whorehouse. I never imagined. I'm starting to realize that I—I can't imagine what you've been
through."

The tension seemed to melt out of him. He smiled,
and she realized how very much she had missed him.
"That's a relief. I had feared you would be distressed by
my decision to stay."

Her skin prickled with sudden dread. "You've stayed
for three months," she said, puzzled. "Why's now any
different?"

"Stay here. At Artistic." His eyes grew wary again as
her frown deepened. "Velvita says they will pay me to be
an actor with their company."

"You—*what*?" Her mouth fell open.

"Now that I am no longer invisible, I can perform in
the guise of an ordinary actor. Or, if the story calls for it,
I can draw upon my incubus powers. We shall see what
the camera can capture. As you know, when we enter
what you call demonspace, we vanish from this world
until you achieve climax."

She found herself on her feet, staring down at him in
shock. "But—but you're out. You're human again. I just
got you out."

Slowly he got to his feet and took her hands. "Jewel, I
beg you to understand. This is a tremendous opportunity for me."

"Screwing skanks for a living?" she yelled suddenly,
and drew her breath in sharply, surprised at the sudden-
ness of her rage.

With dignity he said, "They are no less deserving than
any other woman I have satisfied. No, that's not what I
mean." He took her hands, squeezing them painfully. "I
was a long time in that brothel. A dozen girls came and
went. But not one, not one could I please. It—" His jaw
tightened. "It hurt me to fail."

Jewel pulled her hands free and tossed her hair over

her shoulder. "That bitch, your mistress. She meant you to fail."

"She meant me to learn that I was already a failure," he said soberly. "Those girls taught me so much. I couldn't put their teaching into practice before the place burned down and the brass bed passed to a new owner."

"I didn't know it burned down." *There's a lot I didn't know*, Jewel realized. That didn't feel nice in her tummy.

His voice was full of self-loathing. "I thought them unworthy of my consideration. I learned otherwise. I thought myself a more-than-adequate lover. This, also, was untrue. In time, I pleased more than a hundred other women. Yet I could not give what they could give themselves with their bare hands. I owe them this." His voice shook. "And I can never repay them."

Her mouth opened but no sound came out.

"Don't you see, Artistic and Velvita have given me a chance to settle my debts. I held the whores in contempt, and I can never take back that insult. But I can respect *these* women. *Now* I can give enough." He pleaded, "I beg for your understanding, Jewel. Let me earn my keep with the one skill I have. Even now, in my soul, the earl does battle with the incubus. I—I don't know which one I want to win."

Jewel blinked. *Holy split personality.* "I guess I don't know which one I would want to win, either." Tears sprang into her eyes. "I really don't feel good about this."

"I know you don't. I understand." He squeezed her hands again, hurting her, and she pulled away. "Let me beg your tolerance yet awhile?"

She felt sick. "I suppose I have to." Her throat was raw and painfully tight. "If you get stuck, Velvita can always sneak me in here."

"If you grant me your permission to stay," he said, "I doubt I shall get stuck."

My permission! She felt even sicker as she admitted

that, yes, she had loved owning him. *I'm always saying he has no right to complain about my multiple sex partners. How can I ask him for more than I want to give?* Yet the thought of him coming home from "work" every night, back to her bed, nauseated her.

"You'll be careful about disease?" she said over her shoulder.

"These women are tested monthly. They have only a dozen or two sex partners, all of them professionals." He said gently, "They take more precautions than you did before you met me."

Well, that was a nice slap in the face. She stiffened.

To her back, he said, "Do you—would you prefer I did not sleep at your apartment?"

She kept her back turned. Rage and pain made her say, "Yes, thank you, I would prefer it. If you have somewhere to stay."

"Very well."

Oh hell, oh ugh, was it that Velvita girl? Or would he turn invisible and hide out in demonspace?

At the moment she didn't give a red rat's ass.

She looked back. He looked stricken, his black eyes huge with worry, as vulnerable as she had ever seen him. *And yet he's holding out on me.*

Backbone. Damn. The one thing he needed to make him irresistible, and he was using it to sleep with "a dozen or two" gorgeous, skinny, sexually Olympic porn stars.

She licked her lips and swallowed a jagged lump. "Call me if you need anything." God, was she pathetic or what?

But he only nodded again. "I will. And you."

"Oh, yeah."

She picked up her purse and shoes and walked out.

CHAPTER
 21

Clay was in his suite at The Drake Hotel when Jewel called. "I'm coming over." She sounded upset.

"I'll come to you," he said, looking out at the wet streets.

"I'm on my way over in a cab now from the Artistic Building." She hung up.

This was promising. She must have seen His Lordly-buns. It must have gone badly.

Clay's hopes were realized when she arrived.

"I'm crushed," she moaned. "This is awful." Then she told him all about it.

Clay was careful not to comment while she obsessed over Randy's defection. If he agreed that Randy was a poop, she would defend him. If he defended Randy, he'd be in deep poop himself.

"Let's walk back to your place," he suggested.

That got her out in the night air, surrounded by milling tourists, but even a smoggy moon couldn't deflect her.

"I've been treating this guy like a—like a *dildo*."

She explained Randy's trauma over being forced to become a boinkmeister. Then she explained it again, with girl footnotes. Then she started blaming herself.

Clay clenched his teeth to keep his mouth shut.

"He knows so much about me from crawling around

in my head like he does, and he's been so patient. Always there for me. And how he talked about those women at the brothel! I felt like a brat. I wasn't even nice about it. I just sent him off to work with that—that *girl*, that Velvita. If he's not staying at her place, I'll eat my new shoes." She added sadly, "I shouldn't hate her. She's actually been really nice to me."

"Tell me," Clay said, hoping to stem the flood of Randychatter. "What is it about her that bothers you?"

They stopped to wait for a walk signal at the Nordstrom's pedestrian overpass. Hordes of tourists stopped with them.

"Besides that she's screwing my sex demon?" Jewel plunged her hands into her hair and pulled. "Listen to me! I *don't* own him. I don't. Plus she's skinnier and younger than me, and she can probably do fifty things in bed that I've never heard of."

"Now that would surprise me," Clay said, and felt wounded when she shot him a dirty look.

"What's that supposed to mean?"

"Hey." He took her hand as they crossed the street. "When I met you, you bragged about being the slut-de-la-sluts. Your words, not mine. Those women you work with—well—" He'd better tread carefully. "You and your gang have this whole wham-bam-grrl ethos. I don't pretend to understand it." He shrugged. "I would think you would be glad to meet a real porn star."

She looked glum. "If you had read his diary, you would understand. Do you want to see it? It's on my computer at home."

"I don't think that would be fair to Randy," Clay said hastily. Besides, he'd been hearing about it for twenty minutes.

They walked under the pedestrian bridge over Rush Street and slipped between the chain-link fence and the

KEEP OUT ROAD CLOSED barrier blocking off the Trump Tower construction site.

"Anyway I said something like that to Velvita—about how people treat porn stars. And she said men are mean to male porn stars out of jealousy. God knows," Jewel said bitterly, "I've had to confront my jealousy. What a *bitch* I am!"

"I think you're a decent, honest person," he said.

She blinked at him and stopped in mid-rant. "Thanks."

"I think your decency is not about who you go to bed with, but who you are inside."

Her chest heaved a shuddery sigh and Clay relaxed a little. He smiled. "It's possible that this Velvita person is also decent and honest in her own way. She's still not you."

"That matters to you," she said gloomily. "God knows how Randy will feel after a week or so of—of—"

"Did you want to keep him?" Clay blurted and winced at his error.

She looked him straight in the eye. "I thought I wouldn't ever have to face up to it, because *he* was the one who stuck to *me* like glue." She scooped up a rock and threw it overhand at the scoop of a bucketloader, making a hideous clang in the night. "But, yeah. I thought he was mine for life."

Ouch. "Is it the sex?" Clay said. Another error. He handed her another rock.

She seemed to think about that one, and then raised an eyebrow. "Well, it's a lot. And now I know about all this horrible shit that happened to him in 1811. And probably worse, if I only knew. He's such a good guy inside. He totally melted my heart. By *leaving* me." Her face crumpled. She dropped the rock on Clay's foot.

Oh, for cri-yi, he thought.

But he bumped hips with her and got his arm around her. "Hey, hey. Come on. He'll be back."

"Oomp," she said. "Why? Oomp."

"Because he knows he's left you alone here with me."

Her head came up at that.

"Antler-clashing, remember?" Clay said. He pulled up his shirttail and blotted her face. "We know what we've got."

She squinted at him. "You don't have me. Neither one of you has me."

"Oh, please. You've been faithful to us for three whole months."

"I am *not* being *faithful* to you!" she bellowed.

"Hey, you can't be on this site," said a voice out of the darkness. A flashlight played over them. "Oh. That you, Jewel?"

She waved. "Me, Alfonzo."

"You alone?" Alfonzo asked invitingly.

"Uh, no. Sorry."

Another ex-boyfriend of Jewel's. Feeling conspicuous with his hand around her back, Clay strolled past the guard, out of the restricted area, and up the steps to the Corncob Building.

"I'm not being faithful to you," she repeated. "I'm just slowing down a little." She sniffled.

"Whatever," Clay said. "All I mean is, Randy knows who you are, and he'd rather eat his old brass bed with butter and gravy than leave you to my attentions for too long."

"Why?" she said again. "It's not like you want me."

"You'd be surprised what I want," Clay said suavely.

"Yes, I would. Because I never do know what you want."

Thank God for small favors. "I don't have two hundred years of mystery going for me. I have to play up all the mystery I've got."

That made her laugh.

But she still wouldn't let him come upstairs.

Jewel met Clay on the front steps of the Kraft Building late the next afternoon. Her eyes bugged out at the double armful of big white bags he carried. "Is that what I think it is?" The air filled with the scent of toasted butter and cinnamon, and her mouth watered.

"I thought we should test our hypothesis about the connection between the porn, and the bakery, and O'Connor's little friend Wilma," he said.

"At the department? Do you think that's smart?" But she had taken a bite out of a cow plop before the elevator doors opened. "Mmmm!" Crisp, cinnamony, buttery yummyness! Her bruised heart began to scab over.

The office was buzzing. Ed was out. It seemed every investigator who wasn't actually undercover had showed up for work in a rowdy mood. Jewel remembered that the OED assistant commissioner was due to visit, and that the mission was to make the place look crowded. The whole gang seemed to be on board.

Merntice took the white bags and laid out the pastry at the coffee station. The investigators pounced with animal cries.

Jewel grabbed Clay and a couple of cow plops and coffees and led him into Ed's empty office, where they could hear themselves think. She sat behind Ed's desk and marshalled her thoughts.

"Okay," she said, "this is what I didn't tell you last night because I was too busy being a big baby. That guy Steven Tannyhill, who may have put Viagra in the coffee and started that office orgy? He's connected up with a bunch of other shit." She told Clay about Steven's plan to sell the Artistic Building out from under Onika.

Clay whistled. "How'd you find this out?"

"Margaritas with the girls," she said briefly.

She took a deep breath. It took guts and patience to tell him, next, how Steven had brought her home and then uploaded naked pictures of her, but she did it. "I'm thinking it was a preemptive strike. It's about that night. Something he thinks I might have learned then."

"I'll be sure to look 'em up," was all Clay said. "So what does he think you know?"

"Beats me. It was only one night." She avoided Clay's eye. "He picked me up in the bar at the Doral and two hours later we were in the sack." Memory began to stir. "Oh. And he took me to dinner with some of his friends."

"Who were they?"

"I don't think he said. I think he introduced me to them, but he didn't introduce them to me. It's all pretty cloudy. I was drinking when we met, and he kept feeding me more drinks."

"Did he know who you were?"

"Yeah, we did the dance, what do you do, blah blah blah. He said he was in real estate. He was so impressed with my job. That would have tipped me off, if I'd been sober. Nobody thinks Consumer Services is cool."

"What did they talk about at dinner?"

Jewel shut her eyes against raucous laughter coming from the staff room outside Ed's office. "Steven was on the defensive, acting macho. But I could tell he was tense. He kept reassuring these guys that their investment was protected. They kept saying the window was closing, and Steven said he was taking steps to speed it up. One big fat guy winked at him. Steven kept giving me a bedroom smile, as if I understood. But I didn't." She opened her eyes. "I was so plowed I can't even remember how we ended up in bed."

Clay's blue eyes crinkled. "So can I see the pictures?"

Breezing smartly past that topic. "That reminds me, I want to make a list of everything in these cases that starts with the phrase 'two years ago.' It's beginning to haunt my dreams."

Clay took a pad and a pen off Ed's desk. "Shoot."

"In no particular order." She leaned back in Ed's chair and stared at the ceiling tiles. "Two years ago, John Baysdorter died. Two years ago Lena Sacker took a job as Steven's assistant, Steven hit on her, Lena complained to her mom, and her mom stonewalled her. Whereupon instead of calling the EEOC on Steven, for fear of endangering her mother's job, Lena went to work at the Artistic to get dirt on Steven, because that was the company occupying the nine-sixty west Washington building, which Steven has a permanent hard-on about."

"Slow down. You ended that sentence with a preposition."

"Write faster. Lena and Maida haven't spoken in two years. Although Lena walked in yesterday just as Maida was saying, 'I have no daughter,' and asked her mother to take a stand about something, and Maida said 'I can't.'"

She looked at Clay's pad. "Oo, shorthand. You could be employable in the pink-collar ghetto. Where was I?"

"Two years ago."

"Right. Two years ago, coincidentally, Bill Tannyhill, owner and Adult Uses registrant at Artistic, dies and leaves his daughter Onika in charge. Two years ago, Steven Tannyhill, nephew of Onika and part heir of the company, has a plan to sell her building out from under her, only something goes wrong." Jewel paused.

"Got it."

"What else?"

"How about this one?" Clay said. "A bit less than two years ago, City Council approved final plans for the Circle Line, a new elevated train line running in a big arc from the north side all the way down to the Eleventh Ward."

"The Eleventh Ward," Jewel echoed. "Mrs. Othmar!"

"And last week her house develops a pocket zone and then misplaces it."

"So Ed came through with the lists?"

"I had them yesterday," Clay said reproachfully.

"Only I was too busy having a cow about His Lordship to listen," she said remorsefully. "I'm sorry." Nevertheless, excitement bubbled in Jewel.

A burst of raunchy hooting came from the staff room outside.

She said, "It connects! Steven's at the Artistic and finds out about the hinky porn. He gets hold of the properties list somehow, and he gives the list and some hinky porn to someone bent in Inspectional Services, who plants hinky porn on the target properties and then goes in and scares the crap out of the homeowners. The homeowners decide to sell. Steven buys the properties up, launders the titles, then resells to the city for a fat markup. We've got him!" She slapped the conference table.

"Not quite. We need material facts, officer," Clay said. "Gotta trace the money from the city back to the conspirators."

"He'll be using a secret blind trust," Jewel said positively. "Illinois still has them."

"We need to identify the bent IS inspector and connect him with Steven," Clay said. "Oh, and find out who leaked the property list."

"Your job," Jewel said. "It'll give you a chance to get acquainted with IS. Mostly a nice bunch of guys, with the exception of the guy with the biblical name on his windbreaker."

"That ought to narrow it down," Clay said.

She punched the air. "We're detecting shit! Is this cool or what? Let's tell Ed."

The door opened on a roar of hilarity and Ed walked in with a double fistful of cow plops, looking red in the face. "Tell Ed what? Whaddaya doin' in my chair?"

CHAPTER 22

Jewel moved out of Ed's chair and talked. Ed wolfed pastry. Clay read him the list of "two years" items.

Ed cut to the chase. "You need facts. Taylor won't ask for an indictment without."

Jewel shook her head. "It's hinky. Right to the bone, Ed. We can't prosecute in the normal way."

"Then why you bringin' this to me?" The boss seemed unusually impatient. "You're the Hinky Division!" He finished his last cow plop and licked all ten hairy fingers, one by one.

Clay said, "We may need the Chief Attorney to back us up, if we get them cornered." He coughed. "Somehow I don't think Steven Tannyhill is impressed with Senior Investigator Heiss."

Jewel glared at him.

"And he'd be even less impressed with me," Clay added. "I can present it to the Chief myself if you don't have time."

"Fuck that. You, presenting to the Chief, right." Ed breathed heavily for a moment. "Okay, I'll brief Taylor. I ain't promising him nothing until you got evidence."

"Even evidence we can't use in court?" Jewel said.

Ed rose. "I need another danish before this putz from OED shows up." He drained his coffee and stumped out. A wave of locker-room chanting came through the open door.

Jewel slammed it shut. "Maybe we can search Steven's house or his car for porn."

"We need Randy's hinky radar for that," Clay reminded her.

She flushed. "We'll get it. But he's not to drive without a license again. And I want you to get him those ID papers!"

Clay looked his most innocent. "Absolutely. Right now. Say, did Ed just say the OED guy was coming?" He got up and fingered a peephole in the venetian blind. "Hm."

Jewel went to check the street outside from Ed's exterior window. "Yeah." She peered through the smeary windowpane. A huge fat guy was finishing his cigarette on the front steps of the Kraft. From above he was practically spherical, a cartoon of a city-hall fat cat. "In fact, this is probably him."

A sound of smashing glass came from the staff room.

"Uh-oh," Clay said.

Jewel's head whipped around. Clay was hunched, transfixed, peeping through the blinds. She came to peep, too.

The staff room was a scene of ribald revelry. Britney was standing on a computer chair, stripping, throwing her bra at a mixed gaggle of roaring investigators.

"Holy shit!"

Possibly because the chair was a swivel job and wildly unsafe, Digby was kneeling in front of the chair holding Brit's legs, while Finbow steadied the wobbly chair from behind, and Sayers tried to stuff a folded bill into Brit's underpants.

"Yike!"

Someone dashed past the office window, too close and

fast for Jewel to identify her, but it was definitely someone female with a beach tan.

Someone else female passed the window, followed by
someone who was probably male, although, with that
paunch, who knew.   •

"Oh. My. God. And the OED assistant commissioner
due any second! Where the hell is Ed?"

"Uh—" Clay pointed downward, and Jewel crammed
herself against the crinkling venetian blind to look at the
staff room floor. Under the conference table, a familiar
pair of hairy ankles stuck out, tangled with a pair of
brown legs ending in sensible pumps.

Jewel seized Clay by the arms. "Listen. You have to
get out there and stop them. I'll go down and head off
Bing Neebly."

Clay's eyes were glazed. "Do I hafta?"

"Clay! Snap out of it! Bing Neebly is downstairs and
he'll be here in about thirty seconds. I'm gonna try to
stall him. You've got ten minutes. Get this place cleaned
up before he walks in, or the whole department is
toast!"

With that she jerked open Ed's office door and bolted
through the staff room, trying not to look right or left.
This was not easy. Discarded clothes and shoes lay everywhere. She tripped over two naked people lying in the
aisle by the coffee station, bumped against two more
who were putting a stapler to unauthorized use, and
ducked as someone swooped naked overhead, cackling,
nearly braining her with his roller skates.

Then she escaped the staff room and hurtled down the
stairs.

She needn't have rushed. Bing Neebly still stood outside the Kraft. She opened her navy polyester pantsuit
jacket a little wider, tugged down the matching shell as

low as it would stretch, and tucked it into the matching stretch pants. Then she stepped outside.

He was flicking his still-smoldering cigarette butt down the steps where pigeons milled at his feet. Quick as thought, Jewel whipped out her cell phone and took three pictures.

Bing Neebly turned. And, by golly, he was the fat guy from the bar last night! Steven's co-conspirator!

"Hey, you didn't just take my picture, did you?"

Jewel threw her head back and uttered a squealing giggle. "Isn't it a scream? Da mayor would shit if he saw!" She slapped Bing on the arm. "How are ya, buddy? I haven't seen you since that night at the Doral, what, two years ago?"

Her cleavage shone like snow in the late morning sunlight. *God, I'm subtle.*

"You're gonna delete those pictures, aren't you?" Bing seemed really bent about them.

She put her phone back in her pocket. "Nah-ah-ah. First you have to have a beer with me. You look great!" She beamed. "I hear you got promoted."

Bing blinked, but he started to smile. "Assistant Commissioner this year."

"How cool is that? Wow, you're becoming Mister Big Shot!" she gushed, channelling Britney. She tee-heed and let her breast touch his arm. "Let's go get a beer."

"Uh, sure."

She could make a beer last twenty minutes, easy. God help poor Clay. On this pious thought she towed Bing to Dick's Last Resort, which was dead empty at this hour.

"Just one pitcher," she told the waitress. "I'm cutting back. Gosh, was I snockered that night at the Doral!" She laughed hilariously. "How come I haven't *seen* you?" She slapped Bing playfully on the arm.

The pitcher came. Jewel tossed a ten to the waitress and Bing brightened. He sucked down the first glass in one swallow and refilled it. Apparently free beer cheered him up, but he wasn't chatty. He seemed to have something on his mind.

Those pictures, I bet.

Jewel pretended not to notice. She chattered happily about their last meeting, pretended she remembered what he'd been wearing, and claimed he'd lost weight since then. Bing drank four beers in six minutes. Jewel asked if he still liked oysters.

"They're okay." He eyed her cleavage cautiously.

This was tougher going than she'd expected. Why the hell was Bing hanging with her if he didn't want to be here?

Duh. *Steven sent him!*

Double-duh. Steven had spotted her on that first day in Maida's office. That night he'd looked up those nasty Internet pix. And the next day he called Bing and sicced him on the department. *What do you bet?*

And now she also knew where Steven got a list of all the properties on the Circle Line. Where else but from an AC at OED?

She signalled for another pitcher. Bing swallowed and emptied the first pitcher into his glass, looking mellow.

"See much of Steven Tannyhill these days?" she remarked.

Bing foofed beer all over his hand.

Jewel leaped forward to mop it up with her napkin, making sure not to obscure his view of her chest. "That bum. One night, and he dumps me for two years. Now he's all, 'why are you stalking me?' "

That got Bing's attention. The whites of his eyes showed.

"I'm like, dude, I don't stalk last year's one-night stands. I got 'em coming out my ying yang. But does he believe me?"

Bing heaved a visible sigh of relief. The dope. "Say,

you ought to delete those pictures off your phone," he said, apparently convinced by now that she was harmless.

"Sure, okay." She got out the phone and squinted at it, as if she was too drunk to read the numbers. "It's one of these buttons here." She put the phone down to look across the pitcher at Bing. "You know, Steven's kind of a putz," she said confidentially. "I know he's your friend and everything, but." She winked. "Where did you meet him anyway?" She went back to playing with the phone.

"Uh, fundraiser for the governor, three years ago."

"At Navy Pier ballroom," she said, nodding five times.

"Right."

"Steven's a poop to women. Of course he is a hunk," she said, pressing buttons on the phone. "Darn, that's not it."

"Here, let me," Bing said, reaching for it, and she snatched it out of his reach.

"Nobody touches my phone. I bet you don't realize it, but I'm almost a co—*op!*" She hiccuped. "That one got away. Where was I?" With another squint at the phone, she said, "Oh, yeah, Steven's mojo. I dunno how impressive it is, really. Do you see much of him? Is he always after blondes?"

"Uh, sometimes. Are you sure you know how to do that?" Bing persisted. "You seem, uh, kind of tight."

"Where else do you go besides Bennigan's on Michigan? Have you guys been to Friar's Pub since they remodeled?" She turned a completely sober, sharp eye on Bing.

He said, "No." His eyelids were sweating. When she kept up her "cop" stare, he blurted, "Mostly we go to Corbett's on North Wacker or Little Corporal on East Wacker."

"Huh." She turned back to her phone. "Make sure you try the Little Corporal's fresh doughnuts."

With a little hip action, she could make her breasts wiggle while sitting in a chair. And while she was wiggling and jiggling, she managed to E-mail the pigeon pictures to herself.

"Oh, okay, here! Watch this!" She turned the phone to show him his rotund self, flicking the butt. Her camera was so fast, it actually caught the butt in mid-air, then falling among pigeons milling hopefully at Bing's feet, then the scrum as they fought for possession. "This button here—" She pointed to it. "Now I press it—" She pressed the button. "And the evidence goes away forever. Bye-bye, picture!"

Bing seemed to relax. "You're not snooty like Steven's other girls."

"That's 'cause I'm not a Steven's girl." She faked another hiccup. "Shit, what time is it? I gotta be in the office."

On the street, she did a little dance. *I did it! I conned somebody! Plus now we have provable evidence of his opportunity to meet Steven and pass along the Circle Line lists. Clay would be so proud!*

Bing, now probably convinced she was drunk *and* crackers, said, "I can't believe you got tight on two beers."

"I am not tight, I'm high on Hoby's pastry. That stuff makes a girl loose as a goose, did you know that?" She shimmied.

"Really?"

"Hell, yes." She started to sing, doing a wave with both arms. "I LO-OO-OO-OO-OVE Hoby's PAAAAAstry!"

She led him back to the Kraft and dragged his lard butt on a totally uneventful tour around the building. Per Ed's instructions, the halls and rooms thronged with investigators, all apparently trying to find room for boxes of whatever. Everywhere was crowded except for the DCS staff room. There they found Merntice, sourly washing a wall with a sponge, and some guy nailing plywood over a broken window. No other sign remained of the orgy.

CHAPTER 23

Lena had kind of hoped Onika would never find out about last night. Fat chance. Friday morning, bright and early, Onika was unwinding in her office and Lena was tidying up and Onika said, "So you brought company to the building."

Harry, the night security guy, must have blabbed.

Lena sent her a guilty look. "Just showing some people around." She put the ice bucket on Onika's desk, dropped an ice cube in a clean glass, and measured rum and coke into the glass. "That DCS guy who was here the other day? He wants a job."

Onika blinked. "Doing what?"

"He wants to be in Hot Pink movies."

Onika leaned forward, put her elbows on the desk, and put the end of her cigarette holder between her lips. "Does he, now. Well, that's interesting. Maybe he's a plant."

"A what?"

"Maybe," Onika said, dragging on her cigarette, "that DCS woman sent him here to spy."

"I doubt it," Lena said guiltily. "I think he's just gotten sucked into the place, same as I did."

"I suppose he's waiting for an interview right now."

"Harry tells you everything."

"Everybody tells me everything. That's how I stay a step ahead."

So Lena phoned down to the lobby and told Randy to come up.

He walked in looking like he owned the place, his too-long black hair like a mane around his face and his jeans fitting nicely.

"Onika, this is Randy. He'd like to work at Hot Pink."

He stood very straight and stiff, like a butler or something. "I'm very pleased to meet you." He sounded so English.

"Is that so?" Onika fitted another cigarette into her silver holder with the diamonds on it and squinted at Randy. They exchanged names and handshakes, and Lena went to the door.

"If you're his reference, you can stay," Onika said.

Obediently Lena came back in.

"You got a green card?"

Lena had coached him on this part.

"I shall have one within the week."

Lena could tell Onika was impressed with his accent. "Well, Randy, are you comfortable taking your clothes off in front of people?"

Randy bent his head and looked at Onika, and Lena felt the room heat up. He started unbuttoning his shirt. Onika watched him with her cigarette holder halfway to her lips. Randy folded the shirt neatly and laid it on the corner of Onika's desk. Then he unbuttoned his fly—he wore those old 501s—and stepped out of his jeans. No undershorts. Lena swallowed. She hadn't even noticed him take off his loafers. He folded the jeans and laid them on top of the shirt with a chink of loose change.

A lot of guys looked smaller naked, but not Randy. He was built like one of those old Greek gods, with a big deep chest and bulky shoulders and serious thighs, like Ahnold's, and a meaty, muscular butt. And of course he was hung like nobody's business.

While they watched, his cock slowly rose and saluted.

Onika wasn't to know that all of this, nice as it was, didn't hold a candle to his real qualifications. If Lena had her way, nobody would ever know except her.

"Well," Onika said in a squeaky voice. "That's certainly useful." She cleared her throat, sipped her drink, and said, "Let me ask you this, Randy. How long do you think it would take you to make a woman come?"

His eyebrows went up. "That would depend on the woman."

"How about Lena here?"

He looked at Lena, and darned if she didn't feel a blush creeping up her neck.

"Do you object to this question?" he said to Lena. Right then she knew that there really was such a thing as a gentleman.

She smiled. "Nope."

Randy said to Onika, "In recent years I have never required more than ten minutes. Conditions vary." He exchanged a glance with Lena and said no more.

So we're not telling Onika about the magic part. Good.

"Lena, you know him. How's his manners?"

Meaning, his manners in bed. "First rate."

"Clean?"

"I'll vouch for him," Lena said, mentally crossing her fingers and hoping it was true. Could a sex demon get STDs? She had no idea.

Onika sent her a shrewd look. To Randy she said, "We'll try you for one scene. That's two days' shooting. Show up at six AM for makeup call. We'll draw blood then, and if you test clean you're eligible to work with somebody besides Lena. Shooting lasts anywhere from eight to fourteen hours, depending if we have to wait on wood. Will we?"

Lena had prepared Randy for this question, too.

"I anticipate no difficulties in that realm," Randy said, his smile quietly confident, and Onika turned toward Lena and raised her eyebrows.

Lena nodded.

"Dandy. Okay, you're in."

"Uh, Onika, can he possibly get a little advance for the first scene? He's kind of broke."

Onika watched Randy get dressed with visible regret. "Hell, I'll spot him fifty just for the strip." Lena noticed Randy's lips tighten, but when Onika pulled out her purse and handed him a bill, he took it. She smiled over her cigarette holder. "Congratulations, Randy. You're gonna be a porn star."

Jewel met Clay at her place for pizza. She felt whipped, but satisfied with her day. "Well?" she said, throwing her purse on the pile of mail on the front hall table. "How'd it go?"

"How'd what go?" Clay was reading a Lou Malnati's menu.

"The orgy at the department, dummy. I guess your experiment proved you right. How did you break it up?"

He looked odd, sort of thoughtful and blank and twitchy. "Don't ever, ever ask me to do that again."

Her eyes danced. "You realize I'll ask Britney tomorrow and she'll dish."

"Then she'll dish," he said. "No guy should be asked to walk into a roomful of naked, willing women and make them stop."

"It was your idea to fill them full of aphrodisiac pastry."

He shuddered. "I've learned my lesson."

That made her smile. "Did you do any work this afternoon? I sure earned my paycheck. Wait 'til you hear."

Clay drank beer and turned over the pizza menu. "You first."

She told him how she'd handled Bing Neebly, and what she'd learned. "Now we have a provable link between the two of them."

"And this is good because?" He handed her the pizza menu. "Sausage, ham, and pineapple for me."

"Euw! Pepperoni, sausage, and anchovies for me. It's good because Bing must have got those lists for Steven. We have to prove they met at a time when Bing had an opportunity to leak the sensitive info. What did you get?"

Clay smiled for the first time. "On the CTA Circle Line project, out of approximately eight hundred properties the city has bought to demolish to make way for the 'L' tracks, twenty-one properties changed hands within eight months before the city bought them."

"Holy crap. That's a lot of money." Jewel took his beer off the coffee table and swigged. "Coincidence?"

"I doubt it. It's almost eighteen million dollars." He paused while she phoned for the pizza. When she'd hung up he added, "Here's another little surprise. Follow the money back far enough, almost all of those sales went to or through the same blind real estate trust."

She slumped onto the sofa, pressing the cold beer to her forehead. "Shoot. We'll never crack one of those."

"Ahem."

She glanced up. Clay managed to look modest and smug at the same time. "You cracked it? How?"

"Not only that, but the physical side of the trust is managed by Baysdorter Boncil," he said, skating over the "how" part, she noticed.

"Wow." No wonder Steven was the blue-eyed boy of BB, harassment or no harassment. She thought of something. "Is Baysdorter Boncil bonded with the city?"

"Yup."

"As what? You almost have to have WBE or MBE certification to do that much city business on a single project these days."

"What's WBE?"

"Women-owned business enterprise. Or minority-owned business enterprise, MBE. C'mere and rub my feet and I'll pay for the pizza."

"Baysdorter Boncil is certified WBE," Clay said, coming to sit on the coffee table across from her end of the couch.

She frowned. "You're kidding. Upper management is all men. Who in hell's name are they certified under?"

Clay picked up her left foot and started rubbing. "Some woman named Sacker."

Jewel's mouth dropped open. "Holy frozen shit dipped in chocolate."

"You know her?"

Her head fell back on the sofa. "She's the office manager at BB. Mistress to old John Baysdorter—listen to me, I'm calling him 'old John' just like everybody over there. But she sure as hell is *not* the owner." She smiled unpleasantly. "Well, well, well. I can see I owe Ms. Sacker another visit. Y'know, for someone in as much deep doodoo as she is, she sure hasn't opened her heart to me yet."

"She will. Everyone does."

Everyone but you, she thought.

Clay's hands were a miracle on her sore tendons. Jewel moaned. "Oooh. You're killing me. I was freakin' brilliant today. I figured out that Steven arranged for Bing Neebly to visit the Kraft." She relaxed on the sofa and slowly tipped over, groaning like a dog, as Clay massaged her feet.

He said, "What's with this guy Steven, anyway? You talk like he's evil."

"Oh, he's hot, but he has no idea what it's for. And he's alpha. He's packed full of energy. Okay, he's kind of mean, and I could tell that even two years ago, that night in the bar. But you don't see that kind of—of *vitality* in every man. It's like a bright light, leaking through all his cracks."

"What do you mean, alpha?" Clay's hands got rough.

"Ouch. Leader of the pack. He's a dominator. I was sort of into that in those days," she admitted. "Only I kept getting these utter pricks, and I realized what a bad idea that was in the long run. Sooner or later, one of them would do me harm. Steven proved me right there, I guess."

"You got what you deserve, then." His tone made her crane her neck.

"You're touchy tonight."

"A good con artist doesn't praise one guy to another unless she has a motive for gain in mind," he said primly.

"I'm not praising him. Like you said, he's evil. Steven schtupps his office girls to prove something to himself."

"So your motive for gain is?" His blue eyes went crinkly.

Boy, Clay's ego was getting as sensitive as Randy's. "I'm telling my partner about a suspect."

The smile came back into his voice. "That's kind of weak, but I'll buy it."

"Since when do I have to treat you like a sensitive plant?"

He squeezed her arch. "Because you want to keep me happy?"

Suddenly she felt alert. "Do you want to be happy?" She wriggled up on her elbows and looked straight at him.

He looked at her across her feet, and a boylike expression of fear and guilt crossed his face, before the mask of what he liked to call his "Buddha-calm" erased it.

Now what?

"Do you mean to tell me," she said, "that now *you're* gonna be jealous about men I talk to? Because I get enough of that from Randy."

He didn't say anything.

"You are. You're jealous." If it had been Randy, she would have felt exasperated. She studied Clay's blank, good-natured face. *Well, this is a new development.*

She lay back on her back, staring at the ceiling, and he began working his thumbs into the sole of her left foot.

She shouldn't be surprised. They were always competing. Clay gave a good impression of a passive-aggressive beta male, but around Randy he got territorial. *When he's around Randy—and me.*

Boy, how dumb could she get?

"You're too quiet, Officer. What are you thinking?"

No point discussing this with him. He wouldn't tell her the truth. And she wasn't sure how she would feel about the truth, whatever that was. In his slippery, ex-con-artist way, Clay had become a rock in her life, something sane and predictable and normal in a maelstrom of hinky sex and fierce, gut-tearing jealousy.

Now it turned out he'd been hiding something big after all.

And she couldn't handle it. With Randy making porn, and her insides all stirred up like this, she just didn't have room for more confusion.

She said abruptly, "I'm gonna go turn over my laundry." She sat up and pulled her feet out of his grasp. "Tell you what, you can read Randy's diary. It's on my computer in his folder. Maybe it'll explain some things for you."

CHAPTER 24

When she had disappeared into the rear of the apartment, Clay went to her computer, drawn by horrific fascination. One of his few advantages was that Randy never talked about his past to Jewel. *If he's gotten over that—*

He found the folder. He found the file called "My First Month." He read the file.

Widescreen dread with shark music slowly filled Clay. *No wonder Jewel can't let go of him. I can't compete with this.*

Even more nervous, he wandered after her and found her in the bedroom, changing the sheets. "Aw, you didn't have to do that for me." He attempted a leer.

She sent him a not-lewd smile. "Back off, Bowser."

"Oh, now I'm a dog?"

"A horndog." The smile warmed up.

Was it sisterly? Or more than that? Clay leaped on the bed on hands and knees and started howling and barking, bouncing on his knuckles like an over-excited poodle.

"Hey!" she protested, laughing. The sheet fell out of her hand. "Down, boy!"

He tumbled headfirst off the bed, making it funny and clumsy and, still kneeling, snuggled up to her.

She shrieked with laughter. "And no leg humping, or I'll have you neutered!"

He stopped and looked reproachfully up at her. "You know, some of us have enough inferiority complex without help from uppity women."

Her laugh faded to a shy smile. "You like me uppity?"

Would he be giving away too much if he said yes?

If he waited, he might learn how much his answer meant to her.

Her smile faded, too. "Well, you're stuck with it," she said in a small voice.

The hurt in her face made him want to reach up and touch it. Suddenly he knew that this was not the night.

He got to his feet. "I think I should go home now."

She looked hurt even worse. He felt like a rat, but what could he do? That diary had totally unnerved him. He couldn't compete with Randy's telepathic lay-dar. He needed time to think out his strategy. Figure out what Randy's weaknesses were.

It seemed, more and more, that Randy had fewer weaknesses than he'd thought.

"I guess you're right." Her face pinched. "Maybe you'd better go home."

Immediately, Clay's worst fears came true.

She picked up him and his BB files on Saturday and they spent the whole day tracking the properties that BB had laundered for the blind trust, marking the map as they went. It was slow work, made slower by glacial traffic on the east-west arteries.

Jewel was on edge all day. By evening, she was thumping the steering wheel. "What is the matter with this traffic?"

"Cubs game tonight." Firecrackers and whistling bottle rockets went off over the street, and a pigeon, chasing flying sparks, smacked into a streetlight and dropped onto Jewel's hood.

Behind the friendly confines of Wrigley Field, the fans

roared. "Sounds like they're winning," she said. "Oh hell, there's Buzz." To the indignation of motorists lined up behind them, she stopped the car right in the intersection, put on his flashers, and jumped out before Clay could blink.

She ran across the street toward the ballpark. "Buzz!" he heard her say as she came up to a skinny kid with a backpack, standing beside a bicycle, talking to some ball fans.

A moment later, the kid was skimming away on the bike.

She returned to the car, cussing, and took the wheel again.

"What's he selling today?"

She started the engine and turned off the flashers. "Saltpetre. What the—? Why saltpetre?"

Clay had to laugh. "It's for all those office workers who've been eating too much Hoby's pastry."

Her cell phone rang. "What?" she barked into it.

He sensed her whole body relax beside him. Her closed fists opened on the wheel. Her voice changed.

"Hey, where are you? Oh? Oh." And just like that she tightened up again. "Really. Where? What do you mean, *in* the building?"

Pause.

Yup, that was Randy's voice quacking on the cell phone.

She said, "I guess I could. Okay. I'll be there." She snapped the phone shut. "Oh, hell. We're going to the Artistic Company. Randy's found the source of the hinky stuff."

She was already swerving across two lanes of Clark Street, turning east onto Addison in the deepening dusk.

Clay remembered the pastry shop and, down in the bowels of the printing plant, Wilma's shrine, the feel of Wilma's lips brushing his ear as she promised to help with his woman trouble in exchange for—for what? When they pulled up at the Artistic Building he said, "I think I'll stay in the car."

"Fine," Jewel said. She didn't even glance at him as she strode inside.

Five minutes later a closed stretch van and a black Caddy pulled up in front of Jewel's Tercel and a guy in a suit and five uniformed men got out and went into the Artistic.

Clay frowned. He got out of the Tercel and went to stand in the street, irresolute, watching the front door.

At seven o'clock the front door of the Artistic Building was unlocked, but Harry the security guy was nowhere in sight. The presses boomed under her feet. Jewel took the stairs two at a time to the fifth floor.

Randy was sitting on a folding chair outside the studio. He rose when she entered.

"Okay, what gives?" she said brusquely to hide the leap her heart gave at the sight of him. He was wearing tighter jeans than before and a white dress shirt with the sleeves rolled up. *He dressed up for me.* Her insides went hot and runny.

"Thank you for coming," he said. She blinked. Randy never said thank you. "Please come this way."

He led her to a boardroom with a corner window looking down on Washington Boulevard and the alley. They sat at a conference table opposite one another. She felt odd. In the dress shirt he looked almost corporate. Like he belonged in a boardroom.

"I think I know what's haunting this building," he said.

"Haunt." She looked over her shoulder. "Is it an it or a person?"

Randy folded his hands on the table. "This is rather complex. I've been trying to explain it to Velvita," he said and Jewel stiffened. "But she hasn't the education. In my centuries of contact with magic, I've come to agree with the earliest scholars. Magic, they say, is the life force of the world expressing itself."

She was having a hell of a time concentrating on all the sex-demon jargon. He smelled like himself. Her nostrils flared.

He said, "When human beings are involved, magic expresses itself most through sexual desire. This is why love potions are one of the oldest known forms of magic."

"Would you mind not saying that word?"

Five floors down, the throbbing presses went quiet. Someone far away began shouting.

"I'm sorry," he said gravely. "I must. The theory is simple, if you concede that human sexual desire can be dammed up, or stimulated to flow in excess. Then it becomes fuel for magic. In this building, sexual desire has been the focus for over a hundred years. Men have photographed naked women in situations calculated to arouse. Salacious stories have been printed. Everywhere one looks—"

He waved a hand, and Jewel noticed more oil paintings of Wilma, naked, willing, and wild, on the boardroom walls.

"—One sees images calculated to excite human desire. This place is a powder keg, magically speaking."

This talk made her squirm. "What does this have to do with the pocket zones in people's houses?"

"Attend. Desire is formless, like a mass of water restrained by a dam. It must have reached critical proportions for it to manifest in the pastries as an aphrodisiac, in the magazines as pocket zones. Perhaps the initiation of the film division poked a hole in the dam. The resultant flood—"

The door fell open with a crash. Harry, the security

guy, tumbled in. "It's La Migra—Immigration—they're arresting all the printers!" He wrung his hands. "Miss Onika's gonna be upset."

Jewel leaped like a scalded cat. "INS!"

"Also, I wondered," Harry panted, "does the new guy have papers?"

Her blood turned to ice. She said to Randy, "Run!"

In an instant, Jewel and Randy were through the door into the main stairwell, heading down.

A commotion came from below. "Halt! You're under arrest!" Scuffles and shouts followed.

As one, Jewel and Randy turned and pelted back upstairs. She looked around, frantic. They were on the fifth floor. "Can we go up?"

Randy jerked open a grimy door marked HVAC.

She pushed him. "Go!"

Voices came from the conference room.

They scrambled through the door, Randy first. Jewel shut it behind them. Her foot knocked something on the bottom step, a splinter of wood. She jammed it under the door, wedging it as tight as it would go, and followed Randy upward. All too soon, a heavy body slammed against the other side of the door.

The wind blew fiercely up on top of the building. Jewel pelted behind Randy as he jogged along the block-long parapet wall, looking down over the side. There were no fire escapes coming up to the roof. "Dammit!" she screamed.

She caught up with him at the building's facade, facing down on Washington Boulevard. There was her car at the curb. Clay stood on the sidewalk below, looking up.

Randy looked at her, then down at the street. "Jewel." In the wind his voice sounded hoarse. He took her by the arms. His dark eyes glittered—were those tears?

Her heart clutched up. "We'll get you out of this. Don't panic."

He yelled over the wind, "I have to set you free. Velvita has made me understand that much."

That made Jewel clench her teeth. "I understand, too," she yelled. "About the whorehouse and the girls and you wanting to do the right thing."

"She is a free spirit," he said, digging the knife deep into Jewel's guts. "She doesn't despise herself. I thought I had time to learn that from her—but the authorities have caught up with me. I can only damage you now." He kissed her hard, then pushed her away and hopped up on the parapet wall.

She shrieked, "Randy!"

"It's too late." He pointed.

Over her shoulder, Jewel saw a man in uniform in the roof-access doorway. She turned back to see Randy teetering on the edge, facing the long drop to the street.

"Goddammit!" she screamed, and scrambled up beside him. He tipped forward before she could get upright. She snatched at him, got hold of the back of his shirt, and pulled.

But he was too heavy.

They went over together, he twisting to face her, she clutching him around the waist.

Down there on the sidewalk, Clay looked up, his mouth and eyes getting bigger very, very fast.

Randy's lips touched her ear.

He said, "Are you afraid because you're aroused? Or aroused because you're afraid?"

She never felt the ground.

CHAPTER 25

Clay was standing directly under them. Two cell phones, two wallets, two sets of keys, four shoes, a pair of jeans, a white dress shirt, a three-piece navy polyester pantsuit, and a white forty-two-double-D brassiere with matching panties hit him in the face, one after the other.

He didn't dare look away. Horror froze him.

At length he brushed their clothes off his head and noticed a total absence of mangled human remains.

Uh-oh.

He knew what had happened now.

He groaned.

Then he realized what he would have to do to find them and groaned louder.

Up on the edge of the roof, someone stared down. The night watchman? Clay said some bad words, then ran into the building.

Inside the lobby, men in uniform yapped around a crowd of cursing printers like sheepdogs. A guy in a suit accosted Clay. "You. Do you have identification?"

All became clear to Clay. In his most amiable fake Texan accent he explained that he was a citizen, and he showed his ID, and he stood beside Harry the security guy as half a dozen printers were hustled out into the waiting van.

"Miss Onika, she's gonna shit turkey eggs," Harry

prophesied. "That worthless nephew of hers called 'em on us. Bet you a dime."

The rest of the printers had come upstairs to watch their coworkers leave. Harry offered to help, and they went back to their lair. The noise of the presses started up again.

Clay was left alone with his problem.

He stood under the big portrait of Wilma on the grand marble landing, thinking. His heart hammered in his ears. He wanted to search the place, but logic was catching up with him.

Jewel could always find Randy when he pulled this stunt, because she was his Number One Hundred. Or, wait, was it because she was female? Clay remembered that, when this had happened last month, any woman who slept in the bed where Randy was trapped was guaranteed a good time.

So to be absolutely sure, all he needed was a woman. Somebody to lie down on every single bed in the joint and, well, test it for sex-demon possession.

He had an inspiration. *Someone who knows where every bed is located would be even better.*

He went back outside and collected all the clothes, keys, shoes, wallets, and cell phones. If Randy wasn't a complete idiot, he would have Velvita's number on his cell.

Randy hadn't bothered to label the numbers. *Probably doesn't know how yet.* That would teach Clay to withhold information from Jewel's sex demon.

He started calling at the top of the list, standing in the lobby, fidgeting anxiously, staring vacantly up at Wilma's portrait, and praying under his breath, *Don't let me down, Wilma. Make this be her.*

Wilma must have heard him. The first number answered with a message. *Lena's not here. Leave a message. *boop**

Clay let out a cry of despair. "What do I do now?"

Movement from above caught his eye.

He looked up.

Up on the wall, Wilma stepped out of her picture frame as if descending an invisible staircase. She came straight toward him. She was wearing clothes this time, a corny, country-girlish ruffled blouse and a square-dance-pouffy skirt, but her feet and legs were bare.

She smiled warmly at him. Her voice sounded in his head.

Hey, baby. Let's make a deal.

Jewel found herself alone and naked, in the dark, falling. She screamed until she ran out of breath.

Then it occurred to her that she was still falling.

Off a five-floor building, she ought to have gone splat by now.

This must be demonspace. But if so, where's Randy?

As she thought this she noticed she wasn't falling anymore. *Randy?*

I am here, came his voice in her head.

Why can't I see you? She groped around in the absolute blackness. Her hands touched nothing. *Where is this?* She tried to rub her arms and realized that she couldn't feel them.

She couldn't touch anything.

Panic paralyzed her.

I was falling. Ohmigod, am I dead? Did we hit the sidewalk after all?

We are not dead, Randy said, invisible, intangible.

Well, where are you? I'm scared! She wanted to thrash, flail her arms, clutch something, anything. *Randy!*

Relax. I am here. Let me find you.

She tried to control her rising hysteria.

Out of nowhere, his hand gripped hers.

Where are we? she shrieked.

He held her hand tightly. *This place is familiar.* He seemed to be somewhere behind her, not at her side. A moment later he said, somewhere above her head, *This reminds me of the brass bed where I lay so long.*

She reached for his hand with her free hand. It seemed to take forever, as if her arms were miles long, as if she were drugged, as if she had forgotten exactly how her body was connected to her hands. Then, finally, she clasped her hands around his.

Are we in demonspace?

We must be. And yet—do you feel separated from your body?

I remember falling. We were falling straight down on top of Clay. The comfort of his hand in hers warmed her, made her almost sleepy.

His hand tugged both of hers. *Don't fade away! When first I lay trapped in that brass bed—*

In the whorehouse?

There, yes. I felt nothing. I saw nothing. I knew nothing. I almost faded away, as you are about to do.

She woke a little. *Am I cold?*

You have dissociated from your body. Perhaps from fear of—

Fear of splat.

Yes. It would be best if we made love. If you drift off, I won't know how to find you. This is not sleep!

Fear froze her thoughts. *I don't know if I can. I'm afraid we'll come back and still be falling. What if we have sex and I come and we materialize and we're still five stories up?*

I don't think we will. I think we are in a bed somewhere.

You don't know? Fear grew huge. She felt herself retreat from it. Even the touch of his hand seemed to fade.

Don't fall asleep, Jewel! I'll talk to you. It's absurd to fear falling. How often have we flown, or fallen, or floated? Stay with me and all's well. I'm touching your wrist now, Jewel. Do you feel it? Answer me.

Yes. She felt his hand slide, inch by inch, up her wrist. *I feel it.*

Good. Once, when I was a boy, I jumped off a stable roof onto a pile of hay. I didn't pass out. I stayed awake, enjoying the rush of air. The fall knocked the wind out of me and broke my collarbone, yet I wouldn't have traded the pain for safety. I had never come so close to flying. His hand caressed her wrist. *You must never fear to fall.*

What happened to us? Are we both sex demons now?

She felt rather than saw his smile. *Hardly. But you must return to your body, or we cannot get out.*

I'm scared. What if I can't? Why can't I see you? Where are we?

We have come to the place where desire is everything.

What does that mean?

It means you can have anything you want. But you must want it.

That seemed kinda deep. But she began to calm down.

I want to see you.

Again she felt him smile. *Let there be light.*

The first thing she saw after the eternal dark was his smiling face, his eyes soft, his hand coming up to touch her temple. *Let me make love to you.* His voice was gentle inside her head, but his lips didn't move. Instead he bent and kissed her very slowly.

It reminded her of something, this moment of tenderness.

She felt her heart thump faster, louder. Her body was back, clamoring. She tightened her arms around him and kissed back, fear turning sweet inside her.

When she opened her eyes, the familiar stormy night sky had formed around them.

I thought we were going to die.

Shh, be with me here now. Don't go where the fear is. She lay trembling in his arms, listening to her heart beat, feeling his slow approach, watching his smiling eyes. *Brave Jewel. Let me brighten this for you.* Behind his head, a star burst into a million golden petals that shot away in all directions.

She giggled. *Why don't they fall?*

He cupped both hands around her face. Another star burst behind him. His eyes were so serious, she felt small and fast and huge and scared.

He kissed her again, and the frozen, frightened place inside began to thaw. *No one falls, unless they want to fall.*

While she was puzzling that one through, she heard another voice say, *Where are we?*

CHAPTER
26

It won't hurt a bit, Wilma said, walking her fingertips up Clay's chest like some Roaring Twenties floozie. *You'll love it. I know more about sex than any woman alive. We'll have a ball.*

"But—but—"

You need me. I know where they are. Only a woman can get them out—and I'm all woman. She blinked her cartoon-long lashes and plastered herself against Clay. *Try me, sailor.*

He had to admit, she was persuasive.

And that little problem with confidence—? she began.

"What do you mean, problem with confidence!" Clay protested. "Confidence is my middle name!"

You know. The girl who won't look at you? The sex demon she likes? Wilma snapped her fingers. *Poof! With me on your side, you'll beat*, she said, leaning up to lick Clay's chin, *the pants off him.*

So that was how Clay found himself saying yes.

A look of wonder and joy came over Wilma's face. She laced her fingers through his, raising her arms so that he raised his too, and then her lips met his lightly. Cool delight sank into him from her mouth to his, soaking through every inch of skin on the front of his body, a happiness like vanilla ice cream on a summer day, penetrating all the way to the back of him. She was so happy to be inside him. He was happy just because she was happy.

Now let's go get her, she said in his head.

He felt like he was walking on air. They—she—he climbed the handful of stairs from the entrance level to the first floor and pushed open the door to the photo studio. The lights were out, yet he found he could see everything, almost as if he were a blind man who had lived here for decades, aware of every footstep, every scrape of chair-on-floor, every drawer opening or door closing. The studio dais was covered by a white sheet.

Wilma spoke in his head.

Feel that? They're in darkness. We'll need to call them out of there. A picture of Wilma popped into his head, pointing.

He looked where she pointed. It was dark. Duh.

Clay cleared his throat. "Jewel? Are you in here?"

No answer.

Somewhere over *there* he heard a big firework go off, and a million specks of light erupted in a chrysanthemum. Clay moved toward it, following the specks toward their invisible center.

He raised his voice. "Jewel! Randy! I've come for you!" How dumb was this? They were, uh, busy in there. Wherever "there" was.

But with Wilma inside him he laid one hand on the door—no, it was a bed—that made sense, some faraway part of him thought. He poked his head through the opening and called again.

No one answered, but the darkness seemed populated now.

Clay hesitated. Then a surge of pleasure left him weak, and in that moment of weakness Wilma *pushed* somehow and he—she—they stepped boldly through the opening into—what?

Where are we? he said.
Clay? Jewel said.

It was super-weird to meet Clay in demonspace. He stepped through a door from nowhere into their sky. He looked anxious. Poor guy had never walked in the clouds before. He looked down, and his arms started sawing as if he was about to fall off his cloud, and Jewel turned from Randy, catching a look of dark disapproval on his face.

Hold that thought, she said to him, and held out her hand to Clay.

Clay took it. In another moment they were kissing, and she noticed, oh, yeah, he was naked. *Jewel*, he seemed to say, though his mouth was busy, *we have to give you an orgasm. Right now.* She felt the urgency in his throat as if it were her own.

Behind her, the sense of Randy's urgency saturated the night air.

*But I—can we—*she began, torn between Clay and Randy.

Yes, she heard Randy say behind her, *have an orgasm, Jewel.* The mood of the moment changed: fear gone, tenderness gone, leaving a raging lust.

Clay seemed more assertive than she remembered. More alpha. She swooned back in his arms and let him manhandle her, massaging her breasts, hoisting her by her buns to hang her, as it were, on the hook of his erection, biting her throat and nipples, taking control.

Whoa. Clay's been taking vitamins, she thought, and her thought came out loud as a shout.

At that, Clay seemed to calm down. She had breathing space to look over at Randy and was startled to see Randy locked in a position so tangled that it could only be something from a porn flick, with a blonde she recognized instantly as Wilma, the Artistic mascot. He must have created her out of demonspace to salve his pride.

She sent him a pleading thought. *I want you, too.*

Randy opened his eyes and met Jewel's look. He reached out a hand and pulled her toward him, and instantly the four of them were locked together, spinning slowly through the night sky, ignoring gravity, doing things she hadn't done since that frat party. Too bad Onika couldn't shoot this. She giggled.

She would have thought she could tell them apart in a situation like this. Randy and Clay were so different, their moves in bed so like their personalities. But the very effort of trying to keep them sorted out confused her, until a tongue was just a tongue, hands were everywhere, too many hands, and no matter how many ways she was penetrated, whenever she reached out, someone was wrapping her fingers around a warm cock.

Then she realized that Randy's Wilma had got in the game.

The men floated away briefly while Wilma took Jewel by the hands and raised her arms, looking at Jewel's naked body with wide, innocent, delighted eyes. Jewel felt suddenly shy. She hadn't made love to a woman since that long-ago frat party. Wilma's improbably spherical breasts seemed to point at her. Jewel reached out to touch one nipple, and a thrilling wave passed through her just as if she'd been touching Randy in demonspace, sharing his physical pleasure. Wilma drove her fingers into Jewel's hair and kissed her, sweet and cool, long and slow, oh man, that kiss actually felt like Clay for a minute. Randy's unmistakable number-eleven hands slid around her bottom and up her belly and down between her thighs, and Jewel gave up trying to figure it out.

Until she realized that Wilma was teasing her nipples, Randy had entered her from behind, and Clay was gently sliding his cock down her throat. The satisfaction of having all their attention made her reel.

At length she wondered, *Hey, how come everybody's doing me?*

Randy craned his neck in a way that wasn't humanly possible and whispered in her ear. *Because we are all trapped here until you have an orgasm. You are the chosen one.*

She protested, *Chosen for what? To save everybody stuck in sex-demonspace? That's ridic—*

Come for me, Clay murmured.

Come for me, Wilma said in her own silvery voice, and Jewel thought, *Cool, Randy, she has her own voice.* He was so creative.

Come for me, Randy commanded. *Come now.*

All of them squeezed her slightly at that moment, so that she felt crowded and crazy, and then they released a little, so she could expand like a squeezed balloon into licking tongues, stroking hands, and strong members filling her, and then they squeezed again, only to release, bite, drive deeper, tease her skin, and squeeze—

Orgasm finally blinded her.

Then the three of them were lying on the platform in the photo studio, sweaty, gasping, glowing, and kind of embarrassed. At least, she was embarrassed. Clay seemed as calm as usual, and Randy probably couldn't be embarrassed with his clothes off.

"That was fun," Jewel panted. "Let's not do it again." She looked at Randy. "You did that on purpose. Zapped us into a bed while we were falling."

He raised his eyebrows. "It seemed preferable to crushing our skulls on the pavement."

"Oh, totally," she admitted, still shaken. "But how could you be sure I was, uh, turned on?"

"Sex and death are close relatives."

"Shhh," Clay said, cocking his head toward the door.

Not a sound came from downstairs. La Migra had come and gone.

Clay's things were in a heap on the floor. Her clothes were piled up on the edge of the platform, mixed with Randy's. Silently, they dressed as quickly as they could.

"Let's get out of here," Randy said.

CHAPTER 27

"I forgot my briefcase," Randy said, and headed upstairs.

"Since when does he have a briefcase?" she said, looking after his tight jeans and his mane of long black hair.

But Clay led her out to the car to wait.

"Jewel." By streetlight, Clay looked solemn. He picked up her hand. "Jewel, you know Randy's not quitting this job."

She felt her face start to crumple, pulled her hand free, and turned away. *Crap, don't cry in front of Clay!*

"Do you think he's happy?" she said. "Working here?" *Living with Lena.*

"Who knows. I doubt that guy's ever happy."

She faked a short laugh. "He hasn't come to get his stuff out of my apartment yet. He hasn't zapped into a bed either. So maybe the curse is over."

She felt scooped out and hollow. How could he have made love to her the way he had tonight, in the black void, after they fell off the roof, when she was so afraid, and not care?

I'm thinking like such a girl! She'd been wishing and praying for this moment ever since she realized how dependent Randy was on her. And now that he was independent, she hated it. She felt like a teenager, all swoony and sore inside.

"You know, this zapping-into-beds thing seems like something between you two," Clay said thoughtfully. "Not curse-ish."

That made her look. "What do you know about it?"

"I don't know anything." He showed her his palms. "I'm just saying. You've suggested it yourself. This seems negotiable somehow."

"Like it's some kind of weapon he uses against me when he can't get the upper hand any other way," she said resentfully. "I could believe it. He's so sure that sex will get him out of trouble—not that he's wrong, god-dammit—"

"Never mind," Clay said with an edge in his voice. "I'm sure you two will work it out on your own."

She shifted in the driver's seat so she could see him better. By streetlight his blond hair looked orange. For once, his pouty mouth wasn't smiling. "How did you know to come and find us up there?"

He shrugged. "Logic."

"And the part about—about having sex with me to get us both free?" A thought occurred to her. "That *was* you in demonspace with us, wasn't it?"

"Well, duh." He had his con artist face on now.

She eyed him, feeling unsettled. "I just didn't have you figured for a group grope type of guy."

"There's a lot about me you ought to know."

Well, duh. "And *how* did you get into demonspace with us? That was seriously strange, with the Wilma thing and the foursome."

"Maybe Randy's rubbing off on you."

"Rubbing—*off*?" She sucked in a horrified breath. "Oh. My. God."

What if she was, like, catching hinkyness? What if Randy's hinkyness was contagious? Her skin prickled.

"Don't panic. I'm on your side." Clay took her hand again. "Take a chance on me, Jewel," he said softly. "I know I'm not Randy. I like to think that's in my favor, actually."

Somewhere on a nearby street, someone set off a firework. There was a squeal, a pop! and, behind Clay's head, she saw sparks trickle down in a slice of sky between skyscrapers.

She relived the moment when she saw Randy teetering on the parapet of the Artistic Building.

"You want to know what Randy has that you don't have?" she blurted.

He pulled his hand away. "I have a pretty good idea. I did read his diary."

"I'm not criticizing you. I'm explaining. Only now I've opened my big mouth I don't know how to say this."

"Officer, if this is you being tactful, I'm scared."

Great, now she'd offended him, too. She stared through the windshield at the darkened door of the Artistic Building.

"You don't like hearing about Randy. But I'll tell you one thing he does that you could learn. He takes chances. Not stupid break-the-law chances, but emotional chances. You want me to take a chance on you, but what are you risking? Mister Master Con Artist."

"I guess I'm risking what you're risking," he said, but his tongue touched his lips.

She thought, *He's chicken. Heck, it's getting so I can almost read this guy.* It was sheer meanness to keep rubbing his nose in Randy. *This is why I don't do relationships.*

But she had a point to make.

"Randy's not afraid to throw himself off a building to get what he wants. He once let a taxi run him over, to protect me. That obnoxious trick of his, zapping into beds all over the place? He risks getting left forever, every time. I hate it, but at least he's not afraid to put up or shut up."

"Well, you're liable to run me over, but you don't see me running away," Clay said reasonably.

She frowned. "That's doubletalk."

"Not. Every man you've ever had, you dumped. I think Randy and I are going for a record, with no other competitors in sight. I can't speak for Lord Randolph's feelings, but if I fall off it's gonna leave bruises."

She hadn't thought about Clay having feelings. He was always so careful not to show any. *Am I so selfish that I think he doesn't feel anything?* Why didn't she feel anything herself? Besides bruised and ashamed and upset and doomed.

At that moment, Randy came out of the Artistic Building with a tan briefcase, and her guts twisted into a tight knot up under her heart. He got in the back seat. Jewel started the car.

"All okay?" Clay said.

Randy slapped the roof of the car twice. "Let's go."

She peeled away from the curb to the sound of exploding cherry bombs.

Clay watched her face as Randy walked up to the car. Waiting, she'd been tired, depressed, relaxed. Now, as Lord Almighty arrived, she came alive.

She doesn't do that for me.

What do you do for her? came Wilma's voice in his head.

"Shut up," he muttered quietly. He was still reeling from his visit to what Jewel called "demonspace" and a foursome with Randy and this oversexed teen Venus in his head. Body. Wherever.

Have you tried slathering ice cream all over her?

This isn't an ice cream kind of problem, Clay thought back at her. It was hard to remember to keep his thoughts in his head and not just blurt them out. He could feel Wilma poking around inside his body like a puppy sniffing out its new house, and it made him tingle all over.

And, scarily, it felt good.

She seems like she'd respond well to bondage, Wilma said.

"They resumed printing," Randy said. "With half a crew."

The mere sound of Randy's voice made Clay's hackles rise. *I don't know why, but all of a sudden I hate this guy.*

Maybe it was watching him have sex with your girl.

If you don't have anything constructive to contribute—

Wilma interrupted him. *If you could share, you'd have it made. Or don't you do guys?*

Never mind who I do, Clay snapped in his head.

You're too independent. How can I help you if you're rude? Wilma said huffily.

Clay leaned over and turned on the radio.

Jewel turned it off.

"You missed the turn for the Corncob Building," he said as the car zipped across Dearborn.

Jewel swore. "I'll have to go to Michigan and double back."

"Where are we leaving you off, Randy?" Clay said, raising his voice.

You could invite him back for a threesome, Wilma said.

Will you shut up? Clay snarled silently. He felt his body going rigid with the effort of keeping his face neutral. Wilma-in-his-head unplugged all his training. He felt exposed, as if a con had gone horribly wrong. Maybe this was how Jewel felt in bed with Randy, having a sex demon in her head all night.

Sex goddess, Wilma corrected.

Clay noticed suddenly how the silence had stretched.

Jewel turned left onto Michigan and then, in the strained silence, left again onto Wacker going west.

"Wait," Randy said. "Stop."

Jewel screeched the Tercel to a halt, bumping the left wheels up over the curb on the triangular plaza at Wacker and South Water Street, where a fountain played.

Randy put a hand on her shoulder. "Jewel."

She stared straight ahead. "What." Clay hated the hurting look on her face.

Randy said to Clay, "May we speak privately a moment?"

Clay figured he'd done his best. He got out.

You haven't even tried, Wilma scolded.

You're gonna make me a head case. He walked to the fountain, his back to the car, clenching his fists against his chest as if he could silence Wilma by force.

Randy's voice came, low but distinct, behind him. "I have to do this."

"I know," Jewel's voice said tightly. "I read your diary."

"They're human beings," Randy pleaded. "That was what Lady Georgiana meant for me to learn. I think."

"I think she was just being a bitch."

"It took me so long to learn it. This is my chance to pay for my mistakes. They—they're teaching me something."

"I'll just bet," Jewel said bitterly, and Clay gloated.

Randy said, "What they teach me is not about having sex, but about—about *being* a sex demon."

Randy's voice got faint, and Clay strained to hear. *Hang on a second*, Wilma said in his head, and then she did something.

Suddenly Clay could hear Randy's soft voice loud and clear, over the splashing fountain and the traffic on distant Lake Shore Drive.

"We are alike, Velvita and I," Randy was saying. "She is two people, a respectable secretary—"

"For a pornographer."

"—And a woman without reputation. These two selves rub against one another. And the world is not kind to women like her, Jewel. Nor to men like me."

That was cool, Clay admitted grudgingly. *What did you do?*

Just tuned up your ears a little, Wilma said.

Randy said, "Velvita reconciles some of that by donning her paint like a mask. Yet with her reputation she has lost her mother, her old life, and friends—as I have lost everything. Paint cannot cover that loss."

"Would you mind not telling me her sob story?" Jewel grated.

Don't like being on the receiving end, huh, Clay thought.

"I apologize," Randy said stiffly. "It is easier for me to describe her suffering than my own."

Now there's an adventurous guy, Wilma said. *You could stand to loosen up, you know.*

"Will you shut up?" Clay muttered. He stared blindly at the curve of the Seventeenth Church of Christ, Scientist across the street and flapped his suddenly super-sharpened ears.

"Look." Jewel lowered her voice, but Clay still heard her clearly. "I'm not trying to, like, nail you down here. I'm the last person to do that. It's just, I guess I'm trying to figure out if I—I mean, for three months now we've been joined at the hip, trying to keep you on two feet. Are we done?" Her voice cracked. "Am I free to get back to my regularly scheduled slutting?"

"Oh, Jewel, how can I criticize your lewdness when I—"

"Argh!" The car door slammed. Clay turned to look. She stood beside the car, hands on hips, glaring in the rear passenger window at Randy.

"You have done nothing but criticize my *lewdness*, as you call it, since we met. Now all of a sudden you're taking *money* for it, screwing *porn stars*, and you're Mister Liberal! I'd like to paste you one, you hypocritical bastard!"

She stomped to the edge of the plaza to glare across the river, possibly at her own apartment on the twenty-third floor of the Corncob Building.

Randy got out of the car. Clay stood watching, leaning his hip against the edge of the fountain. Their eyes met, and it occurred to Clay that Randy had been screwing women at the Artistic. With a sex goddess on the premises. Plus, Wilma had materialized in demonspace tonight. Randy must have seen Wilma. Heck, Wilma had been doing Randy, doing Clay, even doing Jewel before Jewel had her orgasm and popped them all free.

So he knows. About you. Clay froze, staring disaster in the face.

Of course he knows, Wilma said.

If Randy told Jewel about Wilma before Clay was ready, Clay was screwed. Jewel could dish it out, slutwise, but look how she was reacting to Randy's job. She would not take Wilma well. It would take serious finessing on Clay's part to reconcile her to sharing a bed with the ultimate porn star.

And Randy knows all that.

As if Randy had heard this thought, he gave Clay a tiny nod. He walked over to Jewel, who stood with her back to them, her arms wrapped tightly around herself.

And in that moment Clay realized he was going to win. Randy might be a skilled sex demon, and he might be readier to make grand, stupid gestures to get Jewel's attention, but he was no better than Clay at showing his feelings.

All I have to do is sit tight and let him blow it.

In the back of his mind, Wilma tut-tutted. He ignored her.

Randy was saying in a low voice, "I have great regard for you."

Jewel didn't turn around. "Same here."

Boy, all you people have a serious spitting-it-out problem, Wilma said.

Clay growled in his throat.

"The thing is," Jewel said, her voice lower and softer, "how do we know that what you feel isn't just Stockholm syndrome? Stuck with your rescuer for three solid

months, twenty-four-seven, you could hardly help feeling something about me. Admit it, you have no idea
how you're going to feel without the curse hanging over
your head all the time."

Randy hesitated. "I thank you again for your unremit-
ting care and hospitality."

"Oh, can it. The point is, is it just the spell talking? If
it weren't for the curse, you wouldn't even want to
know me. You've admitted that, in normal lord life, a
lord like you would never even say howdy to a lowborn
wench like me."

"I was a fool to say that. A fool and a boor. It doesn't
matter."

"Never mind. Is it right or honorable for me to be
with someone who has no choice but to be with me?"

"You're angry because of my work at the Artistic," he
said, ducking the honorable question, Clay noted.

"Well, who wouldn't be?" she exploded.

"Jewel. Please," Randy said, and Clay could tell it was
killing him to say *please*. "I need this. In bed or standing
on two feet, I am half a man. If Velvita can show me
how to bring those halves together—"

"I do not care who you screw," she said flatly.

"—then perhaps I can bring you a whole man someday."

Clay held his breath. He caught a glimpse of her face
past Randy's head. He wished he hadn't. She looked
hopeful and scared and angry and yearning all at the
same time.

She put up her chin. "Maybe I won't be waiting.
Maybe I'll marry Clay."

Holy *what-was-that*? Clay's heart stood still.

Randy threw him a glance.

Now was the moment. If Randy ever intended to tell
her about Wilma and mess this up for Clay, he would do
it now.

Randy's eyes, on Clay, were full of danger. He looked at Jewel. "Very well," he snapped. "Commit yourself to a smooth liar."

Jewel reacted badly. "I should prefer your crude, rude stinginess with the truth?"

"I?" Randy's voice rose. "How can I lie to you? In bed—what you call demonspace—we are equals!"

"Not like *out* of bed, where you're a lord and I'm some serving-wench slut." Jewel sounded like she was crying now. Clay's chest squeezed.

"I have never said you were a servant! Yeoman class landowner, at worst!"

She made a noise like a stepped-on rat. "And still a slut, right?"

Randy put a hand out, palm up. "You call yourself a slut, but I am a whore. I beg you—*beg* you—to grant me the opportunity to commune with other whores. I need to regain my self-regard. In whatever way they can teach me."

She drew back. "That's not good enough."

"I don't despise you! I—" He lowered his voice. "I despise myself. As you despise yourself. How can I heal the insults I have dealt you in my boorish ignorance if I cannot make peace with myself?"

"Look, just give me a straight answer. Is this curse over? Because I can't b-babysit you while you're working there."

"I—don't know."

She leaned forward, her voice full of rage. "*Yes or no?*"

Randy stood still. Clay edged closer. Randy's eyes were shut, or maybe he was looking down that long English nose of his, thinking.

Then his gaze lifted and met Clay's, and Clay froze in his tracks.

He said, "Yes."

She took a step backward. "Well. All right, then."

"What seems to be the trouble?" said a new voice, and Clay spun around so fast he almost fell into the fountain.

It was a cop. His squad car idled, two wheels up on the plaza curb, behind the Tercel.

"Uh, just a little domestic squabble, officer," Clay said. Should he let this guy break it up? Things were going so well. "They'll be over it soon."

"Fine, but you can't park here. If you move the vehicle now, I won't write you a—oh, hey, is that Jewel Heiss?" The cop walked up to the domestic squabble, grinning. "Hey, babe, how are you? Haven't seen you around the bowling alley lately."

Jewel seemed to recognize him. "Oh, hell." She collapsed and sat on the curb.

"Well, okay," the cop said, his face falling. "I was just saying hi."

Randy got his briefcase out of the car and walked swiftly away across Wacker Drive.

Jewel looked after him. To the cop she said, "I'm sorry, Ben, I didn't mean—"

"I'll take her home now," Clay said, coming up and getting hold of her hand. He pulled her to her feet. "You okay? We can't leave the car here, you know."

"Yeah, whatever," she said distractedly. She watched Randy stride away, passing the bridge leading to Jewel's apartment, walking westward along the river.

"We appreciate the warning," Clay told the cop.

"Bye, Jewel," Officer Ben said sadly.

Clay got Jewel in the passenger side and drove her home, his heart seething with terror and glee.

In her apartment, Jewel strode up and down, ranting and crying. Clay kept his temper. *I'll win this one*, he chanted mentally, *I'll win, I'll win*.

She yelled, "Three months of day-in, day-out paranoia, and now this! What am I gonna tell Brit and Nina? My roommate left me for a *porn star*? Ugh, ugh, what was I *thinking*, I *hate* relationships, I don't even *want* one, this is making me insane!"

Clay went to the kitchen and silently nuked some cold pot stickers and a carton of leftover General Tso.

She watched, hiccupping. "I hate him."

In the fridge were a few stray plastic cups of sweet and sour sauce and pot sticker sauce. Clay also found a white paper bag on the counter with one and a half cow plops in it. He nibbled his way through the half and gave the other to her.

"He's an arrogant pig of an aristo," she said when she had wolfed down her cow plop.

Sooner or later, she'll notice I'm here.

Oh, yeah? Wilma said in his head.

He almost jumped out of his skin. He thought, *You shut up! Don't talk to me right now!*

The nuke dinged. Clay ladled Thai food onto Jewel's plate.

"I was sick of bullying him to do his own laundry."

Standing, she shoveled chicken into her mouth with her fingers.

Clay kept his gaze down.

At length she looked up from her plate. "I like you. You're easy."

He smiled. "I try to be." His heart thumped. *Maybe I'll marry Clay*. She'd only said that to yank on Lord Randypants, but it made him feel funny all over, in a good way. She looked up and took two steps toward him, putting her greasy hand on his chest and ruining his shirt.

"Sorry I'm being such a psycho. This"—she breathed deeply—"will blow over."

He shook his head, smiling.

"Really." She stood so close, he smelled sex on her. The porn factory, oh yeah, the bed in the photo studio, right. Less than an hour ago. His short-term memory seemed to be leaking away, the closer she came.

She lifted her face and he realized she was going to kiss him and he wasn't ready. Why wasn't he *thinking*? Should he let her kiss him or not? What would let him hold onto the situation? There was no telling where it might go if he let her run things.

While he was debating the point, she kissed his cheek.

Consolation kiss. Not his favorite, but he took it for what it was worth. Her blue eyes had red rims. She looked like a she-Viking in mourning. Clay lost every thought in his head besides, *Beautiful*.

Now will you try the feathers and ice cubes? Wilma said in his head.

Oh, right. His ace in the hole. Clay bit his lip. Looking in Jewel's eyes, he thought, *I'd rather try something hinky. Something to get her mind off the lord. Just her and me*, he added. *I don't think she's ready to meet you yet*.

He turned away and walked into the living room.

Jewel followed. "I'm sorry," she said, breaking in on

the head chatter. "I forgot—I didn't consider your feelings."

Oh, brother, he *had* been indiscreet.

There's a few things I think you should know, Wilma said. *About being my avatar. Because sometimes, if someone needs me—*

I need you to shut up! he thought fiercely. *Whenever I'm with Jewel.* Darn, this was hard, talking to Jewel and thinking at Wilma and listening to them both. Should he be saying something to Jewel now? About considering his feelings, right.

He turned. "It's okay." He put a bit of pathos into it, which wasn't hard, considering his feelings. "I'm a good crying towel."

"You're more than that," she said warmly, and he tightened, thinking, *Am I really, Jewel?*

She smiled shyly at him. He forgot completely to monitor what his face was doing.

Then he blinked. *Okay, Wilma, do your stuff. What kind of fabulous sex hasn't she had yet?*

Wait a minute. I'm going into the archives. Stall her.

Mentally, Clay rolled his eyes. "I'd like to make you happy," he murmured on autopilot. He cupped Jewel's face with both hands and stroked her cheeks with his thumbs, trying to push aside a feeling that she could see right through him.

"Really?" She blinked rapidly. "That's nice."

She was here, and she'd said goodbye to the sex demon, and she was looking right at him.

Terrifying.

Can you hurry it up? he said in his head to Wilma.

"I'm kind of confused right now," Jewel said.

"So kiss confused." He kissed her forehead.

I'm working on it, I'm working on it. I'm not lightning-fast, you know. My, she has been a busy girl. Are you sure you're up to her?

Insecurity clutched at his gut. *Not helping.*

"It wouldn't be fair to you," Jewel said.

Got it! Wilma said. *Now kiss her!*

"Do me a favor, Officer," he murmured. "Be unfair for once."

"But you—"

He silenced her with his mouth, very gently. A tear leaked out of the corner of her eye and he kissed that. He kissed her mouth until his head swam, and then Wilma said *Here we go* in his head, and he felt himself slipping into a beautiful dream.

After a long, sweet, mindless kiss, he realized he smelled fresh-cut grass and hot sunshine and rain on pavement, heard the spatter of water droplets and the distant sound of children playing. He was falling into Jewel's kiss. It felt sweet and solid and real.

Then something cold and slimy fell on the crook of his neck.

Right in his ear, a dog barked.

He jerked his head back. *Oh, for—*

In his arms, Jewel laughed. *She wants you to throw it.*

Looking over his shoulder, he saw a golden retriever staring at him with eager intensity. Behind the dog was a white picket fence, a lawn sprinkler sending up a glittering arc of spray, and a shady tree. And by his elbow on the grass lay a slimy, green, dog-spit-covered tennis ball.

The dog barked again. Clay was lying on the grass, his arms around Jewel. The cut-grass smell mixed with her smell and it smelled like heaven.

He looked into her face and saw her laughter turn to confusion.

That's funny. The dog has a wig on, she said.

It did. The dog wore a mop of blonde curls.

He felt his lips move. *Sex is supposed to be funny.* He didn't dare tell Wilma to stop with the dog, because his thought would come out loud and clear in this weird place.

Jewel heaved herself onto one elbow, frowning *Where? Where—*

"Are we?" Her voice sounded in his head and in his ears.

The next moment, they were lying on her living room floor.

Her face twisted with growing horror. "Oh my *God!* Clay!"

She shoved him away and leaped to her feet. With one hand she swept the afghan off the sofa, and with the other she felt the upholstery, then lay her ear against it. "Randy? Dammit, are you in there?" She did the same to the carpet.

Clay stood beside her, watching disaster unfold.

She looked up at him. "He's not in there." With a puzzled frown, she leaned her knuckles on the sofa arm. Then she slumped onto the couch.

Clay sat with her, putting his arm around her. "I thought that was nice. Except for the slimy wet tennis ball. I don't know where that came from," he added darkly.

Her hands made fists on her thighs. "You said you thought maybe Randy was rubbing off on me. That's how you got into demonspace with us."

His heart stopped.

This was it. She would find out about Wilma and kill him. Plus, she'd never speak to him again. His mouth opened and closed.

"Is that so bad?" he said weakly.

Her eyes grew round, and she filled her lungs slowly, and then she screamed.

"Aaaaaughhhhh!" She slapped her hands over her eyes.

"Maybe it was the cow plops," he suggested. "You've

been exposed to a lot of hinky sex—maybe they affect you more."

"Oh, my *God! I'll never have normal sex again!*"

"Jewel, it's not so bad—"

"Go home," she said from behind her hands. "I have to be hysterical now."

"Jewel—"

"*Go home!*" she screamed.

On the walk back to the Drake, Clay tried to explain to Wilma why her contribution was such a disaster.

She didn't get it. *You don't realize what an opportunity this is*, she kept saying.

"I realize I'm screwed with Jewel if she finds out about you."

He felt sticky and sweaty and used, and his two-hundred-dollar Hawaiian shirt smelled like General Tso.

Jewel might never touch him again.

"Why do I have to be your avatar, anyway?"

Because Steven Tannyhill keeps ducking me, she pouted.

Maybe she could be deflected onto this Steven character. "I can't believe he would refuse you."

He won't stay in the building long enough for me to get to him. He used to come in every week, real early in the morning, before the office staff arrived, and pick up big stacks of magazines from the printing plant. He also bought pastry. That's where I got the idea to—

"To poison it."

No! To remind him of me. He should be my avatar. He would love it. Bill Tannyhill loved it. You love it.

"I'm more in like, I guess I would say."

Oh, come on, I'm on your wood every minute. I would know if you didn't like it.

"My wood isn't the smartest part of me," Clay muttered.

It was no use.

He hated to admit it, but he was broken.

Sometimes a straight question was the only option.

He phoned Randy's cell.

Randy answered on the first ring.

"Why haven't you told Jewel about Wilma?" Clay demanded.

"Haven't you?" Randy said with amusement in his voice.

Clay had to call on all his con-artist training to swallow curse words. "Why haven't you?"

"I'm giving you enough rope to hang yourself," Randy said.

"Why should I trust you?"

"On my honor," Randy said. "You have a free hand."

"Bull," Clay said angrily. "You could get rid of me forever if you told her."

"But I need both of you to survive in this world," Randy said. "It is you who will not share."

Clay snorted. "You've never shared anything in your life."

After a pause Randy said, "I think, upon reflection, you'll realize that I have."

Clay hung up.

Lena was putting the finishing touches on a script for Onika when the doorbell rang. She went to the peephole. Outside, somebody dark hung his head so low that she couldn't see his face. He looked up to ring the doorbell again. Randy.

"What in the world?" She held the door wide. "You have a key."

He shuffled in. "I felt we were insufficiently acquainted for me to walk in unannounced." His head was still hanging.

He met Jewel and she ripped him a fresh one. Lena sighed. If all the ex-girlfriends and ex-boyfriends in Chicago were laid end-to-end, she'd be out of a job.

"Come in and tell me about it."

She got him a glass of wine and sat him on a milk crate. He looked like two cents. "Tell me what she said."

He raised wounded eyes to her face. "You know what we are."

"No. What are you? Lovers? Friends?"

"No," he said, "you and I."

She and Randy had only one thing in common. "She dissed you for acting in porn movies?"

"And for whoring for two hundred years." He blinked. "She complains of it often. At first I thought she must be jealous, but I learned better the night she came for me at the studio."

"Uh—" Lena frowned.

"I gave her the fantasy she wanted, a fantasy about—"

"Should you be telling me her fantasy?"

He shrugged. "I have told women of others' fantasies before. How else could I learn, if I didn't offer them choices?"

Yeah, but you weren't in love with any of them. If he didn't get it, maybe he deserved a fresh one. "Go ahead."

"She wished to be in a porn shoot. She pretended to be a novice. I was her director, her leading man, her crew."

"Tricky," Lena said.

He brushed that away with two fingers, his eyes elsewhere. "Her understanding of our work—it was all wrong. Disturbingly wrong. But I had to deliver the fantasy she wanted."

"You certainly do that."

"A successful fantasy has a hinge where orgasm becomes possible. The hinge is a moment where a woman feels ambivalent."

"Did you find out why she wanted to be in a porn shoot?"

He swallowed. "Shame. The hinge was shame." He covered his face with both hands.

Lena touched his shoulder. "Seems she isn't the only one who's ashamed." He didn't move. "Haven't you met a lot of women with that hinge?"

He nodded behind his hands. "I don't know why it should affect me so, in her case."

Because you're in love with her, you big dumbbell! Lena resigned herself to a long night. "Tell me about her."

He drew his long fingers over his eyes and down his

face. Hunkered with his elbows on his knees and his hands dangling, his white dress shirt open at the throat, his too-long black hair shaggy around his face, he looked unreally beautiful, like a fox or a unicorn.

Lucky bitch, Lena thought.

"She's morbidly fearful and astonishingly brave. She throws herself upon the spears of her enemies and *they* are crushed. What I have seen her do—" He shook his head, his lip curling. "The man she's with now is a coward to his bones. Although, if he can convince himself he has some hidden advantage, he too can perform prodigies. As if a flimsy secret were his shield. That will undo him with her. I have only to wait," Randy said forlornly.

"You were telling me about her."

Lifting his forefinger, he said, "Let me tell you about the porn shoot fantasy I created for her."

Lena rolled her eyes. "Okay."

"The hinge was shame. She had two desires hung upon that hinge. One was the desire to be whole again, virginal, free of shame." He shook his head. "If she only knew that she's whole! She's always been whole. She was involuntarily despoiled in some way. But the despoiler can take from her only what she believes he can take. *She is still whole*."

"That's an odd idea. I don't see how that's possible, but I'm listening."

"She's whole, and yet she feels despoiled. That's the meaning of her choosing to be a novice porn actress."

Lena felt a shiver.

"She walks into the studio—my lair, as she fancies it—innocently, perhaps by accident. But the magic of the fantasy holds her. She pretends to herself she's afraid to admit that she doesn't belong. So, to preserve her sense of control, she pretends she knows what she is doing."

Randy turned his dark eyes on Lena. "This is the other side of the hinge. Power. She wants to be whole, and yet she wants to give up power. She can't see how she can have both those things at once. She comes to me." He shut his eyes. "And I—abuse her." His face pinched up.

Lena thought she understood now. "She wants you to."

"Yes. At some point in the fantasy she has come to the limit of her courage, and she needs my help. So I give commands. And, to preserve the secret that she's still a virgin, she obeys. Do you see? I have taken the reins out of her hands. I drive her as I might drive a team of horses over the edge of her own self-control."

"But she isn't a virgin."

"No. She *is*. She *thinks* she is no longer a virgin." Randy put a hard finger on Lena's knee. "Everyone is still a virgin. What is a virgin? Clean, whole, honest, pure. When is a virgin despoiled? When she feels dirty, broken, dishonest, as if evil has been stirred into her insides."

The way I felt when Mom refused to defend me against Steven, Lena thought.

"The fantasy becomes a trap in which she may capture her virginity. She permits herself to feel innocent only in the tiny confines of her body, which she has brought to the studio to be despoiled, so that she may renew her wholeness, her virginity. Throwing herself on the spear of her enemy." He shook his head.

Lena followed all this with difficulty. "She's doing something that scares her. That seems brave to me."

"As I said."

"So what's the problem?"

"When she wakes from the dream, she's satisfied, but shame rolls back over her. She can't keep it at bay for long. And so she tells herself a lie. It is the man who made her do these things who should be ashamed." Bitterly, he said, "I am he."

"I see." Lena felt like spitting. "I hate when people do that. I could see my mom being hostile to my work.

She's a mom. But if I make the mistake of telling some guy what I do—"

"He treats you like a whore," Randy finished for her. "That is to say, he has an opportunity to make himself whole by laying his shame upon your back. He can't even admit that he mourns his virginity, because he's a man."

Lena eyed him. "You've only been in porn a few days."

He lifted his head. "I've been a sex demon to pious women for two hundred years."

"Well, brother, you've got the whole song, verse and chorus." She smiled.

Every inch an aristocrat, he bowed. "Thank you. It's an honor to be accepted into the guild."

Lena peeked at her watch. "What will you do about Jewel?"

Randy deflated. "I shall wait."

Lena snorted. "I think you're holding out on her."

"Holding—?"

"You expect her to understand you. You think she should know how ashamed you feel. She should know not to beat you up—she shouldn't try to make you feel more ashamed."

Randy's mouth fell open. "How can she not know?"

"Uh, duh, maybe because you don't tell her?"

"We have been together every night in what she calls demonspace. This is merely the vast space inside her mind, but of course she must demonize it, literally, and blame it on me," he added grumpily. "My mind is exposed to hers there, just as hers is to me. We are equals in demonspace."

"Let me get this straight." Lena put up both hands. "You expect her to rummage around in your brain the way you rummage around in hers."

"She could, if she willed."

"Have you invited her to poke around in your demon-space?"

He said nothing.

"You are such a guy."

"Mock me if you choose—"

"Men are so dense. Number one, you're mad because nobody has ever rummaged in your head the way you rummage in our heads. And why is this? I hate to break it to you, but most of us aren't looking past the sex, which is great, by the way. Number two, you are still a lord. You love presenting yourself as a sex demon and you don't want your power questioned."

"I abase myself every night, providing for her desires, without regard for my dignity—"

"Do you hear yourself? Providing for her desires means you have to 'abase yourself.' 'Your dignity suffers.' You dork, my costars don't think it's beneath their dignity to 'provide for my desires.' At least they don't say so out loud, if they want to have any wood to work with." She looked at him with affection. "She's right. You're totally a lord. I think you deserve each other."

After a stiff look down his nose, Randy slumped. "I wish she thought so."

"Have you been listening to me? Because I've been listening to you. On and on and on."

"I beg your pardon." He swallowed. "What should I do?"

"In words of one syllable? Tell her how you feel." Every single conversation she had with a heartbroken guy, she wound up saying the same thing. Why did she bother listening at all?

And, like every other heartbroken guy, he answered the same way. "I can't."

She got up from her milk crate. "Okay, bedtime for me. I have church in the morning."

"Please!" He caught at her hand. "Advise me."

Leaning over his gaunt face and his beautiful, black, heartbroken eyes, she said slowly, "Tell. Her. How. You. Feel. You gotta show some pink, buddy. Write her a letter, if you can't say it out loud."

"A letter?" Slowly, he nodded. "I could do that."

"Don't tell her she's still a virgin, or dump on her for dumping her shame on you. Tell her what you like about her. Tell her how she makes you feel. A love letter. You know what that is?"

He swallowed. "I believe so."

"Right. Okay. Nighty-night." She dropped a kiss on top of his head and crashed out.

He didn't come to bed all night. She knew, because if he had, he would have done something amazing to her, and she would have remembered that.

In the morning she found a few yellow sheets torn from a legal pad on the kitchen counter.

"What's this?"

Randy came in from the shower, rubbing his head with a towel. "My letter to Jewel. You may read it."

She really didn't have time, but she leaned against the counter and sipped coffee and read.

Five minutes later she looked up, a lump in her throat. He was still watching her.

"It's a good letter."

He smiled.

"Now send it."

"I can't."

She put her cup on the counter and went into the bedroom, handing him the letter as she passed. "I'm going to church."

He followed. "I have to let her go. She will tire of Clay. Or she won't."

Lena threw off her bathrobe. "You're wasting my time."

"I can't send it. If I'd thought she would read it, I

could never have written it." He gave a pathetic smile. "It was reward enough to watch your face as you read it."

She looked up then. "Tell me straight. Did you write the letter to her, pretending you would send it, or did you write it so I would read it? Because I'm not getting in between you two."

"For Jewel."

"And you won't send it." She opened fresh pantyhose.

He hesitated. "No."

"So should I burn it?"

"No!"

Lena sighed wistfully and went back to pulling on pantyhose. She put on a suit and her German Army shoes and put her hair back in a french twist, avoiding his eye.

"Would you keep it for me?" he said finally.

She couldn't resist those big dark eyes. "For how long? Because if I make enough money to move, it might get lost."

"Should something happen to me, would you send it to her?"

Yellow-bellied coward! "Oooh, all right. Put it in an envelope and address it and leave it by the toaster. It won't get thrown away there."

Nina called Jewel on Sunday at noon. "Where the hell are you? I got tiramisu thawing on the counter."

Jewel's heart sank. She was dying for comfort, but she couldn't face the nosiness and needling that would come with it. "I have to work. Paperwork."

"Oh, bullshit. Clay didn't turn me down over paperwork."

"You asked Clay before you called me?"

"He's been coming over for three months, what, you expected different? What's the matter? Did you fight with Clay?" Nina said, getting right to the jugular as usual.

"Something like that."

"Be careful. He's too sneaky to put up with the cold shoulder."

"Yeah," Jewel said tiredly, since this was no news to her. And a big part of the reason why she wasn't talking to Clay right now.

"Girl, you need therapy," Nina said, and hung up.

Jewel felt a hundred years old.

The rest of Sunday was agony. She did her laundry. She took out the recyclables. She vacuumed, that was how low she'd come. A boat honked on the river and she remembered her balcony and went to stand there, staring out at the city and the river and the vast empty lake beyond.

What was the matter with her? Was she doomed to be alone? Was that what she'd been hiding from, hopping from man to man since college? *Everybody who loves me dies*, she'd said bitterly to Randy, and he'd told her, *That's my line.*

Randy was a big throbbing sore inside her, so big and tempting and painful that she couldn't bear to think of him. Yet she couldn't help herself.

I don't want him. I don't.

That lie lasted until the next goose flew by.

Okay, she wanted him.

But what's the point? He's done with me. The curse is lifted. Oh, and by the way, he's ruined me for normal sex.

At least Clay took it well. Clay might not mind having sex with a woman with a hinky social disease. But what if she ruined him, as Randy had ruined her? She couldn't do that to Clay.

An unbidden image rose in her mind, of Clay inside one of those glass cases at the Field Museum, naked, looking out at her, with his curly-headed golden retriever by his side.

"So this is it," she said to the wind whipping around the Corncob, shoving the gallery dream out of her mind. "No more sex. No Randy," she added, as if somehow losing him was worse than losing sex.

The loss was so big, she could only feel it one heartbeat at a time. Then numbness, cold, emptiness. Then she'd think of Randy again, and the hot pain came flooding back.

An hour later she was still standing there, her hand ice cold on the balcony railing.

The hell with it. She left the vac in the middle of the floor and went swimming.

There wasn't a soul at Olive Park Beach.

In the cold, cold water, she let her hot pain out. "What

is the matter with me?" she said, over and over, as she backstroked out to the far buoy. *I don't want to feel like this*, she chanted mentally as she crawled back toward the beach. When rage and panic and the desperate feeling inside grew too hot, she butterflied with great white splashes, working her body until the squirrel cage slowed in her head.

As she walked back to the Corncob Building, she saw a pigeon wobbling on the edge of a trash can with a lighted cigarette in its beak.

"Be careful with that!" she yelled, waving her arms. Of course the rat-with-wings launched into the air and dropped its butt into the trash can, which burst instantly into flames. "Oh, hell."

She phoned nine-one-one for the Fire Department and sat down on a nearby bench to watch. Not that she could do much except stop passing tourists from sticking their hands into the fire. She hit speed dial on her cell.

"Ask Your Shrink." The connection sounded different.

"Are we on the air?"

"Sorry, no," said the silvery voice of the radio call-in show host. "Did you want to be? I can record this call."

"No, that's fine! I'm just surprised you answered."

"I'm always here for you," Your Shrink said warmly.

"Great." Suddenly everything stuck in Jewel's throat. The fire truck pulled up. Guys in yellow rubber got out and hauled their hose toward the burning trash can.

"What's the problem? Coral, isn't it?"

"Emerald." Jewel swallowed. "I think I just broke up with this guy, only it never really was a relationship. And now I'm miserable. And I think I hate myself. He hates me. He doesn't need me anymore. I was sick of it when he needed me and now I hate this, too. I'm not a hater, I'm really not. My life is good," she said, choking on a sob.

Water gushed from the fire hose over the trash can, making stinky smoke.

"Tell me straight, doc. Am I crazy?"

"You have a broken heart."

Jewel took the phone from her ear and made a skeptical face at it. "I can't have. I don't do relationships!" One of the firemen looked up as she raised her voice.

"Very well, then, you're crazy."

"I think I liked broken heart better," Jewel said.

"Jewel? It's me, Dave," the fireman said, coming up to her bench with a big smile. "Remember me?" He clearly intended to remind her of their deathless night together. Jewel sighed.

"I gotta go," she told Your Shrink and hung up. "Dave, you're as cute as ever. Don't call me."

She turned her back on his puzzled smile and headed home.

Next morning Jewel signed in with Harry at the desk at Artistic Publishing Company. Her personal life was in shambles. But she had a clue and a contact and she was by-god going to follow up.

The sound of the presses pounded through the floor. "Guess Onika found some more printers," she remarked to Harry.

"Oh, we got 'em back next day. It was just stupidness. Onika's in the still studio on one."

Thank heaven. Randy would be upstairs on five, in Hot Pink. *Don't think about what he's doing.*

She found Onika having an argument with a photographer.

"I know it's traditional, but it's not sexy." Onika jabbed in the photographer's direction with her diamond-crusted cigarette holder. "It looks uncomfortable."

"We can see both her tits and her ass," the photographer explained patiently.

"You could see Mister Gumby's tits and ass, too, if you tied him up in a pretzel," Onika said.

"Really, it's okay," said the nude beauty, twisted on hands and knees under the lights. "I'm used to it."

"I pay your chiropractor bills," Onika said to her, "so don't try to bullshit a bullshitter."

Jewel spoke up. "Miss Tannyhill? Have you got a minute?"

Onika turned. "Oh, it's you." She sent a glower at the photographer. "Traditional. Hmph."

The photographer and his subject resumed work.

"Can we talk about Steven Tannyhill?" Jewel said.

"Let's go upstairs for that."

In Onika's office Jewel turned down a drink. Her hostess poured a tall Scotch. "What about Steven?"

"Someone told me he inherited a piece of the business. Someone else told me he has, and I quote, 'a hard-on for the building.' I want to know," Jewel said slowly, "what Steven has to do with this company and with this building."

Onika puffed, choked, coughed, sucked Scotch, puffed again, and coughed. "Lemme tell you a story. I've been knocking around this place since I was ten. My mother had shit fits, but they were divorced by then, and my father had the money, and she liked to ski in Switzerland, so."

She swivelled back and forth like a kid in her daddy's big leather desk chair.

"My father wanted me to have everything, and I got everything. Switzerland, Rio, climbing the fucking pyramids, boys, cars, diamonds, champagne, the works. And when I'd used all that up, he let me come home and mess around at the company. He always said I would take over someday, but he didn't trust me enough to leave me full power." Slowly and carefully, she drew in smoke and let it out. "He saddled me with a board full of dead white guys, including my nephew Steven. Do you know that Artistic didn't *have* an Internet division until I started one?"

"Really!" Jewel said. "I'm surprised."

"My father was old-fashioned. Didn't take the Internet seriously. He drove us into the ground. He died and I took over. Then that shit-heel Steven convinced the board we should sell, and I had the dickens of a time convincing them to give me two years—two measly years!—to get my Internet division and my women's film division up and profitable."

Two years! Jewel added another item to her list.

"We're almost profitable, but we're also almost out of time."

"Sounds like an ambitious schedule," Jewel said.

"I didn't have a choice. Steven found this scummy porn company to buy our mailing list." Her eyes narrowed. "What he really wants is our building. It's worth a fortune. This neighborhood's going condo as fast as it can go potty."

"How close are you to profitability?"

"Very close. A week, if the launch of Velvita's new movie goes well. Her past four launches bumped sales ten percent each time. The new picture is terrific. It could bump us right over the line."

"Phone, Onika," Lena's voice came from the intercom. "Steven Tannyhill on one."

Onika chuckled. "How does he sound?"

"I'd say the cob is embedded between four and four-and-a-half inches up his butt," Lena's voice said dispassionately.

Onika grunted, then coughed. "Put him on speaker and come in here." Her voice was rough and hoarse. "Too many cigarettes," she said to Jewel. She hit the intercom. "Steven, how's tricks! I'm thinking of renaming the company, did I tell you?"

"What for?" Steven said with suspicion in his voice. "What are you up to, Onika?"

Lena came in and sat at the end of Onika's desk. *What does he want*? she mouthed.

Jewel made as if to go, though she didn't want to.

Onika held up a forefinger. *Stay*, she mouthed. "It's called rebranding. Artistic is a hundred years of fuddy-duddy porn for men. *Tannyhill* Porn—now that's a woman's porn house."

Onika yukked silently. Lena high-fived her.

"You'll lose old customers," Steven said.

"Who wants 'em? You keep telling me the old-fashioned stuff doesn't sell."

"They won't be able to find you online."

"Ever hear of auto-redirect, Steven? Ninety-four percent of our customers will find us just fine. That's how much our revenue stream has shifted in the twenty-three months since the board magnanimously gave me permission for an Internet division."

Silence from Steven.

"Tannyhill Porn," she mused. "Maybe I'll take it public when I finally get full control. Could be bigger than Baysdorter Boncil Tannyhill." She clicked her tongue. "Oh, but you won't get your partnership until you've got your paws on my building. And you never will, Steven."

"You're not profitable yet," he snarled.

"Did you call about something special, or were you just hoping to gloat about our lousy numbers? How disappointing for you." Onika laughed again.

"You old witch!" he said, and swore.

Onika laughed harder, then started coughing. "Oh— oh, Steven, you're killing me—" She doubled over and reached for her highball glass.

"I hope you croak!" Steven yelled.

Onika turned red. Jewel reached out a helpless hand.

Lena came to her side with a glass of water and chewed her lower lip while Onika fought for breath.

"I'm—I'm fine—oh, h-hell—" That set off another fit of coughing. After a long, scary moment, her snappy old blue eyes widened and she took a slow, deep breath through her nostrils.

"One sick day, Onika," Steven said over the sound of her wheezing. "You miss *one day* and the board will force you out on a medical. I'll make them do it!"

The old lady pulled in a deep breath and held it, then breathed very shallowly and carefully. Jewel watched her fists clench. "You're a vulture, Steven," Onika said in a weak voice. "You wouldn't dare."

Steven laughed, long and nasty. "Try me."

Another convulsion came on. She slapped the phone dead. "Okay," she squeaked. She signalled for her high-ball and Lena handed her water. She waved it away. Lena put the Scotch in her hand and Onika drank deeply. "That's better."

"I don't understand," Jewel said. "Why try so hard to drive Steven crazy?"

Onika cleared her throat. "It's a strategy. Don't trouble your pretty head. It's all worked out. I know exactly how to corner him on the edge of his personal cliff." She chortled hoarsely. "And then I'm gonna stick out my pinky and push him over the edge." Her chest tightened visibly and she took a slug of Scotch. "Honey, call Harry up from the front door and get out your notary seal. I need two witnesses. You'll witness something for me, Miss Thing?"

Jewel nodded, worried.

Lena went to the phone. When Harry arrived, he and Jewel signed what turned out to be a power of attorney, ceding control of Artistic Publishing to Lena "until I get back from sick leave or I croak," which didn't look legal to Jewel, but nobody was asking her. Lena sealed and notarized the power of attorney. Jewel eyed her. *Onika must really trust her.*

Onika was still wheezing. One hand kept pawing at her chest, while the other clutched the Scotch glass. She signed the letter, let out another squeak, grabbed her throat, and then held absolutely still.

Lena froze, notary seal in hand, her eyes big.

Harry said, "I'll call you an ambulance."

"Sure," Onika wheezed, "In about, oh, ten minutes." She went off into another coughing fit.

"I think now," Harry said.

Lena put a hanky to Onika's lips and took it away spotted with blood. She told Jewel, "You'd better go."

Jewel left, realizing her question was unanswered. What did Onika hope to accomplish by "pushing Steven over the edge"?

When the Consumer Services investigator was gone, Onika hacked painfully for two solid minutes. Then she said, "Time to tell you the rest of the plan, I guess."

"Yeah, explain to me why you want to drive Steven nuts?" Lena watched her anxiously. The wail of an ambulance siren sounded outside the window.

Onika sent her an evil grin. "Revenge, honey. For trying to destroy my company. And for being mean to you."

Lena said nothing.

"Don't tell me you don't want to see him lose his job, his friends, and his sanity. Did you ever go down into the printing plant?"

Lena frowned. "You're coughing less."

"Ever look behind the door marked Do Not Enter?"

Lena remembered tile walls, red votive candles, and Wilma posters. "Yes." Her eyes widened.

"Ever light a candle to Wilma?"

Lena shook her head.

Onika sipped whiskey calmly. Her cough seemed gone. "Guess you were never desperate enough. My father did, though." All the creases in her face reshaped into a smile.

"You faked that attack! Should I send the ambulance away?"

Shaking her head, Onika showed her the bloody handkerchief. "Here's the plan."

It sounded loony to Lena, but she sat holding Onika's hand, listening, while the paramedics strapped her into the stretcher.

As they rolled the old lady across the sidewalk to the ambulance, Lena said, "You didn't tell Jewel Heiss about Wilma."

"And have her shut down my company?" Onika coughed. "No way."

Light broke for Lena. "That's why Steven is afraid of Artistic, isn't it? He's not afraid of you, but of Wilma!"

"You're getting smart, honey." Onika's grin disappeared behind an oxygen mask, and then the double doors slammed shut.

CHAPTER 32

Jewel's next stop was Maida Sacker's office at Baysdorter Boncil. "You'll be happy to know that my case is complete."

Maida narrowed her eyes. "In what way?"

"As in closed, finished. I know what caused your little impromptu orgy. Two things, a powerful aphrodisiac and a toxic corporate culture."

Maida's face showed no recognition of personal guilt. Well, it wouldn't.

Jewel went on, "I guess you personally can't fix the culture, but you could blow the whistle on them."

"Let us shelve your opinions," Maida said.

"For the moment. If you don't want another orgy, however, you can stop ordering Hoby's pastries."

"Stop—*pastries*?"

"The cinnamon," Jewel said, wondering if Clay had trained her well enough at lying, "apparently comes from a shipment tainted with psychoactive fungal spores. Hoby has disposed of the problem cinnamon, but you had best keep your people away from their products for a while. The spores linger in the human system for months. Even a taste of ordinary cinnamon, in the context of a work atmosphere like this one, could reactivate the spores and send somebody over the edge."

At the word *edge*, Maida's eyes flared.

Jewel crossed her legs. "Oh, and by the way, I figured out why you phoned in the anonymous complaint about the orgy. You had been feeling guiltier and guiltier about Steven molesting your daughter, and the orgy put you over the *edge*." Maida flinched. Jewel showed her teeth. "What I don't know is, how long have you been the majority stockholder of this firm?"

Maida froze. Her eyes went deer-in-headlights. "Majority *what*?"

"You didn't know?"

"I don't know it now."

Jewel nodded. "I wasn't sure. So I brought you these." She tossed a thick wad of photocopies across the desk, the results of Clay's research.

With a suspicious look at Jewel, Maida picked them up and glanced through them. The Band-Aid was gone from her hand. Only a faint white mark showed where the bitch had bit her.

"Note the signatures," Jewel said.

Slowly Maida stood up, as if she didn't realize she was rising out of her seat. She stared, riffling pages. "I signed these," she said in a hollow voice.

"Yup."

"He said—he said they were for bonds and securities for Lena. Sometimes he would have me notarize something and he'd stop me before I could read it. I found it—annoying." Her thin lips got thinner. "He did it more and more, the last few years."

"He was making you titular owner of the company and filing for Women's Business Enterprise certification with the city and the county, so Baysdorter Boncil could get government contracts."

Maida looked up. Jewel recoiled from the blaze in her eyes. "Hugh Boncil must have known," she hissed.

Hairs prickled on the back of Jewel's neck.

Maida whispered, "I see," not to Jewel. She seemed to swell up and grow solid in her flimsy little body.

Maybe all she needed was some real clout. Not just sleeping-with-the-boss clout.

Jewel hated to give Maida the benefit of the doubt, but she suggested, "So if you want to kick someone's ass up around his neck like a collar, it would appear you are in a position to do so."

Maida was nodding, again not to Jewel.

Alarmed at the fire in those cold blue eyes, Jewel got up and walked out. *If she kills him in the workplace, I might almost feel guilty.*

"Jewel? Lena Sacker."

Jewel was driving home. She felt tired and fragile and fed up. "I can't talk now, I'm driving."

"Don't talk, listen. I'm going to Baysdorter Boncil tomorrow to get into Steven's files."

Jewel's eyes widened. "If you're planning to break the law, don't tell me."

"It's okay, I'll be his office temp for the day."

"Uh, still iffy. I can't solicit an illegal act from an informant."

"I'm just informing you. What's your E-mail?"

This could be useful, if neither of them flubbed it. Jewel spoke carefully. "You can forward *legally obtained* evidence to me at farmgirl@brusilosis.com." She spelled it.

"Weird E-mail, girlfriend."

"I don't get a lot of spam."

"You will today. Don't delete it 'til you look. By three o'clock at the latest."

Lena hung up, presumably to go home to sleep with Jewel's ex-boyfriend, and Jewel thumbed speed dial.

"Ask Your Shrink. You're on the air, caller."

"Hi, this is Emerald again," Jewel said. "I think I may

have a, a social disease and I don't know what to do."
She was still shaken by her hink-o-weird moment with
Clay. Could she have caught it from Randy? "A *hinky*
social disease."

"*Now, Emerald, you know what to do. First, you ab-
stain from relations with anyone else.*"

No problem there. She'd probably never have normal
sex with anyone ever again. "Of course."

"*Then you go to your gynecologist and get checked
out.*"

"Checked out, check."

"*Then, if you test positive, you contact all your recent
sex partners and let them know. It's the only decent
thing to do.*"

Jewel groaned. "I know, I know."

"*Next, you make an appointment with a psychiatrist
and ask him to test you for grandiose fantasies. Would
you like me to spell that?*"

"What!?"

"*Have you been dumped recently, Emerald? It's very
common for people who are suffering from a broken
heart to overdramatize their condition. What seems hinky
to you is in fact a hormonal condition that has been doc-
umented back to the Middle Ages. Treatment is much easier now, of course.*" Your Shrink's voice stopped sounding
sympathetic and took on her lecturing-the-public tone.
"*Victims of love sickness reported hinky emotional suf-
ferings as long ago as the time of the Holy Roman Emper-
ors—*"

Jewel hung up. She glanced at the grocery bag with
the bottle of Bailey's Irish Cream and half-gallon of
chocolate ice cream beside her. What she needed was
mudslide therapy.

She spent the evening at home alone again. She made
a pitcher of mudslides and a bowl of egg-drop-ramen

soup and holed up in front of the TV, pretending she wasn't jittering to pieces.

Now that she couldn't have it, she felt an irrational yearning for plain old sex.

Poor Clay. He'd been as freaked out as she was.

She wondered if Clay was worried that he could catch hinky sex from her. Ugh. Thank God she hadn't fucked anybody but Clay since she took up with Randy. That would make for an interesting confession. *Hi, I bet you're wondering why I called.*

Ugh, ugh.

No point in panicking before she had some facts. No doctor would be able to diagnose her problem. *So I'd better ask Randy what he thinks.*

Breathing deeply, blushing fiercely, trying to pretend she wasn't making a lame excuse to call him, she opened her phone.

"C'mon, pick up, you're not supposed to go anywhere without your cell." Her heart was thumping louder than the ringing in her ear.

"Yes?" Randy's voice said. Her chest tightened.

"Hi, um, am I interrupting you at work?"

"Not at the moment." Randy sounded anything but pleased to hear her voice. His tone cut her like a razor.

"Um, I had a question for you."

Silence. A woman's voice came from somewhere on Randy's end, in the same room. *He must be at her place. Velvita's.*

Jewel's temperature fell ten degrees and her pulse sky-rocketed. Her insides felt cold and icky and hot. "Look, if this is a bad time, I can call later."

"Tell me what you need." He was so brusque. Never before had he showed her anything but patience. *He probably thought of it as subservience.*

How to phrase this? *Did you give me the hinky-sex disease?*

Velvita's voice came even closer, saying "—glass of wine?"

"Jewel?" he said more softly.

She swallowed. "I'm sorry if I'm intruding."

"Jewel," he said more gently. "Should we not give this a chance to work?"

"You and Velvita?"

"You and Clay."

She couldn't breathe. "I'm with Clay because you don't need me anymore." She waited for him to say, *I'll always need you.* He didn't. He said nothing. Her chest squeezed tighter as she pressed the phone to her ear, listening to silence.

Okay, time for the hard question.

"Did you—" There was no nice way to ask. Through buzzing in her ears she said, "Did you give me a hinky STD?"

"What is an STD?"

She said through her teeth, "A sexually transmitted disease."

"Should you not be asking Clay that question?"

Her eyes flared. "Why?" she demanded. "Did he tell you he had something?"

"Surely Clay would tell you before he would tell me," he said smoothly. That female voice murmured, and, away from the phone, he said, "Thank you."

In rage and pain, Jewel snarled, "At least Clay will talk to me!" Which she knew was a lie. *I'm acting like such a girl!*

"Will he?"

"Don't duck the question!"

But Randy said nothing.

Oh, hell, more antler-clashing. Her heart hammered in her ears. "Well?"

Silence.

"Stop putting me in the middle like this!" Her breath caught on a sob. "You're making me crazy!"

He groaned. "It's folly to try to talk through these infernal machines."

"*You're* the one who won't even talk to me!" she yelled. "I'm freaking out here! If you were in trouble, I'd give a shit, but when I call you with a problem, where are you?"

But he didn't answer.

The phone made a *thwap* noise in her ear.

She heard footsteps, and then a woman's voice. Velvita.

"Hello? Is that Jewel?" Velvita sounded upset. "Oh my God. He warned me this would happen. Oh, no!"

"What would happen?" Jewel said, but she knew.

"You have to get over here. His clothes are on the floor, empty. I think he—he must have disappeared into my bed."

Jewel's cup overflowed. "Oh, did he? Into *your* bed? Well, good luck getting your eight hours." Her self-control shattered. Her voice rose. "In fact, I suggest you plan for twelve, because he's gonna keep you busy for at least four hours *every single night*! For the *rest of your life*!"

She slapped the phone down on the table and burst into tears.

CHAPTER

33

Clay came to fetch Jewel for work Tuesday and found with relief that she was no longer hysterical.

Instead she knifed him with an apology. "Listen, I'm sorry about the other night. I totally lost it. It's not your fault if I'm—" She didn't finish the sentence.

"Shh, shh, it's okay." He was terrified she would ask him a direct question. Then he might blurt out a confession, and she'd kill him.

She seemed to sense his awkwardness. She made him coffee and left him with a cloud of guilt.

While she was in the shower, her apartment phone rang. Clay picked it up.

"Jewel? Lena." Lena was whispering.

"No, this is Clay Dawes."

"Tell her I'm in."

"I'll tell her you're in," Clay said obediently. Girl secrets.

"I'd rather talk to you anyway."

"Really. That's nice of you."

"You have to talk to her. Make her see reason. I don't believe she can read that letter and not melt. Randy's a nice guy and all that, and way hot in bed, but I don't need to have sex all day *and* all night, know what I mean? She doesn't really mean to condemn him to slavery in my bed for the rest of whatever, does she?"

"Randy's in your bed?"

"She didn't tell you? It happened when they were on the phone last night. Just make her read the letter. She'll do the right thing if she reads it."

"Wait, wait, what letter?"

"I dropped it off last night. The guard put it in her mailbox. Make her read it. I know she's a decent person."

Clay made soothing noises until he was pretty sure Lena wouldn't call back. Then he hung up.

"Clay? Who's on the phone?" asked Jewel from the bathroom.

"Phone solicitor," he called back.

What letter?

Clay went to the hall for Jewel's keys and raced downstairs to the mail room. In five seconds he had found Randy's letter. Hand-addressed envelope, in a script so flowing and perfect that it looked like junk mail from an underwear company, except for Randy's full name and title on the return address. There was a stamp on it, but it hadn't been cancelled.

He couldn't believe his luck.

Trousering it, he ran back upstairs and sat on the couch just as Jewel came out of the back hallway, dragging a brush through her wet hair.

He decided to take a risk. "Velvita called, too. You didn't mention that Randy got stuck in her bed."

"Nope."

"None of my business?"

"That's right." She tied her hair back in a ponytail. "I didn't think you would care. Do you care?"

"I thought the curse was broken. I really did," he said, feeling guilty, which hardly ever happened to him, and now it was for something that wasn't even his fault.

It isn't, Wilma said in his head. *But don't worry.*

Soberly Jewel said, "There's nothing you can do. I'm beginning to think there's nothing either of us can do."

You know you never had a chance with Jewel until she and Randy both thought his curse was broken, Wilma said.

Shut up! he thought. This was such a pain, trying to talk to someone he couldn't see, without moving his lips.

"But it's not broken!" he said aloud. Darnit, was he supposed to say that to Jewel or to Wilma? "The curse, I mean."

Don't worry. She won't go back to him. She'll stay with you now.

Jewel looked him in the eye. "I'm not going off to climb into bed with Randy."

"But you always save him," he said numbly, like a dope.

"Not this time." Jewel's chin trembled. When he didn't speak, she said, "Put your arms around me?"

He did. She put her arms around him, too, slowly and gently, and he lay his cheek against her hair, feeling unsettled.

He wanted to say, *But you're the good guy, Jewel. I'm the bum who would just as soon let Randy rot.*

Well, shoot.

If he had to drag her down to his level to win her, that was the way it had to be. He felt a little sick.

Maida's long-lost daughter walked into the office for the second time in a week.

Maida stood frozen at her desk. "What are you doing here?"

Lena closed the door and sat down. She looked so adult in a black suit and skirt, with her hair in a french twist, that Maida felt a pang.

"Hel-lo," Lena pronounced in a sing-song voice. "I'm the temp the agency sent to work with Steven Tannyhill."

Oh, no, not this. "You're messing around with that Heiss woman. Don't. She's a bungler."

"I'm not."

I can't protect her with Steven like this! "What are you up to?"

"You know, I think I won't tell you. Last time I came to you for help, you blew me off. Onika Tannyhill has been a better mother to me than you have, and she made me a porn queen."

Maida bit her lip. "She should be ashamed."

"You mean I should be ashamed? *She* doesn't force me to put up with sexual advances from men I don't like," her daughter said, sounding like a snippy teenager.

Inside, Maida groaned, but she didn't soften her face. If only she had come home instead of to the office! "Steven won't bother you again."

"You're dreaming. He bothers me every time we meet. I see him at the Artistic Building pretty frequently, you know. He especially likes to watch us shooting movies. Don't worry, he's never recognized Velvita Fromage as Lena Sacker."

Lena's hair was confined demurely at the base of her neck. Her white blouse was crisp, with a soft white silk tie under her chin. She looked fresh, sweet, intelligent.

A memory flashed through Maida's mind of that face painted like a whore's in the one movie she'd had the stomach to look at. She shut her eyes.

"Go home. Go back to that woman, or go home. Don't let him find you here."

"Sorry, Mom," Lena said in a hard voice. "I'll only need to stay a day or two."

Maida's eyes flew open. "What are you plotting?"

Lena leaned forward and began to unbutton her blouse.

Her mother shrank back in her chair. "Dear God, what—"

Lena pulled her blouse open, and Maida saw the black box and the wire taped to her skin.

Comprehension flooded Maida.

Lena nodded. "That's right. So stay out of the way, unless you want to go on record as siding with the bad guys." She stood lithely and left, buttoning her blouse as she went.

Maida put her elbow on the desk and shaded her eyes with her hand. "What am I going to do?" she said to her empty office.

There was no question what she should do. If that Heiss woman had told the truth—

Maida slapped open the file Jewel Heiss had brought. It was all here. State filings, county filings, a thick stack of documents for WBE certification, all signed by herself. Even bank statements for a trust fund in her name. The most recent deposit was only a month old.

She felt sick. And very, very angry.

The Baysdorter Boncil office had not changed much since Lena last sat at this desk. Mike's girl, Precious, was the first to recognize her. She drifted by with a distant smile on her lips, glanced oh-so-casually at Lena, scoping her clothes, her shoes, her hair, and at last her face. Lena waited gleefully.

Precious met her eyes and nearly fell off her strappy fuck-me shoes. A quick recover, and she sent Lena a bug-eyed look, then hurried away without speaking.

Spread the word, Precious.

Lena breathed deeply. She wasn't meek little Lena Sacker anymore. She had Velvita-power.

The next one to come by was Geri from PR. Geri bent over the front of Velvita's carrel, looking both ways before she hissed, "Lena! I heard you were doing it with porn stars!"

Lena drew back. "Excuse me?" *I haven't seen her in two years and this is the first thing out of her mouth? Who could have spread the word?*

"Is it true that John Holmes has a twelve-inch thing?"

Lena smiled sweetly. "Is it true you frenched Anna from Accounting?"

Geri stiffened. "Slut," she snapped, and hustled off.

Mike Redpune was next—Radio Precious seemed to be broadcasting. He walked toward her so slowly that she had time to blank her computer screen and get out her steel nail file. He still moussed the front of his hair like a cell phone accessory salesman at Best Buy. She ignored him. He came to a stop with a little swagger and stood there, his hands buried in his pants pockets, smirking. After about a minute she looked up.

"Mr. Tannyhill is still out, Mike."

"Just coming by to say hi."

She looked up. This couldn't be good.

He leaned over the carrel and whispered, "I love your work."

"Do you. You realize it's made for women."

Mike wiggled his eyebrows. "I, uh, still think it's great."

Ah-hah. Mike and Precious must have been watching Hot Pink porn together. That's how she'd been found out.

She sighed. "All right, send Precious over with your red silk boxers and I'll autograph them. I really do have things to do here today," she added with an apologetic smile.

Slowly his face reassembled into a puzzled frown. "How do you know I wear red silk boxers?"

Lena said, deadpan, "There are no secrets here, Mike."

He turned and drifted away, his stride lengthening and getting more decisive the farther he got.

Lena giggled to herself. Then she whisked into Steven's office, locked herself in, and swiftly trolled through his hard drive. He hadn't changed his password, the fool. She soon found what she needed.

At two, Sharisse showed up, tapping on Steven's office door. "Hey. You got here."

Lena let her in. "Shut it and lock it, will you? I'm almost done."

Sharisse hugged her hard. "I'm scared for you."

"Don't be. I have extreme protection. Did you talk to the girls?"

"All but Precious, and she'll never cooperate. She totally believes Mike will make her a corporate star."

"Dumbbell."

Sharisse smiled grimly. "So they're on board. It doesn't hurt that that EEOC agent was here for three days. That put some guts into them." Sharisse hesitated. "Your mom seems on edge."

"She should be. She's as bad as Precious."

Sharisse said dryly, "The difference being she was with the head of the firm for twenty-three years."

Lena drew a deep breath. Her mother's loyalties were, thankfully, not part of the plan either way. She resisted the urge to call Onika at the hospital. *If I can't do this on my own—*

She said, "You'd better get out of here before Steven comes back and starts hammering on the door."

"He's getting worse," Sharisse said. "He's crazy. I mean, he was inappropriate before, but lately—the language he uses to the employees—and the way he talks to Maida!"

"Oh, really?" Lena said with sinister meaning. She was surprised how angry that made her. "How does he talk to her?"

"It's like he's baiting her. Used to be, it seemed like she would snarl back, but not anymore. He's out of control."

That's Onika's fault. Her and her crazy plan to push Steven over the edge. Great plan. Except somebody else wound up paying for it.

"I have a plan." Lena patted Sharisse's hand. "You know what I need from you."

Sharisse said, "Go get 'im." She jerked her thumb up. Lena smiled.

The deeper she got into Steven's locked files, the wider she grinned. She copied all the files she wanted, compressed them, and E-mailed them to Jewel.

Her cell phone rang as she was finishing the last of the mail. Lutheran General Hospital. *Onika's doctor? Oh, no!*

"Everything going okay?" came Onika's gravelly voice.

"Ohmigod, you scared me to death. Are you okay? Did the new test results come back?" Her hands were busy deleting the evidence of her work from the E-mail system.

"I've got mono. I'll have to stop kissing Harry."

"You're kidding." Relief flooded Lena. "Four MRIs and a CAT scan plus bloodwork and exploratory surgery to find out you have mono?"

"Joke. It's lung pre-cancer, but they got it early enough. How's the op?"

"I just got our files. Now waiting for the grenade to go off." Lena glanced through the venetian blinds on the narrow floor-to-ceiling window beside Steven's office door. "I'm locked in Steven's office at the moment."

Onika chuckled weakly. "We'll nail him. You, me, and Miss Thing from Consumer Services." She coughed. "They treating you okay there?"

"No." Lena flushed. She hadn't visited her old friends since she joined Artistic, and now she was realizing how smart she'd been. "They're freaking. They can't get past the porn thing."

"Sorry, honey. I did warn you when you started, it changes your life."

"It does indeed."

"Did your mom warm up yet?"

"No." Lena's tone did not invite comment.

"Hm. Well, remember what I said. Steven's been going up the pole. He'll probably top out on you today. If he does—"

"I know, I know."

"Do you have the ikon?—No, not now. I said, No!—Sorry. The nurse keeps coming in with a fistful of horse pills. I'd be meaner, only he's got a cute butt. Where was I?"

"I have the ikon."

"If he gets violent, if he bats it out of your hand or something, you still know what it looks like."

"Of course. I've been at Artistic for two whole years! Onika, take your meds and get some sleep."

"I'll lie here on my bed of pain, fretting, until I hear from you."

"Great. Something else for me to worry about."

"Phone me when it's over."

CHAPTER
34

Clay talked Jewel into spending the morning in his suite at the Drake. Working. Definitely not having sex. Jewel hadn't referred to the hinky thing again. She was so darned tough, he couldn't tell if she was hiding butterflies or if she'd simply put it out of her mind. He wouldn't be surprised either way.

He'd been pretty good at not thinking about that, himself.

Clay felt he was dancing on a volcano-lip. While Jewel went over the Othmar file on her laptop, he counted his blessings. Randy was still out of the picture. Good. She was still acting friendly to Clay. Another plus.

At this point he ran out of blessings and counted his liabilities.

One. He had one big fat naked major liability.

I am not fat!

Clay's breath clutched up, as it did every time Wilma spoke when he wasn't expecting it. Especially with Jewel present. He had to be so careful of what he said out loud and what he thought.

If Jewel ever, ever figured out that he'd been harboring this succubus, this sex demoness—

I am not a sex demoness! I am a goddess!

—This pain in the behind the whole time, if she realized

that Clay had let her blame herself for their last evening together going hinky—

Jewel's laptop dinged. "Check it out. Lena-slash-Velvita just sent me twenty-two meg of data she snitched off Steven Tannyhill's computer at BB."

Clay frowned absently. "What's she doing over there?"

"Beats me. She said she had a plan to make Steven miserable, but I never dreamed she would, like, cooperate with our—wow. Look at this."

"What is it?"

"Bring me that list of properties for the Circle Line."

Clay got up and brought it to her. "Oh." Looking over her shoulder, he recognized Mrs. Othmar's address. "This is off Tannyhill's computer?"

"The motherlode. Properties. Secret land trusts. How he shuffled the properties between the trusts and then sold to the city, so we wouldn't catch on. All his bank accounts. All Bing Neebly's. Escrow accounts. Wire transfers." Her eyes got big. "We've got him. We've got them both."

"Yeah, but you stole the proof. You can't use it as evidence. Lena doesn't have a warrant to be snooping in Steven's computer, does she?"

"Technically, she could be called 'an informant.' When an informant snitches evidence, it's kind of a gray area." Jewel started printing files. "But I realized a long time ago that we won't need admissible evidence, because it won't get into court. I have a hunch I know how the Chief Attorney will want to handle this."

"Bully." Clay felt no triumph. He didn't give a darn about the case. He'd had three—no, four—shots so far at getting closer to Jewel. And he'd blown them all. He would bet a nickel she was pining for His Hinkyness and his magic mojo at this very moment.

Someday she'll love sex with you just as much, I promise, Wilma said in his head.

Silently, he told Wilma, *You mean sex with us. You know, she used to like sex with me alone just fine.*

Not enough, Wilma pointed out. *You said so yourself.* Not enough to walk away from Randy.

Clay swallowed. It was a hard thing to admit to himself, but he didn't want to win like this.

Like how? Wilma said, eavesdropping on his thoughts. *By dragging her down to your level?*

By getting somebody else to open her up for me. There was a forlorn little girl inside Jewel he longed to comfort.

You would have to be a sex demon to reach those parts of her, Wilma said.

Thanks for zero comfort, he thought.

Or a goddess, Wilma said.

I don't want your help with it!

Wilma sounded exasperated. *Or you could quit lying to her.*

I don't lie to her! Much.

You don't tell her how you feel.

That's when it hit him.

He got up and went into the bathroom and shut the door and sat down on the toilet seat cover, rubbing his forehead.

You wanted to have with her what she has with Randy. Wilma was still lecturing. *You're getting it. We can get even deeper into her, if you'll let me—*

I can't. I can't let you. And now I can't do it without you, either, he thought, *because I can't get rid of you.* Horror filled him.

He groaned aloud, "What have I done?"

Well, that's not very nice! Wilma was clearly offended.

Jewel tapped on the bathroom door. "You done in there?"

Clay raised his voice. "Uh, I think I may have a touch of the flu. Why, do you need the bathroom?"

"Never mind. I have to run out and get a newspaper. You want anything?"

"I'll be fine. I just need a little time here," he called through the door. *See what you're doing to me? I can't talk to her when I have to, because I'm talking to you.*

"Come to think of it, I better hit the Swiftymart for a thumb drive," Jewel said through the door.

"Okay," Clay called.

Her footsteps moved away. He cracked the bathroom door open. Twenty seconds later he heard the suite door close.

He stood and stared into the bathroom mirror, feeling a hot spot like a red hot poker poking his heart. "What's the matter with me?"

It's probably just—Wilma began in his head.

"Can you show yourself? I have to see you. It's too hard for me to talk to something hidden in my head."

I can show you a picture in your head, she offered, and suddenly she was there, a faintly see-through version of herself between him and the mirror, her sweet young face hopeful and worried.

"That's even creepier."

She frowned, and her image vanished.

He sat down on the edge of the tub. "Show yourself, please?"

She oozed out of his chest, about eighteen inches high, standing on nothing, stark naked.

Clay shut his eyes. "Clothes, please."

Well! I hope you realize that it's not smart to insult a sex goddess.

He opened his eyes and found her dressed in a cut-out steel bustier, with shin greaves and spiky gloves and a horned helmet, like a porn Valkyrie. She looked annoyed.

He put out his hands. "Look, I'm sorry, I don't want to insult you. Okay, you're a goddess. I'm confused."

Don't waste that stuff on me, Wilma snapped.

Now he realized that, though she was standing astride thin air, she was actually, really, still inside his body. Inside his head. She knew how he really felt.

He couldn't hide anything from Wilma.

His self-control fled.

"I feel like a rat!" he burst out. "Jewel is this rock. She's straight and clean and decent. Normally. Normally she would never turn her back on somebody in Randy's position, no matter what her relations with him were like. I only wanted a fair shot at her!"

There was nothing fair about taking a sex goddess on board and letting her fool around in Jewel's carefully guarded mind. Nothing decent about making her think she'd become tainted with Randy's magic. He groaned and ground at his temples with the heels of his hands.

You could just tell her the truth.

He raised his head. "What, that I'm possessed by the—the spirit of the Artistic Publishing Company? That I want her for keeps, and it'll be just the cozy three of us until I can figure out how to get you out of me?"

It's not that big a deal.

"You don't get it. This is her job. She'd have to, I don't know, condemn me, or have Randy take me out to the hinky dump. Maybe you and the Tannyhill guy had a cozy thing going over at the Artistic where people are used to you, but I have a job, and my job is the same as Jewel's job, and it's all about keeping stuff like you covered up. She hates that part. She's too honest for the work. I have to be here to help her with it." He stopped ranting because he'd run out of breath.

You don't like me, Wilma said, her lower lip drooping.

He closed his eyes and heaved a long sigh. "I like you. You're adorable. But I'm not cut out to be a goddess's whatever—"

Avatar. You're my worldly manifestation.

"I'm a walking pocket zone. If I can't shift you, I'm screwed, and Randy knows it. He's known all along." The pit of his stomach turned over. He slumped. "I'm screwed."

Wilma looked concerned at last. *That's not as good as fucked, is it?*

"I was so eager to get the jump on him and his sex demon mojo." Clay shook his head. "No wonder he hasn't said anything to Jewel. He doesn't have to. I've lost her. Plus, now I'm as cursed as he is." He laughed a hacking laugh. "He's probably been sitting in that bed at Velvita's, laughing his rear off, just waiting for me to realize all this."

Wilma frowned. *Why should you lose her?*

"Once she knows about you, it's over for me. It's over anyway," he admitted bleakly.

You are so negative! How do you expect to keep a hard-on like that? Wilma said in a scolding, motherly tone.

"Look, amazing as it seems, I do not need sexual help from you."

She sniffed. *That's not the song you were singing before.*

"Never mind. I've got you twenty-four-seven now, exactly the way Jewel's got Randy."

Wilma put her hands on her tiny armored hips. *I don't understand this. Bill Tannyhill and I had sixty glorious years, and he loved being my avatar. He had lots of girlfriends and none of them minded me.*

"Bill Tannyhill was divorced, and apparently a sexual omnivore. I don't want a girlfriend. I want a wife." The sound of his own voice saying it gave Clay a shiver. He'd made it to thirty without getting stuck. And, now that he was stuck good and tight, the girl was out of reach.

Jewel would be back from the store any minute now.

A totally unfamiliar urge gripped him, an urge to be

honest and decent and do the right thing, whatever it cost.

He hauled out his cell phone. "Did you get back to my suite yet?" he said when Jewel picked up.

"Where the hell are you?" her voice demanded.

"I got tied up. Listen," he said around a lump in his throat the size of a golf ball. "Do me a favor."

"When you get your ass back here. I've been on the phone with Ed. He's scheduled a debriefing with the Chief Attorney late this afternoon."

"I'll be there," Clay said. *I hope.* He stood up to improve reception. "When you get back to the suite, go in the bedroom closet and find the chinos I was wearing yesterday. They're hanging up."

"I need you here."

"Humor me. There should be a letter in the pocket. It's addressed to you."

"To me? Clay, what the—"

"Just look for it, will you? I don't have a lot of nerve left, and I'm using it all up on this phone call."

"Are you running out on me?" she said with discovery and anger and disappointment and I-knew-it in her voice.

Clay, Wilma said, *I think I hear someone calling me.*

His courage failed. "Read the letter and get back to me." He thumbed the phone off, feeling like he had triggered a bomb. "Well, that tears it," he said over the ringing in his ears. "Just when I'd got rid of Randy, too."

Clay, this is important! If someone calls me, I have to answer!

He felt dizzy and unsettled and far away from his feet. He sat down on the toilet lid, pressing the heels of his hands to his eyes. A feeling of outrageous well-being made his head swim.

"It's over."

This didn't feel so bad. Maybe doing the decent thing carried unadvertised benefits.

As he thought that, he felt a sexual rush so strong that it rippled over him like a dip in an acid bath, from the soles of the feet up.

He looked at his unwelcome visitor. "Is that you doing that?"

Wilma's tiny eyes grew round. *I have to go now.*

Out in the suite, he heard the front door open and close. Jewel was back.

The room spun around him. The rush reached his scalp and popped, with a musical note that he heard in his head, not in his ears, like a soap bubble with a song inside it.

Without warning, he passed out.

The buzzer came again and Lena nearly jumped out of her skin. Taking a deep breath, she answered.

Sharisse whispered, "Steven's here. He's screaming at your mom in her office."

Lena set her teeth. "I wish she would scream back."

"Geri from PR looked through the window and said your mom looked like she was ready to blow. I've never seen her do that."

"And you won't," Lena said. "Thanks for telling me." She hung up, feeling her anger fizz.

I don't have to go out there. She could leave and call Jewel and Jewel would come and bust Steven. Onika's plan was stupid. What was the point in getting him to crack up? He'd been wacko for ages. Onika was just being vindictive.

But she found herself holding her breath, listening for shouting. Why would her mother put up with that?

The answer popped through her mental guard.

She's holding him in her office so I have time to get away.

And he was screaming in her face.

Lena slapped Steven's desk.

For that, he would pay.

She leaped up, slammed open the door, and nearly marched smack into Steven, who indeed looked dark with fury.

He bounced off her as if he'd hit a wall. All the color drained out of his face.

"Hello, Steven," she cooed.

Mademoiselle Heiss, Corncob Building I, on the Chicago River, Jewel read in Randy's beautifully loopy handwriting. Standing at Clay's closet door, she put the envelope down. The letter was handwritten on sheets torn from a yellow legal pad, closely covered with the same loopy writing. A phrase caught her eye, *in your strong buttocks* and she stood up straight as a shiver passed down her spine.

She realized she still had her phone open in her other hand. She shut it.

She sat down to read.

My dearest Jewel, the letter began.

What did he mean, his *dearest* Jewel? Her heart was pounding so loudly she couldn't hear the yellow sheets rustle in her fingers.

She squinted, heart thundering. *He's never spoken this many words to me, ever*. And, *I wonder what he wants to tell me*, although that was a lie, she already knew, or she knew what she hoped, anyway.

My dearest Jewel,

I am brushing your hair. The brush travels down your back, brushing your skin as well as your hair. Tense muscles ease in your back. You arch against me, then away from me, so that the brush can touch more bare skin. The brush moves lower, smoothing away the hot angry day in your strong buttocks, your right thigh, down the back of your right knee, tickling your Achilles tendon at the ankle. The brush passes over the sole of your right foot, tickling, then soothing. Your toes curl.

And again from the scalp downward, this time on the left side. You lie facedown on the bed, smelling sunshine on the sheets, and feel the brush sweep slowly down your body in long, soft, upward-flicking strokes. Stroke by stroke, the brush sweeps away distress. You feel lighter.

The backs of your knees relax. Your aching feet and ankles give up their pain, until your skin tingles, as if it was once dark and now glows. You arch your feet. You are ready to turn over.

The brush returns to your beautiful bottom. Your life is packed into this part of you, although you are only sometimes aware of it. Tremendous power lies dormant here. You begin to feel it stirring as the brush passes over your bottom, stimulating your skin, bringing up the fine down, making you tingle. Deep inside, your inside is growing bigger than your outside.

You are ready to turn over. I place one hand on the back of your neck and the other hand at the base of your spine. Lie still.

You lie still.

Deep in your flesh, something like a belt of emeralds dangles from your hipbones down into the curls below your navel, the girdle of Venus. Although you lie perfectly still, this girdle moves inside you like a sleepy snake. Your right buttock clenches, then your left. You relax them but the emerald snake still moves. You feel my hands, hot on the base of your neck, hot on your tailbone, pressing down. Ever so slowly, the snake turns over. You want to turn over.

The brush begins its slow stroke again while my hands hold firm. From the crown of your head down your neck, your shoulders, lightly along the backs of your arms, into your palms, the brush raises a tingle on your smooth skin. One hand, then the other. Thus you can focus, anticipate.

Your right hand commands, so the brush dips into the hollow of your right palm, teasing the fingertips, making your hand lie still and yet filling it with a fizzing lightness.

Your left hand receives. It is the vulnerable hand. The brush moves slower over your left palm, drawing the need from your belly up into your sensitive fingers, sending a message into deep places: Lie still.

You lie heavier on the bed, while bits of you become light.

Deep inside, the girdle of Venus writhes.

He really does know how it feels. Jewel squirmed a little. *He doesn't know how I'm reacting to this.*
He can't. Can he?
She turned to the next page.

It's no use, I can't make love to you without my own voice. Yet all I would do is give back to you what you have given me: yourself, a single remarkable star in the night of my long life. To your courage I can only bring endurance, not brave endurance, but the endurance of a dog at the spit, chained forever, running within smell of the roast. Your honesty I answer with reticence, bred into me from birth, for the earl was not taught to tell his love nor had much love to tell, and the incubus has held his tongue for two centuries. You must know that you are brave and honest. These are your duties as an officer of the law.

But do you know how your imagination has set me free? In my dark prison, I hungered for flight, and you gave it to me. For another woman I could be a priest, a long-dead lover, a stableful of lusty grooms, but only you could make me a Pegasus, a dragon, a swan, a lightning bolt.

In the dark, below the edge of your awareness, I hold congress with your fancy. You endow me with powers I could never invent for myself. If I have known you, it is because you are honest enough to stand naked before me; if I have flown you to paradise, it was you who gave me wings; if I am ever to do these things again, as my heart hungers to do, it will be because you are honest enough to want me and brave enough to come for me.

Any man would want you for your beauty.

But who would carry you shrieking into the stormy sky, cradle you in cloud, tickle you with rain, soak you with sunbeams?

Come for me, bright Jewel.

Breathless, she turned the page. The folded paper rattled, and something shiny fell out and tinkled to the floor. She picked it up. It was a key.

She looked at the next page.

Again I must struggle to match your honesty.

I have many wants I do not speak of.

I want to be free. I want to restore my name and style. Also to regain my property. Also to pursue my enemy, for I haven't forgotten the woman who damned me merely for being bad in bed. These are ungenerous wants, but they have kept me sane, years in which there was no light, no occupant in my bed. For all I want only your pleasure when prone, perpendicular I am a selfish creature.

Thus the importance of being prone with you so often. Sex may be a poor tool, but it is all I have to woo you with.

I should tell you more truths. But what?

That I have felt lucky to be sharing your life. I shared many unhappy, bitter lives, many of them near their ending by the time I found them. Whereas you are happy and brave and young enough that I have time to give you everything I have and know. Thank God you are young. I have your lifetime to repay you for your gifts: drive your oily chariot under the sun, load the dishwasher with my own two hands, scold and be scolded in the grateful daily bickering of lovers. For these simple things I would give up your gift to me of flight.

To be human again, I would give up . . . much.

I should confess that I respect your lustiness. To perdition with all my criticisms; they are only my jealousy, ill-cloaked. In truth I treasure how deeply desire wells in you. Not only does your fire please me, but it is good for your health, your life expectancy, and, I believe, your honesty and courage. Only someone who has found her own life-source, burning white-hot like the heart of a smoking mountain, can stand as you stand, strong but not hard, sweet but not weak, in the face of this city, this world, this century.

If I have said otherwise, I take shame.

I should say that I would change the past for you if I could. I would make up for all the nightmares I have witnessed in your sleep: grant you sunshine in place of night, warm skin for snow, happiness, not dread.

Let me pretend I can give you a dream now.

Are you ready?

That was all on that page. She read it twice, and then stopped because her throat was tight.

She turned to the next sheet.

You turn over in your sleep and smell your own hair, freshly washed, on the pillow. Your body is clean and sweet from the bath. The sheets smell of sunshine.

You slip into a dream that you are younger, although you know this cannot be. In your dream you are walking along the river at university, feeling young and safe and foolish, and the sun pours a path of gold before you, gold on the glittering river beside you, gold on the greensward at your feet, the fragrant, gilded trees arching overhead like the bones of a cathedral. Behind you come clouds like years, full of regret, but although you know they await you, for this moment you are free. In this moment you walk on sunshine.

I know this.

I stand among those clouds, holding them by their leashes.

I want to walk on that sunshine with you.

CHAPTER 36

Steven's eyes bugged out at Lena. "You!" Behind him stood a gathering crowd of office girls.

"Me."

"What are you doing here?" he sneered. "A slut who spreads her legs for the world?"

Lena looked around at the girls. "Did you hear what he called me? I think that constitutes sexual harassment in the workplace. I can sue this firm into the ground for that."

"Nobody says anything." His face radiated heat. He'd known along!

She felt icky but she wouldn't look away. "Let's vote, shall we? All in favor of shutting up for Steven, say aye."

Stony silence from behind her.

"All in favor of blowing the whistle?"

Sharisse's voice called out, "Aye."

"Fuck him," said a voice far in back.

"Been there, done that," said Geri's voice, and Tonia laughed her braying laugh.

Now what was she supposed to do? Oh, yes, Onika's wacky idea. Lena pulled the ikon out of her skirt pocket and held it faceup in her palm, where only he could see it.

He looked down and did a double take. A weird gurgle escaped his throat, like a coffeepot sucking up the last drop of water in the reservoir.

Lena raised her voice. "Let's hear 'em all together. All in favor of blowing the whistle on Steven?"

"Aye!" said many voices.

Lena shouted, "I can't hear you!"

"*Aye!*" A chorus of laughter followed.

"Shut up!" Steven screamed. He looked past Lena, his eyes rolling. "I have something on every one of you. Pictures. Nasty, slutty pictures. You're all in my power." He was dark red, weaving on his feet, his chest heaving, his fists opening and closing at his sides, foam flecking his lips and shirt. He threw his head back and howled, "I'm covered, and you bitches are *toast!*"

"Thanks for the confession," Lena purred. Yikes, that ikon really worked.

Steven laughed long and nasty. "They'll keep quiet. So will you, for your mother's sake."

"There's the recording." Lena tapped her chest and winked.

Steven's face turned purple. He reached out, grabbed the front of her blouse, and ripped it off, exposing the wire she had taped between her breasts.

Lena was ready. She leaped backward. There was lots of room between her and the crowd now.

Steven lunged.

She kneed him hard in the groin.

He went down, retching.

"Don't hurt me, my dear," said a voice behind her. Lena flinched, still full of adrenaline, and turned.

Hugh Boncil was watching.

The senior surviving partner stood over Steven's retching body and said with sorrow, "I'm very disappointed in you, Steven. This is not acceptable behavior. I'm afraid you may have irreparably prejudiced your chances of staying on in the firm."

"Who's—augh—gonna—uhv—stop me—aughughgh—"

Lena backed away. Now for the rest of Onika's plan.

She glanced at the ikon. *Ikon, shmikon. It's a nekkid girlie playing card.* On the card back, Wilma was painted with her hands on her dimpled knees and a smooch on her lips.

Lena shook her head. *This is crazy, but okay.*

She pressed the card to her forehead. *Wilma, Wilma, come to me, come to me, Wilma, Wilma, help me, help me, Wilma, Wilma, he's gonna kick my ass if he ever stops throwing up*—That wasn't in the script, but it was heartfelt.

Hugh offered his hand to Steven to help him stand.

Steven was a mess. His tie was half-undone. Drool ran from the corner of his mouth.

"You're nothing," he said hoarsely. "You prance around, fucking in front of everybody in that hellhole building, and you're *nothing*. I'm gonna have that place *gutted*." His hands made fists.

Lena pressed harder on the card. *Wilma, Wilma, come to me, come to me, Wilma, Wilma, help me—eek!*

Clay came to himself slowly, hearing Wilma's voice.

"I have an avatar now. Like it?"

He felt himself stand and pirouette, and a weaselly, nasal male voice said, "What the fuck? Who are you, lady?"

"I'm Wilma. You prayed to me, remember?" her voice said cheerily. The voice came out of Clay's own mouth.

The room swam into focus. It was small and smelly and oddly familiar. Tatty curtains. Ratty sofa. Naughty posters thumbtacked to the wallpaper. Stacks and stacks of magazines piled four-, five-, six-feet high against the walls.

And against one of those walls, his eyes rolling in his little ferret face, stood a total stranger with his pants down around his ankles and panic in his voice. "Don't come any closer!"

Thrown over the back of a chair was a blue nylon windbreaker with *Inspectional Services* printed on the left breast in white, and *Zachariah* on the right breast in red. *Ah-hah*, Clay thought.

Wilma pouted. "Don't you recognize me?" Clay felt his hands slide over his own chest and waist, and he realized that the body he occupied was female. As in, va-va-voom female.

Evidently, when Wilma took over, she redesigned.

"C'mon, sugar. You wanted it." Wilma squirmed and posed and flung out her hands. "Come and get it."

"Uh." Ferret-faced Guy tried to back away, but he was already against the wall. His eyes got bigger.

"You prayed to me and I came. So what's on your mind?"

Wilma cozied up to the guy until her breasts—Clay's—no, he wouldn't call those things his. They were all Wilma. Wow.

"What were you thinking about when I manifested?" She laid her hand on the guy's forehead. His eyes fluttered and he slid down the wall.

"Uh-bah-uh-bah—"

She murmured, "Tell me."

"Just how I'm gettin' screwed out of my cut."

"Your cut?" *Kinky*, she thought.

Clay heard her thought. Apparently now it was the opposite of how it was when he had the body and she was just a passenger. He could hear her thinking. But could she hear him?

Clay said, silently because he was trapped inside her head, *He's a criminal. His accomplices are cheating him out of money. Can I have my body back, please?*

Not until I answer his prayer, Wilma thought. Silently, Clay groaned.

She laid a hand tenderly on the guy's unzipped crotch. *Euw!* Clay protested in vain.

"Those bastards," Ferret Face said dreamily. "I do the heavy work. They get the money and blow me off. Broke my back luggin' magazines. For chicken feed! They made millions!"

Darn it, you're right, Wilma said silently to Clay. *I never know what to do about these requests for money. What's money compared with a good fuck, or true love, or a reliable boner? Doesn't he even pay attention who he's praying to?*

Let me talk to him, Clay suggested. To his relief, Wilma quit fondling the guy and her own amazing attributes and retreated enough for Clay to pilot her—his—no, still her body.

He looked around the depressing room and spoke to Zachariah. "Do you think they might double-cross you? Uh, sugar?" Boy, it felt funny, hearing Wilma's high, girlish voice when he talked.

Zachariah nodded. "In a heartbeat. One of 'em's with the city and the other fucker's in real estate. He tried to hide his identity from me but I followed him and I found out. But what can I do? I'm in it deeper than them. People saw my face."

Clay examined the piles of magazines. Yup. Artistic Publishing product. *So he kept it all.* "You sneaked the porn into the houses. Then you inspected and found the pocket zones and threw a scare into the owners."

"You know everything," Zachariah said, not sounding particularly surprised.

"I'm a goddess," Clay said curtly. "You're screwed, all right, buddy."

"I could probably handle sex now," Zachariah said faintly.

Clay put a pink forefinger on Zachariah's lips and pressed, and Zachariah slid farther down the wall, smiling, his eyes rolling up in his head.

Clay hunkered down beside him. "I bet you could, sweetie," he felt his mouth saying. His hand reached out on its own to pet Zachariah on his greasy little face. *Am I handling this or are you?* he said furiously inside his—Wilma's—head. To Zachariah he said, "You'd better move quick if you don't want to be left holding the bag."

Zachariah opened his eyes. "You think?"

"There's a city team on your trail right now. Your friends will hang you out to dry. Your only hope is to turn state's evidence and get out from under, before you become the fall guy." Clay took a ballpoint pen out of the windbreaker pocket and picked up Zachariah's hand. "Call this number." Clay wrote his own cell number on the palm. "Do it first thing tomorrow. Tell him everything. He'll set you up with protection."

And now, Wilma said, *get out of my way*. She took control of Clay's body and reached for her worshipper's crotch.

Clay tried to shut his eyes. No luck. They were Wilma's eyes, now.

"Everybody gets a prize," Wilma breathed into the crook's hairy ear.

Clay burrowed into Wilma's mind, trying to find a corner without widescreen live-action coverage of Wilma's divine benediction, but he was no Randy. *I gotta get me some skills*, he thought, as her worshipper moaned happily. *Or else a mystical paper bag to put over my head*.

He would die before he ever admitted that it was, well, kinda fun.

Five minutes later, Wilma's worshipper was out cold, apparently from an overload of divine blessings, and Wilma walked to the bathroom, placed her hands against the mirror, and planted a kiss on it.

Clay found himself slipping into control of his own body like a man putting on his favorite jeans. "Ahh-hhh."

He resisted the urge to find clothes. Instead, he went through the wallet lying on the dresser. With the handy ballpoint and the back of an unpaid phone bill, he made notes of Zachariah's full name, driver's licence, social security number, credit card numbers, and Chicago Department of Inspectional Services badge number. Then he found Zachariah's cell phone in his pocket and went through it methodically, writing down phone numbers stored in its memory, placing an X by recently called numbers. Then he went through the wallet again. Yup, here was a password list. Phone, E-mail access, and—jackpot—bank passwords.

Really, this could be quite a racket.

Jewel counted off the blocks until she found Lena-
slash-Velvita's place. It was a basement apartment in a
four-flat off Lake Street, a few blocks from the Artistic.
Its front stoop glittered with broken glass. The "L"
screamed past every few minutes. She checked her watch.
Only two-thirty. Looking up at the building, she decided
to try the back door.

Probably only half the tenants were home right now,
feeding their pit bulls. Maybe Velvita had one. *If I was
in porn, I'd have a pit bull*. Of course, Velvita now had
Randy.

Who was stuck in bed. Not much protection for a girl
living alone.

Jewel located the door, hidden in the gangway between this building and the next. *Randy?* He wouldn't
hear her, inside. Panic welled up in her.

She pulled out the key that had come enclosed with
his letter.

"So what was with the poppets and the hinky pastry?" Clay said as he tried on a pair of Zachariah's cargo
pants.

They're invitations to be my new avatar. A poppet-
sized Wilma sat on the edge of Zachariah's bed, kicking
her legs, her blonde curls falling into her eyes.

"Invitations?" Clay pictured an engraved envelope with a little RSVP card inside. "You are cordially invited to let a sex goddess hijack your body?"

More like a message in a bottle. I need an avatar to help express my goddessness. I wanted Steven, Wilma pouted, *but he's been avoiding me.*

"Jewel says he's a jerk."

Oh, he's highly qualified. If you could look at a person without their body, you could see the sex. It looks like— like lightning. Steven's just packed with it.

"Apparently, he can't keep it packed," Clay said dryly.

I've been very lonely, Wilma mourned. *The printers knew what I needed, but none of them would say yes. They cut way back on the offerings, too.* She sounded hurt. She smiled at Clay with trembly lips. *I'm sorry you don't like me.*

"You know darned well I like you. Who wouldn't? The thing is," Clay said, sitting beside her on the bed and nudging Zachariah's sleeping hand out of the way of his feet, "you can't just send out aphrodisiacs wholesale. Bad things can happen if they get used inappropriately. Like, your precious Steven and old Zach here used your porn-poppets to cheat old ladies out of the value of their homes."

Her tiny face crumpled. *You're angry with me.* He felt her unhappiness like an invisible whimpering puppy in his middle.

"I'm not against cheating. Broadly speaking, it's my job. Was," he remembered belatedly. "I just think it's a shame you can't call back all those messages in bottles. Now that you're, uh, visiting me."

Her face cleared. *Of course I can call them back!* She leaped to her tiny tippy-toes. *Watch this!*

Her eyes closed. She spread her arms and wiggled her fingers. Her teensy hot-pink lips moved, and he read the words they shaped:

Come on home! Come back! Come back!

Clay felt a rumbling through the mattress, through the floor. The room seemed to judder around him. He slipped off the bed and tumbled over Zachariah's sleeping form. "Hey!" He struggled to his feet on the shifting floor.

You want me to recall them! Wilma yelled, her miniature curls whipping around her face in a wind that somehow did not ripple the posters on the walls. She stretched her arms farther. *Rats! I can't do this if I'm outside your body!*

"Well, don't take mine over again," Clay began to say.

But in that moment she turned and leaped at him, and he put up his hands instinctively, uselessly. She sank into his chest, and he felt the rumbling a thousand times stronger.

"No! I want my body!"

Whatever you say, came the silent voice inside. *But here they come.*

And here they came. Dozens of little translucent Wilmas ran through the apartment walls from all directions, some naked, some dressed in thongs and pasties, some dressed in black leather, some like nuns, some like cheerleaders, some like slutty schoolgirls in plaid skirts that didn't cover their perky pink buns, and every one of them was charging straight at him.

Breathless, Clay felt them splat into him: two, five, ten at a time. He reeled and fell onto the bed. With each impact, he felt a fizzing in his nerves, a ringing in his ears. He began to believe what Wilma had said about lightning. For two bits he could reach out and zap something.

He was also horny enough to boink a sheep.

After a busy ten minutes, the flood of Wilmas subsided. *I knew you would like that*, Wilma said complacently in his head.

He remembered hazily what he had to do. "Jewel. I

have to call her. She must be wondering where the heck I went." Dazed, he used Zach's cell to call his suite at the Drake.

No answer.

"Uh-oh."

Jewel must have read the letter already.

This could only mean she was on her way to find Randy.

He sat down carefully on Zachariah's bed, feeling like a train wreck with a ten-foot erection. "I knew this would happen."

You didn't have to give her the letter.

"Yes, I did."

He tried Jewel's cell. It rang five times. He pictured a hundred horrible things happening, beginning with her deciding to hate his guts for swiping that letter.

Or she might hate him for letting her leave Randy in Velvita's bed.

Or there was always his gutless *faux pas*, letting her think she was hinky in bed.

"What if she—oh there you are."

"Clay?" Jewel didn't sound mad.

"I'm here. I mean, I'm not here. I'm, uh, at a suspect's residence." He clenched his teeth and crossed his fingers. What had she thought when she found his clothes, shoes, wallet, keys, and phone in a heap on the suite's bathroom floor? He could only imagine, and none of it could be good.

She said, "What in the world are you doing there? I came back to your suite and I got that letter and, well, I started to read it, but you didn't seem to be around, so I—"

Clay let out a whoosh of relief. "Listen, Jewel, I don't have time to talk. Can you come get me in a cab?"

There was a pause.

"Um, actually, I'm breaking into Velvita's apartment."

That stopped him.

Right. Everything goes on hold when Randy's stuck in a bed.

"Good letter, was it?" he said, aiming for Buddhahood.

She sniffled. "The best."

"I guess so," he said mildly, but his voice cracked. "Jewel, I haven't mentioned this before, but I love you."

"I know."

She knew! Even when he'd been so careful! He felt simultaneous despair and joy. She knew his secrets. She knew about his love. A big hot breath filled his chest.

I think I should warn you, said the unwelcome voice of the goddess in his head, and he almost blurted out, *Shut up!*

Jewel said, "Clay, this is so hard for me. The way I feel about you—" She paused.

His breath caught. She was finally going to tell him.

"Yes?"

Look out, I'm being summoned—Wilma said.

Just wait! he thought at her savagely.

"I'm sorry." Two words nobody wants to hear. "I should have been more honest," she said, breaking his heart all over again. "You make me feel—"

Whoops! Wilma squealed.

Clay heard no more.

With plunging grief and an unnerving sense that his dick was being squeezed, stretched, and boinged like a rubber band, he felt the familiar wild rush as Wilma took possession of his body.

Then everything went black.

"Hey, sugar," Wilma said in babytalk. "Who calls me?"

Clay was woozy with Wilma-thrill, so it took him a moment to see where they were. An office somewhere. He stood—well, Wilma stood—on top of a desk, the keyboard of a computer tickling the soles of her bare feet. Summer sunlight slanted in the windows.

They had quite an audience.

A sharp-looking executive was staring at him—well, at naked Wilma—with amazement and horror.

So was the girl Onika Tannyhill called "Honey." Her suit jacket hung open, its button dangling by a thread, and her virginal white blouse was ripped.

Where is this? Artistic Publishing?

Wilma smiled down on them.

"Greetings, Velvita Fromage," she said with affection, using Clay's mouth, or what used to be his mouth.

Clay stared. It was the same girl! *But we're not at the Artistic!*

We are in the lair of my destined avatar, Wilma thought, and Clay heard her thought.

An older executive turned around slowly. A chorus of office girls stood watching with open mouths and goggling eyes. One of them shrieked, "My God, she's naked!"

Wilma beamed. "Glad you noticed. Did *you* call me?"

Velvita's mouth fell open. "Uh, I did."

Clay realized that a brilliant glow surrounded Wilma. Light streamed out of her, a light so bright that it felt to him like a high-pitched electrical hum.

Slowly, Velvita got down on one knee.

Wilma reached out a hand. "Steven Tannyhill," she intoned. Clay felt the hum in his chest.

Steven nearly fell over his own feet.

Wilma spoke sternly. "Steven, you've dodged me for two years. Are you ready to fulfill your destiny?"

He faced Wilma, one fist clenched, the other on the crotch of his trousers. "You're that slut from the porn factory."

She smiled. "That's me. And you're the heir to the Tannyhill mojo." It felt weird to Clay, feeling those words coming from his own mouth, feeling Wilma's power hum in his body. "Come forward, Steven Tannyhill, and join the ranks of the mighty."

Steven was panting. He backed up a step.

"You knew I was looking for you. I sent so many messages."

He shuddered all over, like a frightened horse. "That porn shit made me crazy. In my closet. Tapping. Calling me." His face convulsed. "Get away from me!"

"You didn't eat my pastries?" she said, her face falling.

His head shook. "No way!" He gave a nervous cackle. "Hah! It worked great on Mike's rollout though!"

The office girls murmured.

"I'm going on a diet," one said.

"I'm not," said another.

Wilma pouted. "You misused my gifts!"

"Get away from me."

"C'mooon," she coaxed. "It'll be fun."

He backed farther away, putting his hands behind him. "Nnnuh-uh. No way. Nope."

She stamped her foot. The computer keyboard shattered under her bare feet, individual keys popping everywhere. "Come here!" The lights dimmed with the force of her command.

"No!" White slobber flew off him.

The hum rose in Clay's chest.

Wilma leaped off the desk, sailed ten feet, and landed practically on Steven's toes. He thrust his hands out as if to push her away. She grabbed his hands in hers.

Steven struggled. He was a good foot taller than Wilma. He should easily have been able to throw her down.

Instead, he froze, gasping for air.

This time Clay was a spectator to a Wilma invasion. Through their joined hands, he felt everything Steven felt. He felt Steven's heart hammering so hard it was skipping beats. Steven had both a terrible hard-on and a terrible pain in the balls.

Clay hadn't known you could do that.

Thanks for noticing, Wilma said, and suddenly the pain disappeared, and Steven's body filled with the rush of ecstasy that was becoming familiar to Clay.

Steven writhed. Bad things were happening inside his head. Clay took one look at the colored spears of agony, terror, and rage banging around in Steven's darkness and decided not to go there.

"Submit, Steven Tannyhill. You will be the perfect avatar, and we will spread my benediction throughout Chicago."

Wilma amped up her power. Clay felt it move effortlessly out of his and Wilma's body, into Steven. The glow pulsed around her, the office lights dimmed, a couple of computer monitors popped, and a fluorescent tube overhead shattered inside its plastic housing. The office girls screamed.

"Let me in, Steven," Wilma commanded.

"No!" Steven screamed aloud. "Get out! Leave me—augh! Get—*No! No!*"

Wilma leaned forward, standing on tippy-toes, to kiss him. "We belong together."

And then she slid into Steven's body, taking Clay with her.

Or not.

It was like running full tilt at a mirror and bouncing off.

Dimly Clay heard the office girls gasp and shriek.

Suddenly he was watching from a comfy five feet away.

Wilma's brilliant light surrounded Steven now. Steven crumpled to his knees. He clutched at his head, tearing out clumps of hair, making horrible animal noises.

Then he began to flicker. Streaks of light whirled in a circle around him. In the lightning-spiked haze, Clay could make out Steven throwing punches, Wilma's goddess-sized tits swinging, the sound of clothes tearing.

Suddenly the Wilma-light snapped out.

The office seemed to go dark. Sunlight from the windows cut dusty yellow slits in the blackness.

Kneeling naked and alone on the carpet, Steven raised his fists, and a long scream broke from his lips. "*AAAAAAAAUGH!*" Then he collapsed.

Clay realized he was naked, standing over Steven's body.

Snot and tears dripped off Steven's chin. There was no visible sign of Wilma. She must have stayed behind.

"*What* is going on here?" demanded a woman's voice, and all the office girls turned and gasped at the same time.

Clay didn't waste another moment. He turned, shoved through the crowd of rubberneckers, and ran for it.

In his birthday suit, of course. Nothing's ever perfect.

The big thing was, he was free.

He made it all the way to the elevator, blundering past office workers, the receptionist, a pizza delivery boy, and the UPS guy, tripping on the carpet in bare feet, panting and sweating, before he heard a familiar voice, felt a familiar cloud of ecstasy burst inside him, felt Wilma's poppet *boing* into his back like a hinky rubber band on a sign saying Kick Me, and he tottered, faint with pleasure, against the closed elevator doors.

I'm sorry. He simply wasn't going to work out, Wilma said in Clay's head.

Clay groaned.

You're much nicer.

"I'm so glad," Clay said dully.

People were coming into the elevator lobby. Snatching a frond off a potted fern, he figleafed himself and edged past the pizza deliverer, the UPS guy, and the gaping receptionist, back into the office he'd fled.

Office girls gabbled everywhere. They paused as he passed, checking out his bare behind, and made remarks.

Clay tried to shuffle past them with his back to the walls and his fern clamped over his family jewels.

Where are we going?

"Somewhere in here, there's got to be clothes," he muttered.

Steven wasn't wearing his when I departed.

"You mean you left that poor schmuck naked, too?" Clay didn't bother to say it in his head. As Flash Titty would have said, they weren't watching his lips move.

A gorgeous blonde with a kind face came up to him. "I'm Sharisse." She led him into a private office. "Lena said you might want something to wear."

"Sharisse, you're a woman in a million. Lena's right."

CHAPTER 39

"*What* is going on here?"

Lena froze at the sound of her mother's voice raised in anger. Considering what she'd just been through, it surprised her that the scariest part was Mom showing up mad.

Steven lay folded up on the shreds of his own clothing, passed out, naked, and drooling.

A movement beside Lena made her turn. Precious was holding her cell phone out at arm's length, pointed at Steven. So were Geri and Tonia.

Lena's mother snapped, "Don't you have work to do?"

The girls scattered in all directions.

"Hugh! Get over here this instant!"

Hugh Boncil was at the telephone. He, too, jumped at Maida's voice.

She brandished a fistful of papers. "You have some explaining to do," she said in her most sinister voice.

The senior surviving partner peered at the top sheet in her hand. "Oh. Yes. I was meaning to tell you, your share of the profits is being deposited in the trust fund John set up for you. It's all there," he twittered. "We've been doing very well."

"The trust should have been revealed to me at John's death."

"I meant well, Maida," Hugh said in his nice-old-guy voice.

"You meant to hold onto all the power. Illegally."

Lena cringed at her mother's tone. "Uh, Mom?"

"Come into my office," she said to Lena. To Hugh she said, "And *you* bring the trust fund statements to me in half an hour, if you want to keep your job."

"But—" Sharisse stood beside Lena with big eyes.

Mom whirled. "Yes?"

Sharisse was looking at Hugh, who was looking at his own shoes. "How can you fire Hugh?"

"He and John Baysdorter made me senior partner, on paper, four years ago, so they could establish BB as a woman-owned business and take city contracts, and John left me his share. And he never told me," Mom hissed. Her voice ripped holes in the air. "Hugh owes me my share of the profits. More than that, he owes me two years of waiting on him like a servant—looking the other way when he screws my girls—being condescended to in meetings. *That's* how I can fire him." She looked Sharisse up and down. "Can you do his job?"

Hugh's head came up at that. "Maida. You wouldn't."

"I control the firm," Mom said, deadly quiet. "Sharisse?"

Sharisse blinked. "I suppose so."

"Sharisse, honey," Hugh bleated.

Sharisse stood tall in her high-heeled shoes. Her chin was up. "Nobody likes having to do it, Hugh. Not under threat."

"I never threatened you," Hugh said.

She leaned over and patted him on his bald spot. "You didn't have to." To Lena's mother she said, "Yes, I can do his job. What about Steven?"

Mom turned to Lena. "I thought *you* might take over there," she said, as if she were doing Lena a favor.

Lena frowned. "Let's talk in private."

"No, but what about Steven?" Sharisse said again.

On the carpet, Steven rolled over onto his back and sighed. His eyes opened. Only the whites showed.

"Better call an ambulance," Mom said coolly, stepping over him.

Following her mother, Lena whispered to Sharisse, "What did you do with that other naked guy?"

"He's in Steven's office, putting on Steven's spare suit. Is it true? Do you think Maida will keep me on? Because Hugh has been paying for my son's daycare."

"I'll see to it," Lena promised, wondering how she could.

In her office, with the door shut, Lena looked Mom in the eye, and she had a rare view of her mother as a person: a faded blonde with hard, sharp blue eyes and the kind of figure that costs thirty hours a week at the gym. And a whole lot of grit.

Mom also looked worried. She wasn't pleading or apologizing, but at least she was explaining. She put one palm on her desk.

"Listen to me. I was very young when John got me pregnant. I didn't have college, like you. I thought it was my only path to advancement. You went into an office and you found the right man and he married you. Only John was already married, and he wouldn't leave her for me. I got pregnant right away. He was thrilled to have a baby, and he adored you, but he wouldn't leave his wife, and then his wife found out about you and forbade him to see you. He really cared about you, Lena."

"Yeah," Lena said flatly. "He paid for everything."

"He took me into his confidence at work, made me his right hand."

"Mom, I don't care. That was at work. I wasn't there. I was here, at home, wanting my mother—"

"And I wanted you, sweetheart." Mom reached out and stroked the back of Lena's head before she could pull away. "You were my life."

"No," Lena said in a hard voice. "The office was your life. I was a bid for power that didn't pan out."

"I was born to be a businesswoman," Mom said simply.

Lena shut her gaping mouth. *Well, that's blunt.*

"I had no education, no training, I didn't even have the clothes at first. John made me his assistant for your sake. But when he found out what I could do, he gave me opportunities nobody else would give me."

"Mom—" Lena swallowed. "This was what, the late eighties? You could have gone to college."

"Not with a baby. Girls who do that have families to help."

"Your parents—" Lena was aware she was on thin ice. Mom had never spoken of her parents. But, at this point, Lena had nothing left to lose.

"You never knew my father," Mom said with finality.

I guess her father was a bad parent. Lena pressed her lips together. *Or at least a good excuse.*

"You're pretty critical for someone who's had life handed to her," Mom said, as if she had spoken aloud.

"Well, jeez, Mom." The word stuck in Lena's throat. "You decided your only ticket to a business career was the casting couch. Fine. That worked for you. The thing is, those girls out there didn't sign up to become office sluts. You've helped the men abuse them."

"It's the workplace reality."

Lena put her fists up. "Steven molested me right there in his office! And you wouldn't do anything!"

"I hated it. Believe me, I did," Mom assured her. "I've

been doing what I could to put him on notice. If he wouldn't shape up, perhaps I could get him to overstep, and he'd be forced out."

You, too, Mom? Who doesn't have their knife into Steven?

"I suppose times have changed." Mom looked at her desk, then at an award plaque on her wall, blinking. "You hate reality and you learn to live with it and then one day it changes, and girls are leaping ahead in business the way I never could." She raised her eyes. "Give me credit. I'm promoting Sharisse."

She looked at Lena and her face changed. With revulsion, she said, "*You* have no excuse for what you have done with your life."

Lena took a deep breath. *Here we go.* "I could try to blame you, but why bother? My life is good. Unlike you, I enjoy sex. I feel good about myself. I'm spending my good-looking years getting paid for them. Onika wants to leave me her shares of the company, and she's only sixty-five. By the time she retires, I may know enough that I can handle it."

Mom said eagerly, "But, darling, if you want to go into business, you could work with me! I own the controlling share of Baysdorter Boncil."

Lena made a face. "Thanks, but I have Onika's power of attorney while she's out sick. I'm needed at Artistic. Besides, I don't like the culture here."

"But *I* need you!" Mom clutched the bosom of her pastel blue power suit.

Now you say it. Lena appreciated the gesture, but it wasn't enough.

Mom must have seen rejection in her expression. "You'll keep making smut. Just throwing my sacrifice in my face."

"Sacrifice."

"You're young. You don't know how important appearances are. Appearances are everything, young lady, and they cost a lot."

"I'm beginning to understand," Lena said, feeling sick. "Thanks for explaining it."

"You're entirely welcome," Mom said crisply.

CHAPTER 40

Jewel checked her phone. Clay had hung up.

Heart in her mouth, looking up and down the dark gangway, she let herself into Velvita's apartment.

The kitchen was a single counter with a single cabinet, sink, and microwave—really just a corridor leading to the bathroom, left, with the building's basement beyond, right, to a single living and sleeping room.

Holy crap. The kid lived like a nun.

Jewel had expected porn posters on the walls, but instead she found texts on accounting and business models, a computer on a card table, a folding chair, and a twin mattress tilted against the wall. Two milk crates. A crappy old TV.

She went back to the kitchen. There were two closets, one small, containing a broom, and one big, containing clothes, two pairs of shoes, and some underwear in cardboard boxes.

And, in a separate box, Randy's things, neatly folded.

It wasn't an apartment. It was a safe house. A runaway's bolt-hole.

Jewel's pulse hammered in her ears. She locked the doorway to the gangway. She double-locked the door to the outer basement. Then she went back to the single room, stacked the milk crates against the wall, laid the mattress on the floor, and, with misgiving, got out of her clothes.

This was it. Either he'd come back or he wouldn't. No, he would come all right, eventually. But would he come back to *her*?

She'd finally faced a few things. Like: it was, too, a real relationship, and she wanted to keep him, and she wanted to treat him better, and she wanted—God help her—she wanted him to want her. That was a lot of things to want that she might not get.

She'd got by for a long time by carefully never wanting anything that she had to count on someone else for. Mudslides, a swim in the lake, a good pulse-thumping orgasm, she could give herself. This stuff, not so much. Oh, Britney or Nina would come if she yelled for help. They would always *choose* to come for her. But it would be a choice, weighing her urgency against their own.

She didn't choose to come for Randy. She just did it.

"I guess that's why I'm here," she said aloud.

She lay down on the mattress.

On second thought, she got up and turned on the window air conditioner, feeling guilty. The kid probably couldn't afford to run it. But the unit was noisy, which could be useful right now.

She lay down again.

Her eyes drifted shut.

There was a thunderhead under her feet, and more storm clouds above and before her. Warm, damp air buffeted her. She stood solidly on her cloud. This was one of his favorite places.

She called out, *Honey, I'm home!* The clouds echoed back to her like mountains.

No answer.

With a sigh, she sat down on a cloud and dangled her legs.

He'd written her the letter. But he probably hadn't sent it. She was almost sure he hadn't included the key.

That would have been impolite to Velvita. Her sex demon had a mannerly streak.

Soooo. He wanted to tell her stuff.

She had to stop thinking a moment and just feel, remembering stuff he'd told her, the clouds in his letter
like the clouds around her now, and the sunshine and
the freedom and the innocence he'd written for her. After a hot sigh, she resumed her train of thought.

So he wrote the letter. Then she'd called him.

Then he'd zapped into bed.

Frustration welled in Jewel. He was always doing this.
Trying to jump off a roof, zap into a junkyard somewhere, get out of her life so she could have it back.

Out of the cloudy darkness his voice said, *Yes.*

*Randy, I have my life. How can I not have it? I'm in
it.* Her throat felt hot with messages for him. *Stop wor-
rying about me. I'm too selfish to sacrifice myself for
someone else.* Her throat clogged up.

No.

Had she said that? Thought it? She rolled over on the
cloud, which puffed up around her like a cloudy armchair, and looked over the edge. *Randy?*

*You are not selfish. You don't know what you have to
give.*

She heaved a steamy sigh. He must be near.

*When you are older you will know more about who
you are. Then you will notice, whenever you open your
heart. As you do so often.*

The sky below her was full of nothing but thunder-
heads.

Don't you mean, whenever I open my legs?

Something touched her between her breasts, not on the
skin but inside her. The touch made a little *ting!* sound,
and left a pearl of heat that simmered comfortingly
through her chest.

I mean your heart, bright Jewel.

She lay back in the armchair cloud. He was back! She'd always worried that somehow, sometime, he would vanish into this desolate space and never return. Her cloudy footrest tilted up to cushion her lower legs, and the headrest cloud cradled her neck and head, and she stared up into the blue-gray boil of storm clouds with tears of relief trickling into her ears.

You don't know what you have to give either.

Silence.

You always say you're two men, the lord and the incubus. The lord doesn't bend, but the sex demon gives until he bleeds. You've let me walk all over you. I thought that was why you went to porn school. She stopped, surprised at the insight. *To get some pride in your gifts.*

A fat, warm raindrop landed on her shoulder.

Maybe there's some things that can't be given unless someone knows you are giving them, she guessed.

Another drop splashed on her right breast, then one on her belly.

Maybe we both kind of suck at accepting what's being given. She swallowed a lump. Warm rain spattered all over her. *I'm more of a hit-and-run giver. Saves having to wait to get nothing back.* She thought of the gallery full of old boyfriends, some arrogant, some crying, and all of them begging for more.

Suddenly she thought she knew what Randy wanted.

Will you come back to me? she said. She had thought it might kill her to ask, but the words came out easily.

The sky cracked across. The clouds opened. Rain flooded down on her, drenching her bare skin, slipping between her lips.

It tasted salty.

She reached into the sky.

He formed over her so gently that she hardly noticed. The rain beat down, and he grew solid in her embrace, a being of thundercloud-gray warm water, his surface pocked and rippling with every drop that bulleted through him.

Still shy. She touched his shimmering, translucent face. *Show me your beautiful eyes.*

He smiled, and her tight chest eased, and his big solemn black eyes appeared in his cloudman face.

Okay, that's a little weird. She laughed, and tried to tickle him, and warm salty water splashed wherever she poked, and very suddenly he was quite solid indeed, heavy with muscle and bone and a nice, hard, solid kiss.

In her head, as they kissed, she heard his voice. *Honey, I'm home.*

As they found one another and Randy slid between her thighs with a sigh, the clouds parted. The two of them shot into a blazing, brilliant world of silver and gold light.

She refused to look down. The sun drew her.

He entered her, rattling her bones with each stroke, and she wrapped her legs around his waist and threw her head back, cackling with delight at the sunshine on her face.

Kiss me, he said. They kissed. His cock did that thing again, swelling and shrinking inside her, stretching her, turning her inside out, making her cross-eyed.

They flew higher, arrowing toward the sun.

Her skin shrank and swelled. Her pulse sent her nerve endings out until she filled the sky. He filled her mouth with his tongue, asking with kisses for everything, and she gave it. She opened herself to him, making more room, and he grew bigger, and the sun drew nearer, until sunlight filled her from the inside out.

Oh no, I'm coming already! she thought, sorry to return to reality just when their flight might carry them into the heart of the sun. Then she came like a freight train barrelling into a hole in a mountain, with huge rhythmic pulses of joy.

But demonspace did not dissolve around them. They didn't fall, sweaty, to bounce on a mattress.

They kept flying upward, faster and faster. The sun drew near, not unbearably hot but unendurably bright. Randy drove in and out of her. She felt every millimeter of friction between them, his cock in her sheath, her muscles closing around him, his silky-hard length rubbing her swollen, sensitive tissues, his thumb twitching on her trigger, until she came, came again, came with each heartbeat, over and over and over.

Higher and higher they flew. At last they seemed to plunge into the sun itself. It was like sinking into a sweet custard of light, like a scream, like dying. So much light! With each pulse, every cell in her body seemed to burst at once, unable to contain such light. Yet his climax came like waves of rain, a moment of relief like a blink of utter darkness that she could sense as clearly as she felt her own climax. She knew how he died with each throb. She felt each squeeze of her muscle around his cock, and she felt him rise again, born inside her, a heartbeat later. First the unendurable light, then the total darkness, each an answer, an echo, a gift from one to the other.

Thank you, she managed to say, even while they kissed.

How long this continued, she didn't know. The universe disappeared in a thunderclap, and burst into existence with a heartbeat, over and over and over and over and over.

She must have passed out, because it seemed forever before she woke from the deepest, blackest, safest sleep she'd had in years. "Hey, sleepyhead," she said to the demon lump beside her.

Groaning, Randy sat up, then clambered to his feet.

"Clay's gonna be really unhappy," she guessed, as she put her clothes back on.

Randy dressed. "Possibly."

That reminded her. "Hey, do you think I'm contagious? I guess what I mean is, do you think you're contagious?"

"Contagious?"

"You know. Can I catch hinky sex from you?"

A smile transformed Randy's face. "No. Why?"

"Uh, because I wondered. If you must know, I kissed Clay and it—it was hinky. I got scared. I mean, what if *I* can't be normal in bed anymore?"

"I have no idea," Randy said, poker-faced. "Is that what Clay suggested?"

She frowned. "Kinda, yeah. Like, we'd done it so much that when I ate a cow plop it affected me worse than most people."

Randy shrugged, as if to express mistrust in Clay's opinion. "Perhaps it was the cow plops then."

"Huh." That was the comforting explanation. "He told me where he'd hidden your letter."

That made Randy look up. "Did he?"

"Yup." She gave her hair a lick with a hairbrush, tied it back, and called it good. "Something not right with our con artist partner. He's usually so focused on the main chance."

"Your good influence, no doubt." Randy's tone told her it was time to stop talking about Clay.

Am I the only one who dreamed of sex in the sun? Maybe he would be a tender, vulnerable lover only in bed, always a lord out of it. He looked grim. *I can't handle another fight with him right now.*

At that moment her phone rang.

"Jewel? Clay. I brought that stuff you got from Velvita to the debriefing with Ed and the Chief Attorney."

Oh fuck! The debriefing! "How dare you do that meeting without me?"

"Don't worry, I covered for you. Taylor wants to call

a showdown tomorrow morning with Bing Neebly and Tannyhill. He thinks he can wrap this up." There was a pause over the cell phone. "We'll need Randy at that meeting."

She glanced over her shoulder. Randy had tipped the mattress against the wall and was putting the milk crates back where Jewel had found them.

"No problem. Is Taylor gonna arrest Bing?"

"I gather he thinks a civil invitation will suffice. You seem to have put the fear of Officer Jewel into him."

"What about Steven? One word from Bing and he'll skip town, with all his assets in the Caymans."

"Uh, I don't think he will. He's been neutralized. So come back to my place as soon as you can. We need to organize that stuff Velvita sent us."

Holy shit. "I have to get back to work," she said apologetically to Randy.

He turned off Velvita's air conditioner. His face was a dark mask.

Now what?

They left the apartment.

"Are you pissed with me?" Jewel felt sore and tender inside.

Shaking his head, he took Velvita's key from her hand and locked the door. Then he pried open the mail slot and pushed the key through. She heard it fall, tinkling, to the floor inside.

With a small smile, he put his hand on her back and escorted her through the gangway, back to her car.

Guess we're roomies again.

She felt a little breathless.

CHAPTER 41

Jewel spent Wednesday morning in the Chief Attorney's office at the Kraft Building, listening with appreciation while the Chief put the bite on Bing Neebly. Clay was wearing a designer suit for the occasion. A seedy-looking guy in a blue nylon jacket marked *Zachariah* sat beside Clay, looking scared. Ed tipped his chair back, arms folded, chewing gum. Randy sat at the far end of the table in custody of a large cardboard box.

Steven Tannyhill was also present. Pale, wobbly-chinned, with one eye looking left and the other wandering, he looked like a total head case. Beside him, wearing a dark suit and a frown that screamed Big Nurse, if not Dominella Whiplash, sat Maida Sacker.

The Chief had been laying out the charges.

Bing sweated. He avoided looking in Steven's direction and he hadn't met Jewel's eye once. "You can't prove anything. I have friends in high places."

The Chief smiled and pulled a stack of file folders toward him. The top folder was the result of a long night between Jewel, Clay, Ed, the Chief, and Steven's computer files. God knew what was in the folders under it. Old deli menus, maybe.

"*Au contraire*, Commissioner Neebly," Taylor said. "Mr. Tannyhill has graciously opened his records to us, in exchange for immunity."

The Chief flipped open the top folder and started reading off bank account numbers and dates and sums. "Your greed placed the entire city in danger when you violated the Hinky Policy, and you've embarrassed the city government. You don't have friends."

Bing wilted.

"—But this won't go to trial," the Chief said finally, and Bing brightened. "So long as you and Mr. Tannyhill are willing to pay back to the property owners the difference between what you paid for their homes and what the city paid you, I think we can keep the whole thing quiet."

"To hell with that!" Bing burst out. "You don't dare prosecute. It's hinky from top to bottom. The government would send in the quarantine bulldozers, and bye-bye Circle Line."

At that, the guy in the blue nylon windbreaker shot Bing a scared look, then glanced at Clay. Clay put a finger to his lips.

Clay had miraculously produced the Inspectional Services weasel, complete with confession and plea bargain, only that morning, and refused to tell Jewel how. The deal Clay said he had made was that they would prosecute Zachariah only if Bing or Steven stonewalled.

"I think Mr. Tannyhill would like to say something," Jewel observed.

The former First Senior of Baysdorter Boncil pulled his eyes around until they both looked forward. "How can the sandwich have any meat?" he said huskily. "Without laundry marks, you're screwed." He squinted his eyes shut and shook his head violently.

The Chief looked at Jewel.

Jewel said, "I think he's trying to question our assertions." She faced Steven. "We know your pocket zones were portable."

"There's no such thing as a portable pocket zone," Bing said.

Jewel raised her eyebrows at the Chief, and the Chief nodded. "Close the venetian blinds, Clay?" As he got up to do this, she beckoned to Randy.

Randy stood and slid the big cardboard box the length of the conference table until it was right in front of Bing and Steven. Then he unfolded the top flaps, reached inside, tapped dramatically, and stood back.

A Wilma poppet, eighteen inches high, jumped out like a dancer erupting out of a cake. She twirled, laughing silently, tossed her blonde curls, and stroked her body up and down with tiny pink hands, showing off every charm of her body. Then she reached out to koochie-koo Bing Neebly.

Bing's eyes got big and round. He pulled his neck back until he was all chins.

She reached out to Steven next.

With a cry, Steven leaped backward, knocking over his chair, and stood, quivering, his eyes rolling randomly again.

Maida came up behind him and righted his chair. Then she pressed down on his shoulder until he sank back onto it.

Jewel said, "You see, Bing, there is a caterer's truck in the loading dock at the Darth Vader building this very minute, unloading desserts for that fundraiser you're hosting tonight." She permitted herself a brief gloat at the panic in Bing's eyes. "You may not know what happens when lots of people eat lots of Hoby's pastry in an enclosed space. Maybe Steven can tell you."

Steven turned his head to the side. The whites of his eyes were all that showed. A whine escaped his throat.

"And of course the caterers may leave behind a few boxes of printed matter—Randy, show them the printed matter?"

Randy reached past Wilma's capering feet and pulled out a handful of Artistic Publishing porn magazines. He displayed these for a moment, then dropped them casually back into the box, heedless of proximity to the poppet.

Jewel showed her teeth. "It could take you all day to find the stacks they've left—here and there—all around your eighth-floor luxury lakefront apartment."

"Unfortunately," the Chief said, "you'll be here all day. It's up to you—pay or be prosecuted. Twenty years in jail, no job, no pension. You have fifteen minutes before I call the Inspector General and the US Attorney for RICO. Play ball and you get fifteen more minutes to get the money in my hands."

Ed whispered to Jewel, "Eighth floor? Holy shit, ain't that where that woman was carrying on all summer?"

"Yup," Jewel whispered.

Clay leaned over to whisper to Jewel, "And I hear she filed for divorce."

"No kidding?" Ed said. "What cause? He's too fat?"

"Too horny. Something about forcing her to eat doughnuts."

Over her chuckles, the Chief told Bing, "By the time you get back home, the doors will be sealed." That was the Chief, putting bite into a plea bargain as only he knew how.

Bing protested weakly. "When you called this meeting and said bring your checkbook, I thought you wanted a bribe. This isn't bribery. It's blackmail!"

The Chief smiled.

"I don't have the funds in my checking account!" Bing said desperately.

"You can wire-transfer the funds. There's the phone," the Chief said. "Or you can use this laptop and do it online. I've set up an account for your victims." As Bing sweated, he nodded at the clock on the wall. "In five minutes I make the phone call." He nodded to Randy. "We're done with that now."

Bing pulled out his checkbook, looking miserable.

Randy raised his brows at Clay and picked the box up in his arms. Clay went out with him.

Maida gave the Chief all Steven's accounts and passwords. No one mentioned that Lena had sneaked them to Jewel a day earlier. Maida was legally entitled to provide them, since Steven had kept all the evidence on his computer at her firm.

No one brought up what the future held for Steven.

Today, Jewel seemed high on adrenaline, but Clay was pooped out, between cleaning out Zachariah's accounts, and wrestling with Steven's files all night, and having his heart broken, and giving up the woman he loved, and being flicked like a booger around Chicago in goddess form.

He escorted Randy to the freight elevator and helped him get the box of porn into the dumpster. *Thanks for making it look hinky*, he thought.

No problem, Wilma said in his head.

Randy didn't say anything. In the creaky elevator, on the way back up to the Chief's conference room, Clay finally brought himself to speak.

"I've been meaning to give you this." He fished a long envelope out of his inside coat pocket. "Your identity."

Randy took it, looking suspicious.

"It's good. No booby-traps. Just like we talked about."

"Thank you."

"Winner takes all, huh?" With an effort, Clay held out his hand.

Randy shook. He said soberly, "You will need my help with Wilma."

Clay froze. "Uh."

"If we work together, you can be rid of her," Randy said.

"Excuse me?"

Hey! Wilma yelled in Clay's head. *Come over here and say that!*

Clay shushed her mentally. *There is only one way I am ever gonna beat this guy. I've got to let him think he's won, so he doesn't rat me out and tell Jewel about you.*

Randy said, "Come to me when you need help."

The elevator dinged. Eyeing him warily, Clay edged out. "I think we'd better get back to the meeting."

Back in the conference room, Bing and Maida were setting up the wire transfers. Steven leaned in his chair, dribbling. Zach tried to be invisible. The Chief Attorney smiled, benevolent as a Borgia pope.

Jewel smiled at Randy. Her expression hurt Clay in a way he promised himself he could get used to.

It was livable pain. Like shingles. Or migraines.

Or crabs, Wilma suggested.

Oh, be quiet, he thought.

Why so glum, chum? This will be fun! she said in his head. *You liked smiting Steven.*

That was cool, Clay admitted.

And the hinky sex with Jewel and Randy.

I did not! I just . . . didn't hate it.

And you said yourself that sharing the body with me could be quite a racket.

A nice girl isn't eager to aid and abet a con artist, Clay thought primly.

Ah, but I'm not a nice girl. On the widescreen in his head, Wilma appeared in a top hat, cane, heels, and a few scraps of black fishnet. She did a naughty dance step, winked, and disappeared.

In spite of himself, Clay felt a little less heartbroken.

Bing and Steven, their involuntary disbursements completed, were sent into a deposition room while they all waited for the wire transfers to go through. Zach slipped away without remark.

The Chief sent for coffee. It came with a stack of hot, fragrant, cinnamony cow plops from Hoby's. He eyed the pastry askance. "Are you sure," he said to Jewel, "it's safe to eat this now?"

"Pretty much," she said with a guilty look and sugar on her chin.

Oh, great, Clay thought. That was something he'd spaced, between cleaning up the Circle Line scam and playing host to an oversexed teen goddess. A hundred million messages in bottles. *Wilma? Is it safe to eat now?*

Of course it's safe, Wilma said. *Don't you remember? I recalled all my messages.*

Ed paused, his hairy paw hovering over the platter. "Well?"

"We determined," Randy said suavely, "that there was a dangerous buildup of unexpended sexual energy in the building that houses both the bakery and the Artistic Publishing Company."

"Randy's our research expert on magic," Jewel said. "Ed wants to hire him for the Hinky Division." Clay saw her ankle kick Ed's under the table. "He can also do safe hinky waste removal."

"Uh, yeah," Ed said, choosing a cow plop. "That's right."

"We need his skills," Clay said, forcing the words out.

Taylor nodded. "Okay, I'm impressed. I'll recommend it. And the dangerous buildup is under control?" he said to Randy.

Randy bowed in his chair. "The creation of a film division punched a hole in the dyke, as it were, causing a magical flood. We believe at this point that the excess energy has completely expended itself. In any case, the company has suspended use of the affected printing press until it can be proven safe."

"What he means is," Ed said, "the joint had a case of coitus holdin'-onto-us. But they started making dirty movies and then we got the Summer of Jizz. Everybody can use a dirty movie sometime."

"I'm going to tell your wife you said that," Jewel said.

"Feel free," Ed said, daintily stuffing a whole cow plop into his mouth with his fingertips. "I been bringing home foo dovven of vese fings every night." He squinted, swallowed, and aimed a crumb-covered finger at Jewel. "She's gained ten pounds, 'cuz she ain't feedin' 'em to the dog, if you get my drift."

Jewel clapped her hands over her ears. "Too much information, boss."

"You started it. You start something," he said with triumph, "you gotta be ready to finish it."

CHAPTER 42

"So," Jewel said, making chitchat as they stood on her apartment balcony that evening, watching the sun set over the city as the gulls flew along the river below, toward the lake. Ever since Velvita's apartment she'd been dreading this. The Relationship Conversation. This time she dreaded it because she wanted it. Panic and longing fought inside her, old enemies. "Does, uh, does this mean you've finally satisfied that stupid spell-curse-thingy?"

A shadow darkened Randy's brow. "I scarcely know. Perhaps Lady Georgiana never intended me to be free. Do you believe I love you?"

The L-word. So much for chitchat. She gulped. "Yes."

"Yet, even now that you've freed me, *she* is to be the judge of my feelings for you! It's unjust," he said bitterly.

"There is that yuck factor," Jewel admitted. "You know she isn't, like, personally snoopervising. She couldn't."

He shot her a glance. "True. Such a curse would bind the magician as much as it bound the victim."

"That's what I'm thinking. What's the point of a curse if you have to hang around to make it work?" She looked far down on a dark ambulance crossing the bridge from Dearborn, turning east onto Wacker. *He loves me.* The very words weakened her will. "I think your mistress was a genius. Fiendish, but brilliant."

Randy scowled down at the gulls. "How so?"

"She sets it up so that you have to curse *yourself*, because, I don't know, because you *have* to. Because you want something she's giving you so bad, you'll torque yourself into a pretzel to make it work."

He turned the thunder-brow on Jewel. "You agree with her, then? Have I failed to prove my feelings for you?"

"No! I mean yes, you've proved them." God, had he proved them. *Any second now he'll ask how I feel about him.* She was so nervous her ears were sweating. "I'm saying it's not up to me. I think she set up the curse so you would judge yourself. And if *you* thought you didn't measure up, zappo."

"Have we not argued this point to death?" he demanded. "You accuse me of vanishing into beds to inconvenience you." In the last red rays of the sun, he looked harsh and desperate, and she melted.

She took him by the shoulders. "No! No, I don't. Don't you see? This puts more power in your hands."

He searched her eyes. "How?"

"It gives you control over your fate. If you can face it, and take responsibility for it, you can have that control." She touched his cheek. Under her panic she felt this dumb, girlie, gut-level urge to make his life perfect, solve all his problems, fill his every need. She said gently, "The danger is when you won't face up to your part. Then you're giving control back to her."

"No, I'm giving control to you."

"So it's my fault? *I* make you pull a zapper? Oh, for—!"

She pushed him, but he caught her hand and held it strongly, pulling her closer to his big, warm body.

"When I 'pull a zapper' it is because you're angry with me. I fear to lose you. In that moment, all I can think is that you will always come to me under one circumstance."

So much truth. He always got her with the truth.

She swallowed. "If you're stuck in a bed." He nodded. She added, with irony to fight the weakness in her knees, "And when we're in bed, you're in control. So if you think I'm dumping you, you make me get into bed with you, and that restores your—"

"My place in your regard," he said steadily. "You *want* me when we are in bed."

Her breath caught. *I'll always want you.* She'd never said it. Maybe she could now.

She licked her lips. "I want you to have a life, Randy. I've been a selfish bitch and I've used you sexually and I haven't regarded your humanity or your dignity. I didn't treat you like an equal." She sucked air through her tight throat.

The "L" clanked over the Wells Street bridge. He bent his head nearer. "Have I not said you are my equal in demonspace?"

She rolled her eyes. "You don't want an equal in bed. You want to be Lord of the Nooky. You force intimacy on me in demonspace, when you know I can't say no."

"I want to be your lover, not your incubus."

Her heart thumped hard. *You're already my lover.* If she said it, she'd lose control.

He said, "I don't know if I can be your equal. I was not bred to be anyone's equal." He added with half a smile, "It has been my one defense, for two hundred years, that I am Lord Nooky in bed. And now I am Lord Pontarsais out of it."

"This is America, bub," she blurted. "I'm not comfortable opening my heart to a lord."

There it was. She swallowed hard.

"To whom will you open your heart, then?" His eyes were big and bright and quiet. The storm clouds were gone. "May I come in, Jewel?"

He was being so patient. Inside, she thrashed. *I control myself. But how do I make myself lose control?*

As she stood there, choking on her own silence, he said, "I can try to lower the social superiority that is my shield. What then is your shield? Can we ever be close?"

Her heart hammered. "We can try."

His whole face softened, and her heart beat even harder.

Was it fear making her pulse pound? So often he had said to her, *Are you afraid because you're aroused, or aroused because you're afraid?*

God, he knows me so well.

What she wanted wasn't sex, but something she couldn't name, couldn't see, couldn't touch. Even now she wanted to run away, when he was under her skin in a way that made her shiver.

How can he love a wild animal like me?

"I don't know what we're supposed to be doing," she said helplessly. "I've never been in love like this."

"I know," he said, and with that she quit fighting.

He smiled wider. "We shall have to be inventive."

A laugh fell out out her. "We're good at that." She collapsed with relief against his chest, and he held her tightly, as if he knew she couldn't handle his gentleness right now.

He put his chin on top of her head. "I cannot promise I will never again be trapped in a bed."

"I was wrong to ask if you wouldn't." He smelled like home.

His shoulders sank and the tension seemed to leave him. "You will come for me? You'll rescue me?"

A gull flipped past their balcony out of nowhere, calling, and vanished into the deepening blue over their heads. She felt her heart fill with peace.

"Always."

ACKNOWLEDGMENTS

I have the following people to thank for their help in writing this book. If the book contains errors, it is my fault. If I got it right anywhere, it's to their credit.

David Henry Sterry, for his moving memoir, *Chicken*; Candida Royalle for advice and for some terrific women's erotic film (especially *Stud Hunters*); Don Maass for the guy perspective; Betsy Mitchell for not fainting over the first draft; Sue Grimshaw, for wanting more; Rich Bynum, for infrastructure geekery; Ysa Wilce for patience and brainstorming; "Mr. Balantine" for inside dope; Nalo Hopkinson for such sexual diversity retraining as I'm capable of receiving; Eden Robins for patience and multiple reads; Martha Whitehead for clout; Lisa Laing for book trailer magic; Rob Dorn at Three Cat Media for website design; Julie Griffin for the smoking pigeon; the teams at both Del Rey and Ballantine, for dealing with branding emergencies; and my many, faithful, and ever-wise readers: Yvonne Yirka, Kate Early, Hiromi Goto, Pam and Bar Man Mordecai, Larissa Lai, David Findlay, Nnedi Okorafor-Mbachu, Sylvia Halkin, the Cherries, and the multitalented critiquers at Chicago-North RWA.

AUTHOR'S NOTE: The website mentioned on page 118, where Velvita reports misuse of or involuntary internet posting of her image, does not exist, more's the pity. There should be such a service available to consumers.